A NEW FILM

DARKMAN

UNIVERSAL PICTURES Presents

LIAM NEESON FRANCES McDORMAND

"DARKMAN"

COLIN FRIELS LARRY DRAKE

MUSIC BY DANNY ELFMAN MAKE-UP EFFECTS BY TONY GARDNER and LARRY HAMLIN

PRODUCTION DESIGNER RANDY SER DIRECTOR OF PHOTOGRAPHY BILL POPE LINE PRODUCER DARYL KASS

STORY BY SAM RAIMI

SCREENPLAY BY CHUCK PFARRER and SAM RAIMI & IVAN RAIMI

and DANIEL GOLDIN & JOSHUA GOLDIN

PRODUCED BY ROBERT TAPERT DIRECTED BY SAM RAIMI

A UNIVERSAL RELEASE
© 1990 UNIVERSAL CITY STUDIOS, INC.

DARKMAN
ISBN 1 85286 296 3

A novel by Randall Boyll
Based on a screenplay by Chuck Pfarrer and Sam Raimi
& Ivan Raimi and Daniel Goldin & Joshua Goldin
Story by Sam Raimi

Published by
Titan Books Ltd
58 St Giles High St
London WC2H 8LH

First Titan Edition October 1990
10 9 8 7 6 5 4 3 2 1

Printed and bound in Great Britain by Cox & Wyman Ltd,
Reading, Berkshire.

DARKMAN

A novel by Randall Boyll
Based on a screenplay by Chuck Pfarrer and Sam Raimi &
Ivan Raimi and Daniel Goldin & Joshua Goldin
Story by Sam Raimi

TITAN BOOKS
LONDON

Prologue

Eddie

HIS NAME WAS Eddie Black and he didn't take grief from anybody. He was a big man, Eddie was, a dockworker who had spent twenty years hoisting crates as big as Volkswagens, hauling chains as thick as telephone poles, sweating under a hot Midwestern sun with the putrid stink of the river around him and the savage knowledge that he was real tough burning inside. The fact that he was an asshole did not faze Eddie. The fact that his employees generally considered him to be insane bothered Eddie even less. All he wanted at this moment was to beat the living daylights out of Robert G. Durant, and Mr. Durant was on his way to see Eddie.

Eddie was leaning casually against his car, a brand-new Dodge, waiting, not worrying much. The car was parked inside a huge, empty building on a riverside pier. Weary light bulbs burned overhead in a futile attempt to stave off the dark. Shadows moved in the corners of the buildings while empty crates, slowly rotting, stood silent watch. The orange fireworks of burning cigarette tips flared periodically in the darkest recesses of the warehouse. Eddie nodded to himself. Just wait and see what thirteen husky dockmen could do. That punk, Durant, was in for the surprise of his life.

Something inside the Dodge emitted little electronic beeps. Eddie leaned inside and plucked a remote phone from its holder on the dash. In the years since his retirement he had found himself growing fairly rich, at least as far as dockworkers go. As a younger man, he had worked in this very building, sweated and slaved, sweated and saved. By the time he had hit fifty, the mandatory retirement age, he had a nest egg big enough to put a down payment on this waterfront property and the buildings that stretched forty yards on either side of the pier. Handsome little investment, handsome profits. He had considered buying a river barge but came to his senses in the nick of time and bought the Dodge instead. Barges had a nasty tendency to sink, especially if some angry union boss found out that Eddie hired nonunion men and paid them under the table. It was kind of illegal and kind of dangerous, but Eddie had faced danger before. Surely more than that slicked-back greaser named Robert G. Durant.

He put the phone to his ear, feeling smug and important. He loved getting calls on the car phone. He wished he could hang one on his belt. It made people think he was dashingly cool.

"Yeah?" Eddie said.

A tinny voice squawked at him. Reception was bad on this Thursday. Perhaps the tin wall of the warehouse blocked the radio waves. He made a mental note to park closer to the door next time.

It was his secretary on the line, a scrawny, brainless bimbo who was actually dumb enough to work for two dollars an hour. Not that she had much to do except screen his calls, and she wasn't even very good at that.

She rattled off a few names. Eddie ran them through his mental Rolodex. "No . . . because he's an idiot. Tell him no way. . . . Okay, tell him no way too. . . . Him? Tell him to drop dead."

He struggled to get a cigarette out of his shirt pocket while clamping the phone to his collarbone with his chin. The brain-damaged bimbo rattled on and on. He tweezed a crumpled Chesterfield out of the pack and began patting his pockets. The phone felt greasy against his chin, threatening to fall to the cement floor. He tried to elbow it back into place. It was a feat for a contortionist but not for Eddie Black. The phone slipped away and smacked the floor. A piece of plastic popped off and skittered under the car.

"Oh, hell!" he bellowed, dropping down to pick up his favorite toy. On his knees, he stuck it back to his ear. The bimbo was still babbling. "Stop," Eddie barked. "I dropped the damn phone."

She kept on talking. Eddie tapped the phone on the floor. Because the plastic had broken off, a small green circuit board was exposed. He stuck his finger on it. Nothing.

"Mabel," he shouted, "shut up for a minute!"

"Blah blah," she said, after a fashion. "And blah and blah and blah." Eddie realized that he could no longer understand her brainless voice. He hammered the phone against the Dodge's door, digging neat little chips out of the brand-new paint. Seeing this, he attempted to repair the damage by covering it with the phone.

And still his secretary talked, sounding oddly metallic against the door and its peppering of fresh paint holes. Eddie cranked his head back and screamed to the high ceiling, beseeching God to end his suffering. Mabel droned on.

A figure emerged from the shadows and skirted the car, a beefy man in a sweaty white sleeveless T-shirt. He was all hair and fat. He went by the name of Hank.

He bent down. "Trouble, Mr. Black?"

Eddie snapped his head around. His eyes were wild and wet. Saliva bubbled at the corners of his lips. "No, Hank, I'm fine. Durant's on his way to muscle me out of my property and we'll probably have to kill him. This building is costing me a fortune every minute it stands empty, my phone's broken, and to top it off, my secretary has turned into a robot. Why shouldn't I be fine?"

Hank, not the brightest of men, nodded solemnly. "That's really weird, Mr. Black, because you don't look all that fine to me."

Eddie jumped up, intending to shove the now useless phone up Hank's stupid nose when the rectangle of light that was the open doors behind him went dim. A snazzy blue Lincoln Continental idled into the building, its tires crunching over gravel and debris. Eddie threw the phone into the car and motioned to his men in the shadows, no longer concerned about Hank's nose. Rumor had it that Durant was one tough hood for a small-timer, a little dope here, a little prostitution

3

there, a few riverfront property owners roughed up and forced to sell. He was about to learn a lesson in diplomacy from Eddie Black.

Eddie's men formed a line. Each carried a weapon of their choice: six had knives almost as long as machetes, two others had short shovels, one had a crowbar, and the rest had rusty lengths of chain. They leered at the car, whose windows were tinted black.

The car doors popped open and six men got out. Aside from Durant, Eddie had no idea who the others were, though it wasn't hard to tell what they were here for. Backup for Durant, simple as that. But they were very much outnumbered and were about to lose their weapons.

"Okay," Eddie said, smiling with a mouthful of yellow teeth. "Against the car, boys. We're going to do a little searchy-searchy."

They went obediently to the proper stance: hands flat on the roof, feet spread wide. Eddie waved a hand at two of his biggest workers. They ambled over to Durant's car and began patting them down. No one protested. A large pile of pistols grew on the floor as Durant's men were stripped of hardware.

"Don't the ladies look better now?" one of Eddie's men said.

Another nodded. "Bunch of cuties, huh?"

"Put skirts on them and I'd marry one."

The dockworkers laughed. Eddie breathed a small sigh of relief, amazed to find that he had been mildly worried all along, though he hadn't been aware of it. He smiled again. Chalk one up to nerves of steel.

"Well, now," he said, strolling around with his fingers laced behind his back, feeling idiotically like a drill sergeant with a platoon full of recruits, "I believe we have some business to discuss."

Durant nodded. He was wearing what had to be a six-hundred-dollar suit. The aroma of fine cologne drifted on the air. His hair was slightly greased, combed perfectly in place. Eddie had to hand it to him: He looked like a million bucks. A dope for coming here, but a pretty dope.

Dope Durant looked at Eddie. "Mind if we quit holding this car down?"

4

"Be my guest," Eddie said. "Unarmed, you guys are about as scary as Daffy Duck. This shouldn't take too long."

They pulled away from the car. Eddie noticed that one of them was limping. No, more than limping. He was hobbling.

"Bum leg?" Eddie asked conversationally.

The man shook his head. "*No* leg."

"Ah. I was engaged to a girl with a wooden leg once."

Durant's man brightened. "Yeah? What happened?"

Eddie shook his head glumly. "Poor girl. I had to break it off."

His workers howled. Eddie chuckled. How fine it felt to be in charge. "Well," he said, "it's time to cut the chatter. Durant, I've only got three things to say to you." He held up one finger. "First, I'm not selling you my property." Another finger. "Second, nobody muscles Eddie Black. Especially a bunch of jerks like you." Third finger. "Last, if you are unhappy with the previous two, we'll be more than happy to amputate your privates and nail them to the wall. Sort of like a poor man's doorbell."

The workers screamed laughter while Eddie basked in the limelight of his own cutting wit. How great it was to be onstage with an admiring crowd. He turned to his men, good men all of them, every one, and while they howled and screeched and pounded each other, one of Robert G. Durant's goons jumped at the one-legged man and pulled his wooden leg out of his pants. Something metallic flipped down from the wooden calf, a handle of some sort with a trigger. He pressed the wooden foot to his shoulder, took quick aim, and fired.

At any other time Eddie would have found this trick quite laudable; after all, Durant was in the business of high-pressure sales tactics and should be as prepared as possible for any upsetting little detail, such as thirteen dockworkers armed only with clubs and chains. The machine gun blatted, spitting smoke and fire, drilling through the uneven line of men, bowling them over. The machine-gun-in-the-leg trick was absolutely stunning to Eddie, because now he was seeing thirteen men fall in bloody heaps while body parts—arms, legs, guts, brains, unidentifiable red blobs—flapped through the air and spattered down on the cement. There was groaning; there was screaming. Eddie did not realize that it was he himself, Eddie Black, who was screaming the loudest. His fingers had dug themselves into his cheeks, pulling his face down into a mask of insane horror.

The machine gun swung toward him. He dropped to the floor without saying so much as howdy to the cement, and hugged it for dear life, eyes squeezed shut, heart pounding in his throat, sweat beading on his forehead, while the machine gun—*good trick*—hammered away at his new Dodge. Glass exploded and rained down on him. A tire blew with a bang, then farted its air out. The car clunked down when another tire blew. Bullets perforated the shiny new paint with a sound like small hammers hitting steel. Eddie screamed some more, screamed until he realized the gun had shut down and the only noise left were echoes of gunfire and his screams booming off the walls and high ceiling.

He raised his head. Glass pebbles slid off his hair. Gunsmoke as thick as fog wafted in the still air, smelling like burned chemicals and sulfur. The one-legged man was hopping around on his only foot while his leg was put back together. He accepted it and stuck it back in his pant leg.

Feet shuffled. Eddie was hauled upright. He tried to stand but was forced to his knees. His terrified mind showed him a horror house of things yet to come. Knives in his eyes. Decapitation. Strangulation. The cutting out of his tongue. Castration. Any number of new and interesting things.

Durant stood over him, grinning. A hand grabbed Eddie's hair and jerked his head up. Oh, yeah, Eddie thought, wild with fear. Gonna cut my throat. Jesus God, my *throat*!

Durant reached inside his suit coat and withdrew a long cigar.

Burn my eyes out, oh God, oh no, HELP!

He reached into another pocket and produced an unrecognizable gold gadget. It looked like a small guillotine. He thumbed it and a hole appeared. He stuck the end of his cigar into the hole. Snip! A small piece of cigar dropped to the floor. He stuck the clipped end in his mouth and withdrew yet another gold gadget from a pocket. Eddie looked on, his thoughts a chaotic and useless whirl. What the hell did Durant have in mind?

Durant touched a button. A tiny finger of flame burst alive. He lit his cigar. Nice lighter, Eddie screamed inside. Let me live and I'll buy you a truckload of them. What is that, anyway? Electronic ignition? One little button, and presto, you've got fire. Question is, what do you intend to do with it?

Durant went into a squat, facing Eddie eye to eye. The lighter burned. Better blow it out, Eddie was able to think. Blow it out or that fancy gold job will overheat and burn your hand.

"Let us negotiate," Durant said evenly. "I believe we have a sale to discuss in very fine detail. Stop whimpering so. You haven't been hurt."

Yeah? Not yet I haven't. But if you do not extinguish that lighter soon, it will be very, very hot.

Ooops. Hot lighter. Perhaps as hot as, say, a branding iron? Nope.

Durant touched the flame to Eddie's hair. At his age Eddie was not blessed with a bountiful crop, but for a man nearing sixty he wasn't all that bald. His hair crackled alive. In seconds it was a burning cowl. The stench of it filled the building, making some of Durant's boys hold their noses and giggle through their mouths. Eddie, meanwhile, began exercising his voice again. He whooped and bellowed while his hair evaporated as if by magic, leaving only burned stubs and a scalp gone pink and black. He was inclined to get up and run, but the strong hands holding him down changed his mind. Instead he had to content himself with whipping his flaming head back and forth and screaming.

"Jeez," Durant said, looking apologetic. "Did I do that?"

More giggles. Durant blew on Eddie's head, making the last remnants of hair glow brightly before going out. Eddie moaned and gobbled. He was unaware that one of his hands had been captured and was being held out, pointing at Durant.

"Now," Durant said, withdrawing the cigar trimmer, "I want you to consider these points one by one." He clicked the trimmer, making a hole appear. He slid the device onto Eddie's forefinger.

"Number one: I try not to let anger get the better of me."

He squeezed the trimmer, hard. Eddie screamed as the

7

razor-sharp blade dug past his flesh and into the bone. Durant grunted and the blade clicked home.

Eddie looked down at his newly trimmed hand with bulging eyes. Instead of a finger he had a spurting stump. Durant waddled backward, to avoid staining his suit.

"Point number two!" he shouted over the noise Eddie was making. "I don't always succeed in overcoming my anger." He slipped the trimmer over another finger, the second one. Eddie struggled against the hands that held him.

Snip!

Eddie saw everything through a blood-red mist of pain. His screaming was winding down to sloppy chuckles.

"Point number three," Durant said, and snipped again.

Eddie swayed, moaning, drunk with pain.

Durant grinned cruelly as he fitted the trimmer over yet another finger. "Point number three, Eddie, is this: I have seven more points."

Everyone laughed at this—everyone except Eddie, of course. Eddie was too busy with his own problems to see the humor in this, or anything else.

1

Destruction

1

Yakky

FOR YAKITITO YANAGITO—a name so unpronounceable that his friends at Wayne State University called him Yakky, which sat just fine with Yakitito, because he had no idea what Yakky might mean—the first Thursday afternoon as lab assistant to Dr. Peyton Westlake was a memorable one. Westlake was a tall, loose-jointed man just easing into his thirties. Likeable if a bit skittish, he was the kind of guy who might kill you in a basketball game or nail you to the wall with an impossible Chem 101 exam, and then go home and invent Flubber. He could be seen dashing across campus in his white lab coat on some inexplicable mission, deaf and blind to his surroundings or hunched over a microscope at the biochem lab, jammed so tightly into his own little world that there was no room for anybody else. Yakky had indeed heard a lot about Peyton Westlake, even seen him a few times charging from building to building with his lab coat flapping. As a foreign graduate student at the university, Yakky could easily understand what it meant to seem strange, even bizarre, to the rest of humanity; he felt that way all the time.

Standing now at the door to Peyton Westlake's private laboratory, ready to peck at the glass, Yakky felt a surge of fresh apprehension. This place was strange. A two-story red clapboard affair, it was seedy and generally run-down. Some windows were boarded over with plywood that was slowly surrendering to rot, other windows were broken and gaping, even the tin roof leaked. The whole sorry structure was located within fifty yards of a sludgy river that smelled of toxic waste and dead fish. Yakky felt decidedly nauseated as he stared at his own pale reflection in the glass of the door, the only thing around here that appeared to have survived the ravages of time and vandals. He smoothed his hair. He adjusted his tie. He took off his Coke-bottle-bottom glasses, which weighed nearly half a pound, stuck his nose to the glass, and searched his face for pimples until it occurred to him that he had not had a pimple since he was seventeen.

Now or never, he thought in his native Japanese as he repositioned his monster Mr. Ed glasses and rapped on the door. While he waited for a response he polished the tips of his Oxfords on his pants. Someone had told him that Dr. Westlake was notorious for dressing casually: cutoff jeans in the summer, a ratty field jacket in the winter. Still, Yakky had no desire to make a bad first impression. The grant that funded Westlake's research was due for renewal in December, three months from now. In the last six months he had had three different lab assistants; all of them had gotten fed up with this or that and ran screaming into the night. There were rumors of a failed experiment that Westlake had become obsessed with and would not let die. Some spoke of spending hideously long hours staring at a stopwatch. None of it really mattered to Yakky. He needed the credit hours and he needed the money. Postgrad hours for out-of-state students had been jacked up to the sixty-two-dollar mark. Pretty bad, especially when your dad drives a garbage truck in Osaka.

He knocked again. In the distance he could hear some kind of machinery whining. Curiosity gnawed at him, but he did not give in to the urge to take a peek. Besides, it looked dark inside.

Time passed. He knocked again, harder now, as hard as his inbred sense of decency would allow. Sweat trickled down his neck. September in Michigan was an odd mishmash of too much heat or too much cold; nobody was ever satisfied, Yakky included.

Something clunked. Somewhere above, wood crunched. It

began to rain sawdust on Yakky's head. He looked up, squinting against the sawdust and the hot afternoon sun.

The boards on one of the windows were being wrenched apart. Yakky stepped back, his eyes behind the Mr. Ed glasses growing large. He saw hands. He saw the cuff of a white lab coat. He saw a large kitchen clock sail out the window and crash on the hard-packed mud near the river's edge. It burst apart in a noisy explosion of glass and springs. Yakky looked on in horror.

A fist stuck itself out of the window, followed by a head. The fist was shaking angrily up and down. The head was screaming.

"You rotten stupid son of a bitch!"

The fist began to hammer the head, pounding it silly. Yakky blanched. Even for Americans this was strange behavior. He stepped farther back, hoping to dodge any other clocks that might come sailing his way. The man who was upstairs busily knocking himself over the head looked down at him. Yakky tried to force a smile. No good. All he did was grimace.

The man upstairs quit hitting himself. He smiled down at Yakky.

"Yakitito Yanagita, I presume?"

Yakky looked around quizzically, pointing a finger at his own chest. No one else was there. He had a strong urge to deny any knowledge of the poor slob named Yakitito Yanagita, and run away. He had a quick mental glimpse of himself sprinting the eight blocks back to campus while this lunatic hurled clocks at him. For a sensitive soul named Yakky it was a vision straight from hell.

"Come on in," the man upstairs shouted, and Yakky knew, as his heart sank into his shoes, that this was Dr. Peyton Westlake and nobody else. He shuffled back to the door and grasped the knob. It fell off in his hand.

"Minor setback," Peyton shouted above him. "I'll plug it back in later. Watch the steps, though. They might be wobbly."

Yakky pushed the door open, wishing he had not worn this shirt and tie because the shirt was threatening to suffocate him and the tie was about to strangle him, and who really

13

cared when the next three months—longer if the grant was funded—were spent in the company of this madman?

He went in, ready to jump at shadows. It was dim inside, the air heavy and hot. Crates and boxes bulked to the ceiling on the far wall, most of them bearing the IBM logo. A staircase loomed in the dark on the right. Yakky put a hesitant foot on the first step, bouncing a little on the springy, eroded wood, testing it while visions of various fractures flitted through his mind like ghosts. He made it to the fifth step before the wood gave out with a dry snap, and he plunged downward, his hips wedging themselves between the riser and the fourth step. He suppressed a howl as sharp wood splinters dug through his pants; a man with thick glasses wearing a brown polyester suit, up to the waist in stairs.

"Watch the fifth one," Peyton sang out from somewhere up above. "It might give out on you. Death trap."

Yakky pulled himself free while searching his English vocabulary for new and exciting curses. Things ripped as he struggled out, but he was at the point of no longer caring. He crawled on hands and knees to the top, muttering, while his sweaty hair—so perfect before—draped itself over his eyes and glasses like black seaweed. He got on his feet and scrubbed an arm across his forehead. The heat was even worse up here, but at least it wasn't dark. There seemed to be a breeze of sorts, cooling Yakky below the waist.

He looked down, puzzled. His pants were in tatters. His zipper had burst. His belt had opened and hung down from this disaster like a defeated snake. He was covered with dust.

Peyton came out of nowhere and grabbed his hand. He began to pump it. "Yakitito! I'm so glad to see you. What this project needs is new faces, fresh input. What the hell happened to you? Together I think we can lick this thing, make it work. Bomb go off or what? Doesn't matter. Come on in."

Yakky staggered after him into the depths of the second floor, which was nothing at all like the first. It was a little lighter, made that way by a single bulb hanging from a wire. It was spotlessly clean, unlike below. Lab equipment—some of it familiar to Yakky, some of it not—was jammed into shelves that rose to the raftered ceiling. A pale blue centrifuge idled in one corner; in another was a rackfull of beakers and test tubes. Two large tanks, one labled OXYGEN, the other ACETYLENE, sat like squat soldiers, guarding these puzzling treasures. Things were humming. The place seemed alive with electricity. Yakky spotted a strange glass tank about the size of an aquarium set on a metal stand with electrodes jutting out from its sides. It was filled with a weird pink liquid. Yakky thought of mad scientists.

"Have you been told the nature of my experiments here?" Peyton asked while Yakky gaped at the various devices that were the workhorses of this undertaking. Yakky nodded and turned to him.

"Manufacture of synthetic skin. Something about burns."

Peyton smiled. "I'd hardly call it manufacturing, but that will come later, after I've—we've—succeeded here. The burn part is fairly correct."

"Sorry," Yakky mumbled. "Nobody seems to know exactly what you do here." He waved an arm to indicate the whole floor. "Why do you do this on the riverfront, anyway?"

Peyton raised a finger. His blue eyes twinkled. "Yakita—Yatiko—oh, hell, can I call you Alphabet?"

"Most people call me Yakky."

Peyton deliberated on this, tapping his chin with a finger. "Anyway, Yakky, this ramshackle hut helps me keep expenses down. Plus people tend to leave me alone."

I don't blame them, Yakky thought, but simply nodded. There was a moment of awkward silence between them.

Then Peyton spoke up. "Let me give you a brief overview of what we're doing here." He stooped over and hauled a white lab smock out of a plastic bag. "Better put this on. It might get messy."

Yakky put it on, beginning to feel that first tickling of anticipation, the same feeling he always got when embarking on a new project. Of course, this project was hardly new; in fact, it was more than a year old, but for Yakky it was barely a minute old. He put the smock on, glad to cover the ruin of his pants with something decent.

Peyton walked over to a space between the equipment, where a small camera with some decidedly exotic hardware protruding from it was perched on a tripod. In front of it was a chair. "Want to have your picture taken?" he asked, grinning.

Yakky shrugged. Better than having clocks thrown at him. He sat on the stool while Peyton fiddled with the camera.

"Nose, lips, cheek, chin . . . which will it be?"

"Huh?"

"Never mind. Turn sideways, please."

Yakky did, wondering now if that strange camera were some sort of ray gun. Weirder things than that were being invented every day.

The flash snapped. For a millisecond Yakky was deluged with hot white light. He blinked against it.

"Turn the other way, Yak, old boy."

He turned. What the heck.

Foof!

"Now look straight at me. Don't wiggle."

Foof!

Yakky stood up. Peyton moved in front of the camera, which fed him three small photographs on strange, wafflytextured paper. He hurried over to a large IBM computer that was linked with wires to a dozen or so other machines. Yakky tried to make sense of them. No dice.

"I feed them in here," Peyton said, pushing the photos one by one into a slot on the side of the computer. Yakky frowned. This was weird stuff, indeed. The slot in the computer looked as if it had been cut there with a hacksaw.

"Now we get our digitization. See?"

Yakky saw. The computer blipped. A picture of his nose appeared on the monitor screen, then dissolved into thousands of dots.

"Next we transfer it to the Imager."

"Imager?"

"Holographic. Nothing fancy."

A round aluminum plate crudely wired to the IBM began to vibrate. Two inches above its surface, multiple rainbows began to dance and merge. They swam into each other and became a three-dimensional picture of Yakky's own nose, in living color. He stared at it. So what? Holography was not exactly headline news anymore.

Peyton had moved off to another table and another machine. He motioned for Yakky, telling him to come over. Yakky went.

"This baby is my Bio-Press," he said, and indicated a squat machine about the size of a suitcase. Yakky saw that its surface was crammed full of tiny blunt pins. Again, so what?

"Each pin has a tiny servo motor underneath, in the guts of the Bio-Press. Feeding off the Imager, they rise in conformation with the holograph and the computerized digitization. The pink fluid in the tank over there soups itself onto the face of the Bio-Press, in direct contact with both the Imager and the computerized version."

Soups itself? Yakky felt a sudden and desperate need to fly home to Osaka and never set foot on American soil again.

"Like this." Peyton pressed a touch pad on the side of the suitcase thing. Across the room, the electrodes at either side of the tank that looked like an aquarium began to hum.

"Builds a bullet charge of two thousand volts," he said over the growing noise. "Amperage follows with no drain. Don't ask me where I get the juice. The lights blow at Michigan Power every time I do this." He grinned wickedly. The pink fluid began to surge through coils of glass pipe into the Bio-Press. Yakky watched with a mixture of revulsion and excitement as the liquid boiled across the top of the Bio-Press like waffle batter being dumped on a hot waffle iron, sizzling. Blue sparks danced on its surface. In the center the pins rose up to create a perfectly shaped Yakky nose. A twist of smoke rose into the air, smelling badly of burned pork. The fluid turned from pink to flesh color as it cooked. Yakky's stomach gave a lurch.

"You'll get used to the smell. What's happening is that the synthetic skin is being formed at the same time it's solidifying. That way we get maximum time from it."

Yakky frowned. "Time?"

Peyton smiled grimly. He pulled a drawer open and riffled through it, finally coming up with a stopwatch on a twist of string. He hung it around Yakky's neck. Yakky fingered it, frowning.

Peyton nodded. "You saw the clock? No sweat. Before the

year's over, you'll be tossing that stopwatch out the window too. Click it on as soon as the Bio-Press indicates sufficient cooling. Red light there on the side.''

Yakky squatted a bit and found the light. It went on, and he hurried to start the watch. Peyton lifted the sheet of what now looked like soft pale rubber off the press. He bounced it from hand to hand, wincing. ''Hot little honker. Looks just like your nose, eh?'' He fished a pair of old black-framed glasses out of a pocket and slipped them on. ''Hah,'' he said after a moment. ''How'd you get that scar on your septum?''

''Septum?''

Peyton rubbed a finger between his nostrils. ''The thing that differentiates us from the apes but not from pigs.''

Yakky touched his own. There was a tiny scar there from a huge zit that had struck him in this unlikely place when he was fifteen. ''Acne,'' he told Peyton. ''You know.''

Peyton smiled. ''Afraid I've never had the teenage curse. This pretty face has never been marred.''

''Lucky you. Now, what am I timing?''

Peyton's smile disappeared. He put his glasses back, laid the nose sheet on the table, and went to the computer. He tapped the keys, then looked glumly at Yakky. ''Take a look at this.''

Yakky went over beside him and bent to read the screen. It said:

AMINO ACID CONTENT—64.0%
MEMBRANE POTENTIAL—120 millivolts
DNA CONTENT—00.047 millimoles
COLLAGEN CONGENERS—22.8%
ELECTROLYTES—Physiologic

Yakky frowned. ''This reads a lot like a human tissue sample. Skin tissue.''

''Quite right. When your stop watch reads ninety-nine minutes, you'll see what it turns into. That's when I need your input. Myself, I'm stumped.''

"Stumped?"

"Yeah." He made little motions in the air. "Dead end. No go. Finished. Kaput."

Yakky nodded, trying to look as glum as Peyton. He assumed that with time and practice he would actually feel as bad about whatever was going to happen in ninety-nine minutes as Peyton was. It was easy enough now to see what had been going on here and why the last three assistants had abandoned the project. Peyton had failed in his attempt to create artificial skin for burn victims. Such a discovery would advance medicine a hundred years, but because it didn't work, Dr. Westlake didn't need any lab assistants, didn't need any help at all. What he needed was a timekeeper.

Peyton was working himself out of his lab coat. Beneath it he had on a gray suit and an honest-to-God tie. So much for the rumors about casual dress, Yakky thought. Peyton tossed the coat aside and gave Yakky an apologetic smile. "I have to go meet my fiancée—well, girlfriend, actually—I have to meet her for a late lunch before she attends some hotshot meeting. She's a lawyer, you know. Follow me? Anyhow, on the way back I could grab you a pizza, Yak. Any preference?"

Yakky thought about it. Crashing through the stairs must have awakened his appetite; either that or his upbringing was so ingrained that he feared for his life if he turned the invitation down. He shrugged and said, "Sushi and anchovies. Fish eyes, if they have them."

Peyton laughed. "At last a man with a sense of humor. Sausage and mushrooms it is. Be back soon."

He clumped down the stairs, probably avoiding, by instinct and habit, the ruined fifth step. The door slammed and he was gone.

Yakky looked at the stopwatch. But that got old fast. He looked around the lab, hoping to spot a radio, maybe even a small TV. No luck. The only thing here that looked remotely interesting was a toy drinking bird on the table beside the computer. The bird was made of plastic and multicolored feathers, weighted with lead somewhere so that when you rocked it, it gradually dipped farther and farther until its beak

19

dunked into the tiny cup of water. Yakky tapped it, making it bob. Eventually it dipped down far enough to take a drink. By then Yakky had lost interest. He stared at the stopwatch, then stared some more.

There was nothing else to do.

2

Peyton

DR. PEYTON WESTLAKE was not dressed so superbly by accident. He had not awakened that Friday and decided to change his slovenly ways. He had not peered at his reflection in the bathroom mirror and found, to his horror, that he was actually on the low side of thirty, and looking older every day. He had made no attempt to turn over a new leaf. Nothing was unusual, as far as usual things go.

But today *was* a bit special. Today he would have a late lunch with a certain blond lady and pop several surprises on her. That is, if he could find a taxi in this rotten area of town. Since leaving Yakky behind to fend for himself, he had walked nearly to the college campus, where surely there would be a taxi available. But so far, waiting at the curbside of Jackson Street, the sprawling maze work that was the campus just ahead, his luck had become just plain lousy. He stuck his thumb out at a passing car and got laughed at for his trouble: college punks bebopping around in the car Daddy's money had bought, using Daddy's credit card for gas, paying their tuition with Daddy's money. Poor Daddy seemed to take a soaking every time Junior turned around, and Junior did not appear to care even slightly.

Peyton shook his head to clear it. When he thought of things like this, he invariably grew angry inside. He had financed his own way through college less than ten years ago, financed it all the way to his doctorate. While the kids with rich daddies tooled around in new cars, Peyton drove a wobbly antique called a mo-ped. While they bought fancy clothes and kegs of beer, Peyton went to class wearing jeans gone white with age and drank nothing but water with every meal. His part-time jobs had ranged from pizza slinger to summertime corn shucker. The whole ordeal had been tough and no fun at all. Of course, now, as the local nutty professor, he made money, and then some. Enough, maybe, to finance a kid or two through college.

He grinned at his own inanity. He disliked the kids who lived off Daddy but was quite prepared to become Daddy himself.

If things went right today, that just might happen.

He patted the coat pocket nearest his heart, where the big lump was. Inside was a velvet jeweler's box, and inside that was a gold necklace adorned with five small diamonds. It looked like—and was—an expensive gift, but to Peyton's way of thinking (as he saw the ugly yellow of a taxi coming close) the gift was something like oil, to be used to grease his way into his true love's heart.

The taxi stopped. Peyton climbed in the back, pondering his weighty excursion into philosophy. Was he that crass that he would shower a woman with gold and diamonds before . . .

"Where to, pal?" the driver asked, watching Peyton through the rearview mirror.

"Downtown. Bowser's. Know it?"

"Yeah." He gave the taxi gas and merged with the sparse traffic. "It's that fancy effing joint where everybody eats out on the effing sidewalk."

"Patio, I believe." *Effing?*

"Patio, schmatio. It took the caveman a billion years to figure out how to put a roof over his head so's he could eat without getting rained on, and now we're so effing fancy, we eat outside for the effing fun of it. Screwy, huh?"

"I suppose." Peyton wondered if this philosophy thing was spreading. He seemed to have contaminated the cabbie instantly. It occurred to him that all the cabdrivers he had ever encountered had some kind of quirk. This morning the guy had launched into a spiel about how the Chinese had sabotaged the space shuttle *Challenger.* He had managed to work himself into a lather by the time he had dropped Peyton off at the lab, and Peyton had been highly relieved when he drove away. Chinese, indeed—everybody knew it was the Russians.

The taxi ran into heavier traffic, causing the predictable delay. Peyton looked at his watch. Behind the smashed crystal, the hands read four-thirty. Rush hour was barely half an hour away. He had promised this certain blond lady that he would be at Bowser's before five, and smashed crystal or not, his watch worked quite well.

He sat back, resigned to whatever fate the taxi had in store for him. He let his thoughts drive back to the previous night, Thursday, when Julie

Blond lady
femme fatale???

had spent the better part of the evening and night at his apartment over on Walker Street. Peyton had borrowed—filched—an aging slide projector from the university's junk repository and put on a private slide show. Champagne had been purchased and dutifully drunk, along with a pizza, which, during the last year of his efforts to perfect synthetic skin, had become his main source of sustenance.

Julie had been in high humor. She had cracked up and laughed champagne out of her nose when Peyton showed a slide of himself at thirteen, a gawky, skinny kid with over-large glasses, standing in front of his booth at a science fair.

"Look at those glasses!" she had shrieked through a mouthful of champagne, which was about to find a strange exit via her nostrils. "Mr. Ed!"

Peyton had accepted this unfavorable review with humility, never knowing that Yakky had endured the same humiliation, then laughed wildly when the wine blasted out of her nose like a sneeze. He clicked the projector while she dabbed at her blouse with a Pizza Hut napkin. This slide showed a fifteen-year-old Julie Hastings in a swimsuit, posed for the camera at poolside, pretending to be debonair.

"God, your jugs were big back then," Peyton said, and grabbed two handfuls in order to make a more precise judgment. She didn't mind. He was busy with her twin marvels when she asked the question he did not want to hear.

23

"Peyton, how's the skin coming?"

This brought him back to reality, hard. He mumbled something about ninety-nine minutes.

"It'll happen," she said, then dropped another unwanted party favor. "Think the grant will be renewed in December?"

"Hard to say," he replied uneasily.

"Have you meet your new grad assistant yet?"

"Nah. He's coming over tomorrow sometime. Name's Yakitito Yanagita. Japanese grad student. I sure hope I don't have to say his name much."

"You'll get used to it. Think he can add some ideas?"

"Hope so. I'm tired of this quagmire I'm stuck in. Maybe I'll just dump the whole frigging project, stop beating a dead horse. Biochemistry is a dead-end field. We've gone as far as we can."

"Oh, stop that," she said. "You've never been a quitter. We've been going together since high school and you haven't quit on me yet."

"These love bumps are a good incentive." He squeezed them harder. "Going to, ah, spend the night?"

"Do I have a choice?"

"Not when I've got you in this new karate hold I just invented. Just try to escape."

She hadn't. Sometime around two o'clock, when she was sleeping with her face in a cold bar of moonlight, Peyton had stroked her hair, enjoying that familiar fragrance of shampoo and perfume, and made up his mind. They weren't getting any younger; they were both financially secure; and lately, when Julie saw a mother with her children on the street, an oddly pensive expression would pass across her face like a shadow. Peyton knew what it meant, though she might deny it.

"Bowser's, mister." The cabbie wrenched down the arm of the fare meter, startling Peyton out of his memories. "Four-twenty. And just look at them dummies eating on the sidewalk. Effing effers."

Peyton paid him and got out, glad to be rid both of him and his effers. He spotted Julie waving at him from a table and sauntered over, feigning a casual attitude. In reality his heart had switched into a higher gear at the sight of her beneath the fringed patio umbrella. He patted his coat again. Still there, still worth more than seven hundred dollars. How about that business with being crass? Was he still?

He nodded slightly as he walked. Call it crass if you must, but that's one tough lady when she wants to be. The necklace was grease, pure and simple.

Are you that afraid she'll say no?

Naw. Not really.

What if she does? What then?

What should I do? I can't simply keel over dead on the sidewalk, and the earth is most certainly not going to open up and swallow me. How red can a face get? Will people stare?

Aren't you really afraid that if she does say no, your relationship will be over?

Please God, no. Anything but that.

Then don't take a chance.

Wise effing counsel, Peyton decided, and pulled out one of the white metal chairs to sit down. Julie stood up at the same moment. Peyton looked at her quizzically, then at the table, where a glass and a greasy plate sat.

"I'm sorry," she said, and for a terrifying moment he was sure she had been reading his mind.

"W-what?" he managed to stammer.

"Sorry I have to leave. I'm running late already. Big meeting popped up, and Pappas couldn't make it. He sent me instead." She picked up a briefcase from the cement and stuck it under one arm. "This is big, Peyton. Bigger than I've ever handled before."

He slumped in his chair. She cast him a sweet smile. "You're such a dear," she said, and bent to stroke his cheek. "Try the mutton hock today. Sounds like pure puke, I know, but Christ, is it good. See you tonight, right?"

She gave him a peck on the lips, then hustled away. Peyton sat frowning, not quite ready to digest any of this. His eyes widened as it sank in. For God's sake, he was supposed to propose today!

He jumped up and hurried after her. She was hailing a cab,

25

one arm waving. For her, of course, a cab appeared instantly. Peyton rushed to chase her down.

"Julie, wait!" he called. He fumbled at the lump in his pocket as he ran, managing finally to pull it free. He held it overhead like a trophy. "Julieeee!"

She opened the door of the cab and set her briefcase inside. Peyton rushed up and grabbed at her arm. The cabbie looked on, frowning.

"Julie," Peyton said, breathing hard.

She sat down on the tattered seat. "What's the matter?"

"I've been thinking. Maybe we should . . . maybe we ought to get . . . married?"

Her blue eyes became larger. "Marriage? Well, we could do that, I suppose. Of course, there's our careers. I mean, I'm just starting to get used to the firm. And you know I kind of like having my own place."

He shook his head furiously. "We're practically living together now. All marriage means is that we only get one listing in the phone book. What about kids?"

She looked stricken. "I—I can't talk about this now. I'm late. And there's—"

"Just say yes," he implored, practically on bended knee. "Julie, I'm asking you to marry me. Please?"

The cabbie, delighted with all this, spoke up. "Hey, Mac," he said, "have you got a ring in that box, or is that where you keep your dirty socks?" He laughed uproariously at his keen wit.

Peyton straightened. "Ring? Holy Christ!" He handed the box to her and she opened it. She gasped. The driver leaned close to Julie. "If you ask me," he said, "this fellow doesn't show much commitment. Or common sense."

She gave him a furious glare that made him turn back around to his own business. He ratcheted the meter, grumbling, and it began to tick.

"Peyton, I love the necklace, but we'll have to talk later. This is all too fast for me."

"But I love you," Peyton said, panicked. He could see it all crumbling. Why hadn't he waited for a romantic evening to drop this bombshell?

"And I love you," she said. "But I've got to think about it."

That said, she shut the door and the cab pulled away with a brief screech of its tires. One cabbie, highly irritated; one Peyton sinking into despair.

He hailed a taxi. None stopped.

He had to walk eleven blocks before anybody took pity on him, and by then he was so deep in the mental cesspool called depression that he no longer cared.

3

Julie

THE TAXI DROPPED her off eighteen miles out of town, at the
Felix Heights Hunting Club, a nose-in-the-air outfit if she had
ever seen one, very posh and pooh-pooh. The front entrance
was as beautiful as a grand European hotel. Sculptured marble horses the size of merry-go-round ponies flanked the huge
double doors, prancing eternally to nowhere. A fountain was
splashing somewhere beyond the hedges; aging men shambled about in ridiculous-looking jodhpurs and knee-high
boots, bleary eyed, martinis in hand. A fat woman was preparing to tee off on the distant golf course. When Julie saw
all this as she walked to the door, she was suddenly gripped
by the fear that she might not be as well dressed as she should
be. After all, this place was simply crawling with upper-crust
types, most of them ugly and old, no doubt about it, but since
most of them had more money in the bank than, say, Scrooge
McDuck, they could afford to fool themselves.

She looked down at herself, feeling oddly naked and vul-
nerable. She was wearing a corporate power suit, the standard version that Sears peddled through the mail to all those
executive women who wanted to look like small men: shirt,
tie, the works. This suit happened to be green, which she
found strangely inappropriate at this moment. Hadn't she read
somewhere that you never wear a green suit if you want to
impress somebody. God, had she blown it already?

Get a grip on yourself, she thought, snarling inwardly, and adjusted her hair with nervous little sweeps of her hand. She discovered, with a burst of horrified shock, that she was wearing a hat. It was pinned in her hair. It was stylish as hell, but it was also very green. She felt suddenly like a frumpy housewife with a head eternally full of curlers, or the party guest who invariable winds up wearing a lamp shade, much to everyone's disgust. The hat was very heavy, almost enough to topple her over. She quickly unpinned it, looked around, and shoved it into a dark nook in the hedges. The pins followed.

She discovered also that she needed to go to the bathroom. With her mutton hock at Bowser's, she had downed three or four glasses of Zinfandel Auslese, a German import that seemed to go well with anything. Almost anything. Her kidneys were manning the pumps in a frenzy, stretching her overworked bladder inexorably to the full mark on the gauge. She hurried inside, expecting to see the clients standing around grumpily checking their watches. Julie put on a false smile as she entered the foyer of the giant club.

No one there looked even remotely familiar. Two old geezers were examining an ancient flintlock rifle. Three others dressed in colorful plaid pantaloons were comparing putters, one of them loudly arguing that a Glen Cook was the best ever made; whatever a Glen Cook might be, Julie had no idea and didn't want one.

She looked around, her nose picking up the scent of luxurious new carpet and cigar smoke. There were no doors except the ones behind her. Where was the john in this joint, anyway?

She walked up to the men arguing over their putters, cleared her throat, and waited for the clamor to die down. They hesitated in mid-sentence and stared at her.

"Excuse me," she said, smiling uneasily, "but could you gentlemen tell me where the ladies' room might be?"

One of them raised a finger and pointed it at her chest. "She's impartial," he crowed. "Ask her!"

She got a faceful of putters and a demand to choose the best one. She raised her hands and backed away. "I'm afraid I don't golf."

"All the better," one of them roared, sloshing his martini all over his shoes and the thick red carpet. "She's impartial to the bone!"

"Mine's a Hogan original," another said. "Wooden shaft. See?"

She saw without an inkling of interest. "How nice. The ladies' room?"

"Over thataways." He jerked a thumb over his shoulder. "I use the same one as Arnie Palmer, and by God, if it's good enough for Arnie, it's good enough for me."

"What?" number three said. "You mean to tell me Arnie uses the ladies' room?"

They broke apart, howling, coughing, generally getting red in the face. Julie slunk away, feeling very much like the center of attention, which she did not want to be. There was a row of potted palms on the right, and she wished she could dive in. Her nerves had already turned the day sour.

And Peyton, good God, Peyton. Of all the worst moments to pop the question, he had to go and do it today. Her mind was too full of worries and pressing concerns, too filled up with doubt to handle a sticky point like marriage, kids, one telephone listing. Her thoughts were scattering like autumn leaves. For one brief second she wished Pappas were here to guide her. But no, she decided, she had to sink or swim on her own.

She found the ladies' room, much to her relief. While she washed her hands she caught a glimpse of herself in the mirror: blond, slim, attractive, terrified, green. Damn the color, damn the terror. She dug in her purse and hauled her lipstick out, along with an amazing amount of other junk. She shoveled it back in, pausing for a moment to look at the strip of photo-booth pictures for which she and Peyton, just for fun, had posed a week or so ago at the carnival. In the first picture they both sat grim and stony. The next one had them making faces. The third was them kissing while Peyton made rabbit ears behind her head. The fourth was a hand reaching for the camera. Yes, it had been fun, quite hilarious. Looking at these pictures brought back a measure of composure, and she did her lipstick with hands that were no longer shaking. An hour from now it would be over, she would have done just fine, and the deal Pappas should have handled would be wrapped up and finished. Now was not the time to lose her nerve.

She went out and asked a very nice old gent where the kitchen might be found. He was kind enough to take her arm in arm and show her. For his trouble Julie did not smack him when he dug his fingers into her fanny. Instead she thanked him and disappeared inside . . .

. . . and returned five minutes later, just in time to greet her new clients at the door. She was smiling radiantly with what she hoped was a measure of authority—the perfect lawyer, slick, suave, unimpeachable, in command. Of course she felt none of these, but the little excursion through the kitchen had eased her nerves remarkably. At least she had a plan now.

She recognized the elderly Louis Strack from photos Pappas had prepped her with. Tall, slightly stooped, old enough to die but rich enough to hire someone else for the job, as Pappas had joked. Beside him as he came through the doors was his son Louis Strack, Jr., a somewhat short but powerfully built man Julie guessed to be in his late thirties. His black hair was impeccably styled, as opposed to his father's, which was a wispy gray tangle. Strack Senior looked positively grumpy; Strack Junior smiled at Julie as she approached.

"Mr. Strack," she said, offering her hand, "so nice to meet you. I'm Julie Hastings, here from Pappas and Swain to represent you in the Von Hoffenstein negotiation."

"Charmed," he murmured, and for a wild second she thought he was going to kiss her hand. A brief chill rippled up her spine, and she wondered why.

Why? her inner voice chided. *The man's a dream boat and filthy rich to boot. Most women would melt. As it is, you're simply wilting.*

She forced herself to stop wilting. Strack Junior was saying something.

"Please call me Louis, if I may call you Julie. This is my father—"

"Goddammit," his father barked in a rattly voice. "I don't need some fancy-ass woman to do my negotiating. Where the hell's Pappas at?"

Julie flashed him one of her best smiles. "Mr. Pappas is tied up in litigation this week. Don't worry, I've done my homework." She hefted her briefcase. "It's all in here."

"Fine," he snapped. "I'll stop worrying when Von Ball-breaker drops his price down to sixty million."

"I think we can do better than that, Mr. Strack. My figures show—"

"Just get him down to sixty," Strack grumbled. "If he goes lower than that, he's insane."

He stomped off. Two or three aides hurried to follow, all of them looking like hungry weasels, which Julie supposed they were. Hangers-on waiting for a nickel or dime to fall out of the old man's pocket. She turned to the more pleasant visage of Louis Junior, or, as she corrected herself, just Louis.

"Shall we?" he asked.

"We shall," she said.

He walked her upstairs to the conference room, exuding charm and a confidence she hoped was infectious. Inside the conference room an Austrian moneybags named Baron Hugo Von Hoffenstein was waiting, along with his lawyer, Myron Katz. Pappas had briefed her about these guys: They played hardball all the time. At stake was a chunk of riverfront property the good Baron wanted to part with. In return he was asking only seventy-five million dollars. Sums like this were staggering to Julie; she had enough trouble with her own budget. But Pappas and Swain, attorneys-at-law, stood to make a few million of their own from this deal. All of this sat uneasily on Julie's shoulders. Pappas had told her she would do fine, but the tone of his voice carried something rather sinister. Julie read it as a veiled threat: This was do-or-die for her future with the firm, and her career just might go swirling down the tubes if she botched it.

Thus it was that she entered the conference room to face the Baron and his lawyer with her knees knocking together and her mouth as dry as dust. Louis held the chair for her. Whatta guy, she thought crazily as she put her briefcase on the massive conference table. She sat down and prepared to do battle with her nerves and the big fat Baron. Behind him was a huge window, through which she could see the golf course and several bridle paths. Ah, to be out there with no cares, dallying among the sand traps instead of here, where traps big enough to fall into waited at every turn. What a life.

A waiter in red and a wine steward in white came in and placed delicate wineglasses on the table, then stood by, waiting for the Baron to order. He made idiotic faces while he debated what year and brand to choose, finally coming up with an '86 Cabernet Maison Rême. The steward went out and came back several minutes later with a bottle nestled in a chrome sleeve. He stood by, calmly waiting for the Baron to get around to having the bottle opened for the mandatory taste test. Julie resisted the urge to charge over and snatch the whole thing out of its bed of ice and slug it down, but no, her entire future might hinge on that bottle.

Katz propped his elbows on the table and stared at Julie. She squirmed inside. This was one of the Big Guys, hard as Krupp steel. His pale eyes seemed to gleam with a malevolent hatred. Still staring at her, he laid out his proposition. "We want to be reasonable here," he said. "We indicated we were interested in selling the pier frontage, and we are indeed interested. But frankly, Herr Von Hoffenstein will not be robbed. Seventy-five strikes us as a fair price for this parcel. We're ready to conclude a deal here and now at that price. Do you follow me, Ms. Hastings?"

She gave him a false smile, fighting the urge to stick her tongue out at him. "Indeed I do, Mr. Katz. It seems we are missing only one element in this deal."

"Oh?" He raised his eyebrows. "What might that be?"

"An interested party."

Louis pressed a hand over his mouth, hiding a smile. He tipped Julie a wink. The Baron sat looking old and frumpy and fat. He snapped his fingers and the waiter began to assault the cork. When it was out, he poured the Baron a sip and stood back, the bottle wrapped professionally in a white towel, awaiting a verdict. Von Hoffenstein made more faces as he checked it out. He swallowed and nodded. Wine was served around the table.

"Mr. Katz," Julie said, "I've found that in the real-estate business there are three factors which determine a property's value."

Katz seemed interested.

"Number one, location. Number two, location. And three . . . well, I'm sure you've guessed it. Location. Unfortunately you have none of the above. Your price is fair for midtown commercial, not for riverfront."

Katz did not flinch. "It's worth more than that to your client, considering his plans for the area."

"If my client can spin straw into gold, he'll still pay market price for the straw. Our offer stands at forty-eight million."

The Baron smiled, nodding. "Very well, then. Business is business, and deals will come and go. But the world will pause for a beautiful woman and a fine wine. Now, let us toast a sale at the price of sixty million."

The elder Strack started to lift his glass, doubtless glad to see the price just where he wanted it. Julie stomped on his foot and he almost spilled his glass. "You're moving in the right direction," she said, "but our offer stands firm at forty-eight."

She sipped the wine as Katz and the Baron held a whispered conversation. She frowned and turned to the wine steward. "Sir, there's been a mistake. The Baron ordered a bottle of '86 Cabernet Maison Rême. Isn't that right?"

He bowed slightly. "*Qui, madame*, that is what I have served."

She took another sip, frowning harder. "No. You have served us an '87 or '88. California Beaujolais. Pleasant, but hardly worth what you must be charging the good Baron."

Old Strack examined his glass as if a fly had crash-landed in it. He made a face.

The wine steward looked stricken. "But madame! I have served the Rême!"

Strack took a sip. "Tastes okay to me. Let's get on with this."

Katz spoke up. "Ms. Hastings, the wine is fine. You're way out of your league here, and I'm sure the wine steward knows more about fine wine than you ever will."

Von Hoffenstein plucked the bottle out of the ice. He pulled the towel away from the label, then smiled and showed it to everyone. "California San Meduso 1988. The lady is correct. Steward!"

The steward stared at it, aghast. He snapped his fingers at

the waiter, who began snatching up glasses. "Please forgive us," the steward said. "We will bring the Rême at once. Gratis, of course."

"Of course," Julie said, then turned to the Baron. "At any rate, our offer still stands at forty-eight." She pushed her chair back and stood up. "Gentlemen, if we can't toast to a deal closed, we prefer not to drink at all. We have other business to attend to, so if you'll excuse us, we'll go."

The elder Strack got up, grumbling. "I thought I told you to make this deal," he snapped at her as he passed. Louis got up, unperturbed. They went to the door just as the new wine was brought.

"Wait!" the Baron called, and they turned. "As you say, the price is indeed forty-eight million, for this is too fine a wine not to use for a toast." He raised his glass. *"Prosit? Zur Gesundheit?"*

"Zur Gesundheit," Julie said, mentally shaking hands with herself. "And to everything else as well."

4

Stracks

WALKING TOWARD THE lobby, past gilt-framed paintings of
one hundred years' worth of past superintendents of the Felix
Heights Hunting Club, Louis Strack, Jr., was in high spirits.
That cute lawyer, that Julie girl—man, what a performance.
The mistake with the wine—pure genius. Von Hoffenstein
was as good as putty in her hands. Even his shyster lawyer,
Katz, had wound up speechless. Yet Julie had been terrified,
Louis knew. Her hands had been cold and shaking when he
walked her upstairs. She seemed to have difficulty swallowing. But once things began to roll, once she was allowed to
take the ball, some kind of inner resolve had turned her nervousness into authority. She even had been able to make an
ass out of that Katz guy, and did he ever deserve it.

He heard the whisper of feet behind him and slowed. Julie
caught up and beamed at him. "Satisfied, Louis?"

He nodded. "More than that. You saved us twelve million
bucks. Pappas is a fool for not using you before. I assume
this was your first taste of a multimillion-dollar real-estate
transaction."

"How'd you guess?" She laughed when he rolled his eyes.

Louis said, "How much of a bribe did you give the wine
steward?"

She looked shocked. "Well, I never!"

"I'd say you've already started. Down the road to petty crime, I mean."

She laughed again. The wine steward came down the stairs, and she stepped aside to talk to him. Louis saw a flash of green that had nothing to do with her suit. She came back, looking a little too nonchalant.

"Fifty bucks?" he asked her.

"I'm not that cheap."

"Hundred?"

"Do you really think that man would sell his reputation for a hundred dollars?"

"I do."

"Well, he did too."

They laughed together. Louis's father was already at the door, looking no less crabby than he had before the deal was clinched. Louis knew one thing for sure: The old man was getting grouchier and more senile every day. His idea of making money for Strack Industries dealt only with real estate. There was a fortune to be made out there with stocks, commodities, gold, silver, bonds, you name it. The old guy was a fossil, a detriment to the company he had founded so many years ago. If he would ever retire, Strack Industries could branch off in new directions, make bigger profits. Not that Louis needed the money. It was the power money could buy that he was interested in, though he had only vague ideas what to do with it once he got it.

He turned back to Julie. "Could I meet you for dinner tonight?" He looked at her left hand. "I don't see a ring, so I hope you don't mind me being brash like this."

"You're not brash at all," she said. "But I already have plans."

"What's his name?"

"Peyton. Peyton Westlake."

"Weird name."

"Nice guy."

He grinned. "All right, I fold. Maybe in a few weeks?"

"Doubtful."

"Must be one hell of a man. Since you're a lawyer, can I ask if you're into his briefs?"

She drew back. "Now *that* was brash."

37

They laughed again. At the doors, old Strack watched them sourly. A long white limousine drew up and he went out.

"Need a ride?" Louis asked.

She deliberated for a moment, then: "Probably better not. I might . . ."

He frowned amicably enough. "Don't say it, Julie, because then I'll get my hopes up. And I hate having my hopes dashed."

She smiled. "Fine, then. I'll take a cab."

"Good enough. Can I, um, call you sometime?"

"For business?"

He raised his hands. "Strictly business, madame."

"That would be fine." She extended a hand. "Nice working with you, Louis."

He shook her hand. "My pleasure."

He opened the door for her and she went out. Louis watched her go, smiling a bit. If that guy with the funny first name ever let this one go, Louis would be there to catch her; he knew that as fact.

The limousine honked. Louis saw the old man poking the chauffeur on the shoulder, forcing him to honk like some damn taxi driver. He ground his teeth. God, but the doddering old coot was getting cranky lately. Louis made a mental note to buy him a bottle of Geritol, if the old man lived long enough to drink it. It was obvious to everyone that he was failing.

He got in the back with Pop and made himself a drink to wash the anger away. The limo pulled out smoothly, and when he finished his drink, Louis buried himself in a fresh copy of the *Wall Street Journal*. Strack Senior was studying financial reports. The silence between them grew long, but it was nothing new. They had had nothing to say to each other in years, except an occasional brief argument over financial this and financial that.

An article caught his eye. Krugerrands were on the rise again. He read it, almost drooling. Real estate could go to hell; here was *real* money. He lowered the paper. "Krugerrands are looking attractive, Dad."

Strack snorted. "Krugerrands. Bah. Strack Industries will stick with real estate. You remember that, sonny."

Sonny? How swell. Now Pop thought Louis was a kid again. It was a miracle his brains weren't leaking out his ears.

The chauffeur drove into a small, run-down gas station. Strack craned forward. "What now?"

"Flat tire, sir."

"Oh, goody. This will come out of your wages, you know. This vehicle is your responsibility. Got that?"

"Indeed, sir."

The driver got out. He walked to the errant wheel and stooped down. He reached into his uniform pocket and withdrew an ice pick. He drove it into the tire, which was remarkably full of air for a flat tire, pulled it out, then went to the trunk and opened it. A minute later Strack got out, grumbling about his prostate being bigger than a bowling ball. He headed off to find a rest room, stopping long enough to examine the tire.

It was flat.

"Damn tires cost a billion bucks nowadays," he muttered, blinking under the harsh sunlight. "Damn shitty driver."

Off he went. Twenty yards away, a man wearing a stuffy-looking blue suit was hurrying toward the station. He held a rolled-up newspaper in his hand. Strack didn't notice, and if he had, he wouldn't have cared. Peeing in this fleabag of a gas station was his uppermost worry now. What if germs were floating around in the air?

The man in the suit came inexorably closer, not quite so fast now, pacing himself. He was grinning, showing plenty of white teeth. He hooked a cigar out of a pocket and stuck it in his mouth. He was five yards from old Strack now, on an intercept course. In the car, Louis sat daydreaming about Krugerrands.

The man aimed his newspaper, revealing a dark rod of sorts hidden inside. There was a brief orange flash and a small pop! Strack clutched his chest, staggering forward by force of inertia only. The man caught him. They danced a wobbling tango.

Still in the car, Louis looked up. His view was blocked by the station's double pumps, and the driver, who was lugging the bad tire around the car. Louis looked back down to his newspaper, unconcerned.

The man dropped Strack, who landed on the cable of the electronic bell. It began to ring, about once every three seconds. He reached into a pocket and withdrew a gold-plated cigar trimmer, freshly washed now, sparkling clean. He bent over and clipped off the old man's left index finger, squeezed the blood out of it, then stuck it and the trimmer back into his clothes. He ambled away and disappeared around the back of the station.

Louis looked up, irritated by the bell. Why couldn't this dump have a rubber hose you drive over that rings the bell? Chalk one up to modern science: They finally had invented a better bell but, sadly, one that never shut up.

He got out, wincing as the hot September air enfolded him. He walked around the double pumps and saw his father lying facedown in the dust. Had the old jerk-off finally keeled over?

He went to him, knelt, and turned him over. There was a blot of blood on his chest, an ugly flower. Louis stared at it with large eyes.

Behind him, a midnight-blue Lincoln Continental pulled away, not in a hurry, almost soundless. The man behind the tinted windows had lit himself a cigar.

Louis saw none of this. Robert G. Durant and his vehicle disappeared unharmed and unseen.

Louis cradled his father in his arms, lifting him off the electronic cable. He clutched him tight.

The bell stopped ringing.

5

Julie

THE FOLLOWING MORNING in Peyton's apartment, Julie made two rather disturbing discoveries. The first was a short article in the morning newspaper that sketchily outlined what had happened to the elder Strack. The other was a single sheet of paper she found in her briefcase, along with hundreds of less interesting documents. It was obvious that it was not intended for her eyes.

Peyton came out of the bathroom wearing a robe, scrubbing his hair with a towel, while Julie pondered the meaning of this particular memo, the one not intended for her. It was the documentation of an obvious bribe paid by Strack Industries to a certain Claude Bellasarious, dated July twelfth of last year. It was not good news.

Peyton drew up behind her while she debated the pros and cons of spilling the beans or keeping her mouth shut. By spilling the beans, she would embarrass the surviving Louis Strack and most likely lose her position of trust—Pappas and Swain would be dumped out of Strack Industries like so much useless garbage. By keeping her mouth shut, she could expect to have a long and profitable relationship with the firm. Somewhere in between lay her own sense of decency and professional ethics.

"Coffee?" he asked.

She didn't hear him. Christ, a woman busts her ass to make

it big, compete with the boys, and then something this nasty chances along and ruins everything. To remain mum or not to? A hell of a question.

"Coffee?"

She nodded without hearing. Peyton shrugged and got her a cup. By then she had set the incriminating memo aside and had her chin propped on her hand, chagrined, bewildered, basically unhappy.

"Just like you like it," he said, and set the cup on the coffee table, right on top of the memo.

"No!" she cried, but it was too late. She picked the cup up and saw the wet brown ring on the memo. It hadn't ruined it by any means, but it would make weird evidence in court.

"You're being eaten alive," Peyton said, and sat beside her. "Inner demons?"

"Outer ones," she said glumly. "Can you bring me the phone?"

He looked around. His apartment was a catastrophe, obviously the victim of a terrorist's bomb, so piled with junk that the floor seemed about to collapse. He scouted around, tossing old newspapers and pizza boxes aside. His bare foot clunked against something that rang, and he carried it to her. "When the hell are you going to clean up this dump," he growled at her. "Surely you don't expect *me* to do it."

She tried to smile but it wouldn't work. She dialed Pappas and Swain, glad that she was already dressed and ready to go. It might be a long day.

The receptionist connected her directly to Pappas, whom Julie assumed was just on his way out and headed for court. He clicked on. "Pappas."

"Yeah," Julie said, thinking hard. "This is Julie Hastings, Mr. Pappas. I found a memo while I was researching the Von Hoffenstein deal I don't think I was supposed to find. It's from the late Mr. Strack to a guy named Claude Bellasarious. It's a record of payments to various people on the zoning commission."

His reply was curt. "Bribes."

"Well, they do look like payoffs. What I'd like to do is talk to Strack's son first, give him the benefit of the doubt. After that we'll have to decide how to handle this."

"Fine."

Click!

She looked at the phone, chagrined. "Nice talking to you, too, fella."

Peyton laughed. "Someday you'll be a partner in the firm and you can fire old Pappas."

She didn't smile, simply put the phone back together and worked at closing her bulging briefcase. Peyton pressed on it to help. "A good-morning kiss, perhaps?" He turned his head and puckered up. "Just one for the obvious road you're about to be on?"

She stood up, not even there anymore. Her eyes were vacuous, her face dark and set. She hefted her briefcase and made for the door. Peyton tagged along. "See you tonight? The proposal still stands, if you'll have me." He got the door slammed in his face for his trouble. He put his hands on his hips and regarded it, thinking that if he thought *his* job was tough, look at hers. He turned, shaking his head, then saw something that almost made him laugh.

The deadly memo with its coffee stain was still on the table.

He got dressed for another long day down at the river. Before he left, he folded the memo quite neatly and stuck it in his shirt pocket. Most likely Julie would show up at the shack looking for him and the memo, since the lab was closer. She would be pleased to know he was so thoughtful.

He polished off his coffee and went out, already debating whether he should have a sausage-and-mushroom pizza for breakfast, or go crazy and have them toss on some green peppers too.

Strack's secretary allowed Julie in without hesitation, without even ringing Louis. She pointed to a door, a useless gesture because the words LOUIS STRACK, JR. were on an engraved nameplate, and said to go on in.

Julie shrugged to herself. This was better treatment than she got at Pappas and Swain. Louis was one considerate man. A crook, probably, but considerate as hell. She tapped on the door, anyway, got no response, and went in. Louis had his

43

back to her, staring through the huge window to the city below. He was on the phone.

"Yes, that's a buy on the Krugerrands. The price won't get any better. And thank you for your kindness, Franz. It will be difficult to fill my father's shoes."

He turned as he hung up and saw Julie standing half in and half out of the door, looking pretty much like a crook herself. "Julie! What a pleasant surprise! Get on in here and let me look at you."

She went in and clicked the door softly shut, then stood there, feeling awkward. He motioned to a chair in front of his huge executive's desk. "Take a load off, Julie. And for God's sake, let me see that smile again."

She sat down, unable to smile. She put her briefcase on her lap and popped the latches.

"Can I get you something?" he asked. "Coffee? Brandy? Maison Rême 1987?"

Now she did smile. He seemed pleased. "No thanks, Louis," she said. "I've been going over some documents and I came across something that puzzles me. It's a memo from your office to a Mr. Claude Bellasarious. It carries your father's signature. It details certain payments—"

"My father," Louis repeated sadly. "Did you hear?"

She almost slapped herself. "Good grief, Louis, I am so sorry. You've got all the condolences I can offer." She almost stood up. "I'll just go out and come back in, start all over."

He smiled. "Don't feel so terrible. My father had been on death's doorstep the last five or ten years. Bum ticker." He poked a finger at his heart. "It was inevitable."

She frowned. "I thought he got shot."

"Indeed. At least it ended his suffering. The best the police can come up with yet is that a hunter or sport shooter let a bullet fly where it shouldn't. It hit his hand and ricocheted into his chest. Happens occasionally. Last year a teenage girl was shot dead while driving on the freeway. The hunter was almost a mile away." He tapped a finger behind his ear. "Killed her instantly."

"I think I read about that. Please forgive my stupidity."

He smiled. "Your intelligence is not a matter of debate. Now, what's this about a Claude, ah, Bellery? Benson?"

44

"Bellasarious. The memo spells it out pretty clearly." She lifted the lid of her briefcase and soon found, to her horror, that the memo was gone. She remembered the coffee and that she'd laid the paper aside to dry. She had a sudden, almost desperate desire to cry.

"Ah," Louis said, and began to pace his spacious office. "Yes, I know the memo."

"You mean . . . you've read it?"

"It?" He looked slightly ill. "Them, you mean. Hundreds, though not quite so well documented as the one in question."

She frowned. "It seems like a record of some strange payments."

"They were payoffs," he said without hesitation. "Payoffs to the zoning commission. Bribes, to call a spade a spade."

"Then you knew?"

"Of course." He looked at her with an appraising eye. "Does that shock you?"

She sighed. "Actually, it does. But worst of all, I think, is that is disappoints me. But it's not my place to pass judgment."

He continued to pace, his fingers linked behind his back. "That's true, it is not your place. However, as Strack Industries' consulting attorney, I do value your opinion."

"Does that mean you expect me to endorse the practice? Give my okay for bribes?"

"Of course not. You weren't supposed to know about them. That memo was not supposed to circulate, and you can bet your ass my secretary will be pounding the pavement tomorrow looking for a new job." He slammed a fist into his open palm. "God, I wished this had never happened!"

"But it did," she said coolly.

"Right. It did. But I am asking you to have some understanding here. I'm not going to bore you with that old speech about how we all have to swim in the same pond. But you know as well as I do that not so much as one mini-mall ever went up in this city without some grease being applied to the greedy palms downtown."

She deliberated. Did she know? If so, had it never struck her that someday she would be one of the greasers? She shook

45

her head. "I believe in the old saw, the one that says honesty is the best—"

"Policy. Right. But you're not naïve. You know it's just part of the cost of doing business. Ordinarily people don't have to face it, but I face it every day. And I don't let it turn me into a cynic. That's the chicken way out, and I'm tougher than that. I don't let it distract me from my dream. Come here and look at this."

She put her briefcase on the floor and followed. There was a large, thick beige curtain covering most of the south wall. He pressed a button and it slid open. A light popped on. On a huge table perhaps ten feet long was a scale architectural model, fantastically detailed down to the trees and shrubs and tiny cars in the parking lots. It looked like a wonderful toy for a very rich child.

"This is Project Riverfront Development. What you see here is what everyone will see within three years: that trashy, polluted mud flat turned into a jewel. Dust into diamonds. Poverty into wealth. Take a long look at this model, Julie. It is the final touch of a dream. Acres of riverfront reclaimed from decay, thousands of jobs created, a building block—a very *large* building block—laid for the future. Not such a bad dream, as dreams go. And if the price of making this dream come true is greasing a few palms, well . . . I don't run away. I say, 'so be it.' So"—he held his hands out to her, wrists together, palms up—"'gonna book me?"

She smiled in spite of herself. What a guy.

"The point is, Julie, that my father is well beyond the reach of the law, but that memo could embarrass Strack Industries."

"I get the point, Louis," she said. "But the fact remains that I'm in possession of evidence about the commission of a crime, and you can no more ask me to destroy it than I could ask you to destroy one of your new buildings."

He passed his fingertips over his mouth, staring at the floor, debating. Then he brightened. "Let me suggest this. You excuse yourself for a few minutes, go to the ladies' room or some such, leaving your briefcase here. What happens to the memorandum while it's in my custody is my responsibility. Good?"

46

"Very good, and I wish it were that simple. First of all, I don't even have the memo with me. Second, I need to discuss this with one of the partners at Pappas and Swain. Did . . . perhaps . . . Pappas know anything about this?"

He shook his head. "Not a chance. You are privvy to some very secret things."

"Okay, then. I'll talk to Pappas over the weekend."

He darkened. "That would be a very grave mistake."

She flinched, her eyes growing wider. "Are you threatening me?"

He moved with her and touched her arm. "I'm trying to protect you. Does the name Robert G. Durant mean anything to you?"

"Sure. He's an underworld figure. Racketeering, drugs, the usual stuff."

"And real estate, Julie. Robert Durant is a competitor for the riverfront and knows about the memo. Several times he has broken in here and trashed the place trying to find it. We even found blowtorch burns on the safe." He smiled grimly. "He is a very dangerous man, Julie, and he will freely resort to crime to get what he wants. I'm not exaggerating when I say he's dangerous."

"I understand," Julie said, "and frankly I'm not sure what to do. You'll have to trust me over the weekend so I have time to figure this out."

He nodded, looking strangely sad. "Is that the best I can get?"

"For now, Louis."

"All right, then." He offered her a hand, which she accepted, confused. "I'm in your hands now, Julie. Together we'll see this thing through. Coffee now, or would you like that brandy?"

She chose coffee. And then, mercifully both for him and for her, they chatted about other things.

Four hours later she was in her tiny office at Pappas and Swain, attorneys-at-law, who were perpetually busy with other high-paying things, leaving the lion's share of petty legal duties, research, and minor torts to the underdogs, Julie and the like. She had a yellow legal pad on her cluttered desk,

47

and she was writing. Her free hand fingered the gold necklace
as she wrote:

Julie Hastings
Mrs. Peyton Westlake
Mrs. Julie Hastings-Westlake
Peyton's Old Lady

She smiled and threw the pen against a stack of unread briefs
in bulging folders, a stack that crawled all the way up the
wall and almost to the ceiling in the far corner of this oversize
closet of an office. And then she went to lunch, though she
wasn't even hungry.

She got back an hour later and dialed Peyton's lab phone
to see if he had the memorandum, or if it was still at his
apartment.

"Groovy," she said aloud as the phone rang and rang.
"Hey, Peyton baby! This is your old lady calling!"

But no one answered.

6

Peyton

AT THE SAME moment Julie was beginning her discussion with Louis Strack, Peyton was hiking through the weeds and cattails that infested the riverbank, making his way toward the crumbling nightmare that was his cut-rate laboratory. The air was thick and humid on this Friday, the stench of the river blowing off the water like a putrid gas. Peyton reminded himself that as soon as this skin thing was over (for better or for worse), he would conquer pollution. After that he would take a year off in Tahiti.

Yakky was already waiting at the door. He popped to his feet and almost bowed; Peyton suppressed a smile.

"Good morning to you, Yak, old chum. How's the world?"

Yakky looked perplexed. "The world? Well, I believe there is a famine under way in Africa. A jet plane crashed last night and killed everybody. The weather is supposed to be hot today, and—"

"Please," Peyton said. "Local news only."

"Huh?"

"Never mind." He unlocked the door and waved Yakky in. "Today we make a breakthrough, Yak, and may the nasty ninety-nine plague us no more. Stopwatch ready and able?"

"Stopwatch upstairs, Dr. Westlake."

"Peyton, Yakky. Just Peyton."

"Okay, Dr. Peyton."

They went up the stairs. Yakky eyed the ruined fifth step hatefully; Peyton stepped over it as if it had been broken years ago. "Sorry I didn't make it back yesterday," he said. "I got tied up with some personal stuff. I owe you a pizza, I guess."

Personal stuff? You mean, like making a total ass of yourself at Bowser's, where people eat on the effing sidewalk?

"Is no problem, Dr. Peyton. I locked up good."

"I knew you could handle it, Yak. Did you see what happened to the skin at ninety-nine minutes?"

"Yes. It melted. It was almost on fire. Didn't smell good, either."

"Did you cut a slice of it and watch the cell destruction under the microscope?"

"Uh-huh, but I was almost too late. Complete fragmentation. The skin self-destructed. How come?"

At the top of the stairs, Peyton flipped the light on. The lone bulb stuttered on, not seeming sure if it wanted to do this today. "Yak," he said, "if I knew why its life span is only ninety-nine minutes, I would be a happy man indeed."

"Have you tried an alkaline solution?" Yakky asked, slipping into a fresh lab coat. "Maybe ten percent?"

Peyton smiled sadly as he rummaged through the bag for a coat. "You're good, Yak, but yes, I've tried ten percent, twenty, even fifty or more. They all were busts."

"Bust?"

"Failure."

"So what next?"

"We keep on trying, I guess. Any more suggestions?"

Yakky shrugged. "Maybe try some heat?"

"Sorry. Heat speeds up the fragmentation."

Yakky walked over to the lab table beside the computer. He picked up what remained of the nose Peyton had made yesterday. It was mushy and dripping, looking for all the world like wet toilet paper. There were large blisters and holes in it. Yakky made a face. "How about electricity? You use it to make the substance, so why not keep it charged?"

Peyton sat down on a tall metal stool and hooked his heels on the bottom rung. He put his hands together. "That would be defeating the purpose, Yak. This is supposed to be synthetic skin for burn victims. Are they supposed to walk around with a dozen car batteries on their backs? Actually, I *did* try electricity. Results: el crappo.''

"Crappo?"

"Failure."

Yakky frowned. "Some language this English is. You have five words for the same thing."

"Keeps us occupied," Peyton said. "Any more brainstorms?"

"Brainstorms?"

Peyton sighed. "Ideas, Yak. Got any more?"

He thought about it. "How about freezing?"

"What, and keep the patient in a meat locker for the rest of his life? No way."

"Some sort of sealant? To keep the air away from the artificial tissue?"

"And have the patient walk around inside a giant Glad bag?"

"Glad bag?"

"Ah, Christ. Let's just make a batch and see what happens. What would you like today? Lips? Chin?"

"How about a whole face? Have you ever tried that?"

"Just makes a bigger mess when it fragments." Peyton hung his head. "Yak, why in the hell can't I give up on this? Thirty thousand dollars and fifteen months later, I'm back where I started. The vivification process was easy. Tissue rejection? I beat that monster. So what's missing? Why can't I make the cells stable? Tell you what—why don't we chuck everything out the window and see what floats."

He saw Yakky doing mental battles with his vocabulary. "Chuck equals toss, Yak. See what floats means see if anything is salvageable. Oh, no. Salvageable means worth saving. Follow me?"

Yakky took off his half-pound glasses and wiped them on his shirt. "Certainly, Dr. Peyton. In Osaka I was the best English talker of the whole school."

"Any more ideas, then, you English talker, you?"

"Pizza break?"

"Sounds fine. Do you like green peppers?"

Yakky wagged a hand. "So-so."

"Let's find the phone, then." He pointed to the floor. "Follow that wire."

Yakky followed it. The phone was behind the aquarium tank of pink soup, for reasons only Peyton might know. Yakky carried it to him.

"Got this one memorized," Peyton said, bringing the receiver to his ear. He frowned suddenly. "Wait, I forgot my wallet. Have you got any cash?"

"Not until payday."

"To hell with it." He put the receiver back onto the cradle. "Let's make you a new face."

Yakky found his stopwatch and hung it around his neck while Peyton fiddled with the camera. He posed, and after the strange, waffled-looking pictures rolled out, Peyton began to process them through the computer. Yakky looked on without much obvious interest. Peyton guessed he would last about three weeks before going insane. Oh, well.

He fed electricity to the electrodes on either side of the reservoir tank, or, as Julie liked to say, the ThinkTank-PinkTank, whatever that might mean. While the bullet charge built up he switched on the Bio-Press and let it warm up. This one Julie liked to call the Bio-Mess. It struck him that she had pet names for just about everything, except him. Was that a good sign or a bad one? He had no idea.

He put a hand on the pipette that fed into the Bio-Mess, ready to open it after the bullet charge, nearly two thousand volts, whipped the soup into something more respectable. Yakky yawned and stretched, looking like he could use some more sleep. Peyton shrugged to himself. How come nobody got a kick out of this anymore? Even Julie tended to doze off while the ninety-nine minutes crept along toward inevitable cell fragmentation.

The bullet charge arced noisily through the tank, flashing blue and white, heating the fluid to an instant boil. Peyton opened the pipette, making mental apologies to Michigan Power, which was now operating in the dark. Pink soup flowed over the Bio-Mess's face, blue sparks dancing over its surface. The tiny pins raised up, forming a perfect likeness of Yakky's face. When it was dry and the color had changed, he peeled it off and held it up.

"Start timing, Yak."

Yakky snapped the stopwatch on, looking somewhat green. "Is that what I look like?"

"Yeah, but only if you were skinned. Want to put it on?"

"Not really. What about the hair?"

"Please," Peyton said, "only one miracle every few years. For now you have to be satisfied with a wig."

"Eyebrows?"

"Shut up, Yak."

He shut up.

Peyton trimmed a slice from the chin area, put it in a petri dish, and stuck it under the microscope. He checked it once, seeing what he knew he would see: cohesive cells pulsating with artificial life. Not a bad accomplishment; too bad the damn things went haywire every time. What was causing it?

He spread the face on a steel table that already had thousands of faces and face parts on it. He wiped his hands on his lab coat. "Might as well kick back, Yak. There is absolutely nothing to do but wait."

And so they waited.

Ninety-eight and a half minutes later Peyton was horsing with the toy drinking bird, watching it bob, bored to death. He took a quick peek through the microscope, stifling a yawn. His empty stomach growled at him, demanding pizza. As usual, the cells were just fine. In a few seconds they would be dead, and then he and Yak would go to Pizza Hut and check out the green peppers.

The overhead light went out suddenly, leaving the room in darkness save for the dull glare from the computer. "Now what?" he muttered. "Must be a fuse." He clicked the microscope's light switch; the tiny bulb came alive instantly. Not a fuse, then. He looked up at the ceiling fixture, realizing two things at once: The computer was still on, so it couldn't possibly be a fuse because this grand manor only had one; and the elderly bulb overhead was black and dirty-looking.

"Have any new light bulbs?" Yakky asked.

"Downstairs in a box, I think. Can you give me the time first?"

Yakky brought the stopwatch close to his eyes. "Ninety-nine minutes, forty seconds."

"Okay. Put a new light in and we'll abandon ship." Out of habit he looked through the microscope one last time, again knowing exactly what he would see: fragmentation, death.

The cells were busily pulsating, looking very healthy.

"Check that time again, Yak. Something's weird."

Yak checked it. "Ninety-nine—one hundred minutes."

"Baloney." Peyton snagged the watch and dragged it over, towing Yakky along. "Hmm . . . one hundred minutes, sixteen seconds. I need a new stopwatch." He pressed it to his ear. "Sounds normal. Piece of shit."

"Want me to chuck it out the window, Dr. Peyton?"

"Nah, I'd rather smash it with a hammer."

"I could do that. Very gladly."

Peyton smiled and checked the tissue sample again.

Pulsating.

He checked his wristwatch. Hard to tell. "Are you sure you punched that on at the right time? You didn't jump the gun, did you?"

"Gun?"

"Never mind. I saw you click it myself." He looked at the stopwatch again. One-hundred minutes, thirty-two seconds. To the microscope: still pulsating. To the watch: one hundred minutes, forty-five seconds. To the microscope. Yakky was being dragged all over the place but took it like a man.

"Holy cow," Peyton whispered, suddenly too stunned to move. "The cells are stable. No fragmentation yet. Could it . . ."

He pressed his eyes to the microscope.

Alive. Alive and well.

"I've done it," he said, shaking with excitment. "Yak, old boy—we've done it! Take a gander for yourself!"

Yakky bent over and took this strange thing called a gander. The cells were just fine.

"A hundred and one minutes, Yak! I can't believe it!"

Yakky straightened. "But why now? What is different?"

Peyton shrugged, then looked up at the dead light bulb. "Light," he breathed, smiling. "It's the goddamn light, Yak! The cells are photosensitive—have to be. In the dark they don't fragment." He hurriedly snapped off the microscope

54

light. "I'll check it every thirty seconds. Hell, maybe it's just weak light that destroys the cells. Sunlight might be good for them. This will take some research, but man! Think of it! With just an old photograph we can give burn victims their undamaged faces back!"

Yakky smiled, but it looked slightly off-kilter. "Does this mean we're done? I have to look for another job?"

"No, no. This is just the beginning. All we've got is a piece of the puzzle. There's still the big question—how to keep the cells stable in normal light. Once we lick that, consider yourself unemployed. Call me in Tahiti sometime."

He turned the miniature light on, grinning, and peered into the microscope. The cells were slowing. "Baked them in the scope light too long," he muttered, watching them die and fragment. "Time?"

Yakky looked at the stopwatch. "One hundred and two."

"That's three minutes better than ever before. I love it." He pushed away from the microscope. "They're all dead now. Let's knock out the windows and see what sunlight does to them. There's a crowbar or something downstairs. I'll whip up a new batch while you demolish the boards. Mind if I use your face again? No, screw it. I'll make a flat sheet." He went to the computer and started tapping the keys, feeding new instructions to the Bio-Press, lost to the world. Yakky went downstairs and came back a few minutes later with a rusty tire iron.

"Is this a crowbar?"

Peyton looked up. "Sort of. Give me some light, would you?"

Yakky started downstairs again. "Wait," Peyton barked. "Not the package of bulbs. Give me real light, sunlight. And a breeze too. This place is broiling me alive."

Yakky dutifully began to smash the boards away from the windows. Nails squealed and wood splintered. The place began to smell like a lumberyard. Peyton didn't notice; he had jammed himself into his private world again. When the sheet was ready, he had Yakky start the stopwatch, then placed a sliver under the microscope lens.

It died ninety-nine minutes later.

He tried it again, knowing it was useless; the burn victims

would have to spend their lives in a closet. Yakky sat playing with the drinking bird, the only form of recreation available. Peyton put a fresh sliver under the microscope.

It died ninety-nine minutes later.

He told Yakky to board the windows up again, but the phone rang. Julie was calling from her cubbyhole office, and for Peyton and Yakky the world as they knew it ceased to exist.

7

Durant

BY THE TIME the phone had clanged once, Robert G. Durant was at the top of the stairs. The dimness and the ruined step had almost conspired to trip him up, but he caught himself at the last moment and whispered down to his associates—five of them—to avoid the fifth step because there wasn't one.

Moving remarkably quietly for five small-time crooks and one big fish, they ascended the stairway and crammed themselves into the doorway, looking around with slitted, criminal eyes. Skip was there, one-legged Skip, along with Smiley, a borderline schizophrenic with a fondness for wooden legs with machine guns hidden inside. Rudy Martinez was there, he of the crooked nose and cauliflower ears, features caused by seven years as a boxer in his native Mexico. As he often sadly lamented, he could have been somebody, he could have been a contender.

Pauly was there, along with his permanent indigestion, carrying a bottle of Maalox. His lips were white and chalky with the stuff, but he didn't mind that much. It made him feel special.

That left nervous Rick, slugging down Valium by the handful and chasing it with bourbon. He did not like crime at all, had no stomach for it, but his only talent was nonstop drinking and there weren't many ads in the paper for that. As he sadly lamented, he could have been somebody, he could have been a bartender.

Durant saw some Japanese dude trying to board the windows in this dump. Lousy Jap, he thought. He saw a tall man looking around, a telephone cord in his hand, obviously trying to find the phone. That would be Peyton Westlake. It would have made more sense to hijack his girlfriend, Julie Hastings, but she was safe in her office and Durant had no intention of making a scene. Here in this rat hole, though, far from the teeming masses, he could be as loud as he wanted.

He turned and pointed to Martinez. "You handle the Jap," he whispered as the phone rang for the second time. Martinez's eyes registered acknowledgment above his mashed and crooked nose. He reached in a pocket and withdrew a small plastic bag, careful not to make it crackle and spoil the whole shebang.

"Smiley," Durant went on, "you cover our asses in case the dork has a gun or something. Skip, hand him your leg. The rest of you, let's have some fun."

They slunk into the lab, quiet as snakes. The phone rang again. Peyton Westlake found it at last, lifted it up, and moved to snatch off the receiver.

"Don't bother," Durant said loudly. Westlake flinched in surprise, nearly dropping the phone. That made Durant feel good. "Put it down, Doc. We have some business to discuss. Pauly, stop guzzling that chalk water and introduce us."

Pauly stepped forward, jamming the bottle in a back pocket. "Name's Pauly. Hi."

He punched Peyton in the face, knocking him across a lab table. Glassware shattered on the floor. Peyton flipped over the table and landed hard on his back. Pauly hauled him upright and slammed him against a wall.

Nervous Rick, still in the doorway, watched this with huge eyes, began feeding himself Valium.

Durant put a cigar between his teeth and pulled out his trimmer. It glittered savagely on a bright ingot of sunlight shafting through a window. He raised it and expertly snipped a bit off the end, then licked the whole cigar before reversing it. "Havana," he said, feeling tough because he *was* tough. "Castro's grandma rolled it."

His men laughed, except Rick and Martinez. Rick was draining a bottle of Ten High whiskey; Martinez was stuffing the Jap's head into a clear plastic bag, much to the Jap's discomfort and despite his protests.

Peyton had slumped to his knees after the wall banging. Durant made a motion, and Pauly grabbed a handful of his hair, jerking his head back.

"No foolish heroics, Dr. Westlake," Durant said. "Smiley has Skip's leg pointed directly at your heart."

Peyton's eyes, full of fright, shifted to Smiley, who was indeed smiling and indeed did have a leg in his hands. Skip was holding on to his arm for balance, his empty pant leg swinging.

"Now," Durant said, "we have come only for a single document. Tell us where to find the Bellasarious memorandum and we shall disappear like a nightmare before the breaking day." He smiled, full of congratulations for himself at having phrased that so beautifully. "Well?" he asked after a bit. "Who has it?"

"I don't know what you're talking about," Peyton croaked.

Durant made another motion. Rick came in and attacked the lab's sole filing cabinet, tossing papers over his shoulder, sluicing them across the floor. He looked at Durant and shrugged. He seemed immensely relieved, anxious to get out of there.

"Time's running out," Durant murmured. "Pauly, entertain the good doctor."

Pauly grinned. He lifted Peyton and threw him through a rack of glass shelves that almost touched the ceiling. They broke and rained down in shards on Peyton's back. Blood appeared in multiple pinpoints on the back of his white lab coat.

Durant walked over to him. "This is very sad, Doc, but one less Jap in this world will not influence the price of eggs in China. Or Japan. You never can be sure, huh? Martinez!"

Martinez hauled Yakky in front of Peyton. The plastic bag over his head was inflating and deflating as he tried to breathe.

It was cinched around his neck with a huge rubber band. Martinez held his arms pinned behind his back.

"If your houseboy appears to be in agony," Durant said sweetly, "it is because he is. Where is the document?"

"I don't have any goddamn documents," Peyton shouted as Pauly jerked him to his feet. "Yak's only a lab assistant. For God's sake, let him breathe!"

Durant smiled. "Rick, old boy, be so kind as to ventilate the young slant-eyes. The good doctor ordered it."

Rick jerked, looking positively green, but his hand went inside his belt and he pulled out a small nickel-plated pistol. Peyton tried to surge forward, but Pauly gave him a vicious backhand that sent him reeling. Rick shot Yakky in the mouth. He died instantly. Martinez dropped him to the floor. Peyton seemed to be on the verge of fainting. Durant laughed.

"Better than John Wayne," he said, giving Rick a wink. "You're coming along nicely."

Rick turned his head and threw up on the floor. When he was done, he fumbled with his prescription bottle, managing to drop it. It rolled to Durant, Rick staggering after it. Durant crushed it with one patent-leather shoe. Amber plastic crunched. "Nice touch," he snarled at Rick, making him back away. He turned his face to Peyton. "We're out of time, Doc. Give me the fucking paper I came here for!"

"I do not know what in hell you are talking about," Peyton said evenly while blood drooled down his chin and spattered on the floor.

Durant sighed. "I have an appointment in less than fifteen minutes, and I do not expect to have to drag you along. Perhaps if we asked your lady friend? Julie?"

Peyton jerked. He shook his head. "If you touch her, I'll—"

"You'll what?" Durant shouted. "Look around yourself, Doc. We don't horse around. If we don't find the memo here, we'll find it at her place. Maybe even your place. I don't have much time, and I'm not famous for being patient with raw assholes like you."

Peyton frowned, his eyes shifting back and forth. He nodded to himself. "Wait," he said. "I have a piece of paper in my breast pocket. That's as close as I can come to a document.''

Durant stepped forward and ripped open Peyton's lab coat. He slipped his fingers into the pocket of his shirt. The hand came out holding the trophy he had been seeking. He spread it open and grinned.

"I like you a lot better now, Doc. I really enjoy mutual cooperation. Guys?''

Smiley handed his leg gun to Rick. "My turn, boss.''

"Bullshit," Pauly snapped. "He's mine.''

Durant waved his hands. "We're a team, men. You can both have him.''

They lunged at Peyton. He looked quite surprised to be so popular. They jerked him backward, away from Yakky's bleeding body, toward the ThinkTank-PinkTank, where electricity hummed and porcelain insulators stood naked and obvious. Smiley smiled, seeing them. He would have smiled at an enemy battle tank just as much. He and Pauly spun Westlake around and pulled his hands toward the insulators, where naked wire was coiled and exposed. Peyton struggled uselessly.

"Ain't this dangerous?'' Pauly asked Smiley.

"Only if you touch both sides at once.''

"What are you, an electrician?''

"Idiots!'' Durant shrieked. "Shut up and torch him!''

Smiley wrapped Peyton's left hand over the exposed copper wires, then nodded to Pauly. Pauly held on to Peyton's forearm and forced his hand around the insulator. A brief shower of yellow sparks shot across the room. Peyton, electrified and unable to let go, performed a fantastic shake, rattle, and roll, shrieking with pain. Smoke boiled off his captive hands. The skin popped and split, exposing white twigs of bone where the muscle was cooking and bending. He screamed and screamed and screamed.

"God,'' Durant muttered, plugging his ears. "I'll bet that *hurts*!''

Smiley tried to pull Peyton away. He was as good as welded there. Pauly punched him hard in the face, knocking him backward. His hands jerked free from the insulators and burst into flame, sending the stench of burned hair and cooked meat into the air. Rick gagged, standing at the doorway with an empty bottle in one hand and nothing at all in the other, where a prescription bottle usually resided. He looked horrified because he was.

Peyton fell on his face with his hands tucked underneath him, extinguishing the flames. Rick was oh so glad. The stink was enough to kill a buzzard, to his way of thinking. He turned to go, but . . .

. . . but Durant wasn't finished yet. He nodded once more to Smiley and Pauly, and they understood well enough what he meant. They lifted Peyton by the clothes and charged at the ThinkTank-PinkTank. At the last moment they applied the brakes and let Peyton dump headfirst into the fluid. Electricity flashed and popped, hurling sparks in random patterns.

Smiley went into a squat to watch him. Inside the pink stuff, his head was turning back and forth while scream bubbles boiled out of his mouth. Smiley was aware that something was humming that hadn't been humming before. It sounded like a jarful of wasps. He stood up and went to Durant.

"Hear that?"

"Sure. So what?"

"What kind of mad scientist is this guy?"

"Who cares? He played with me, so I'm playing with him. Gentleman's rules. He knows what the scoop is."

Smiley went back to watching Peyton being drowned and fried at the same time. There was a huge blue flash, a bullet charge, and suddenly the pink stuff was boiling, boiling. A chunk of blackened skin floated to the top, and then another. Hair surfaced in a single dark blot, then was dissolved by the heat. Smiley decided that enough was enough. Rick was dry-heaving over in the corner. Smiley jerked Peyton out and let him crumple to the floor.

"Chicken?" Durant asked casually.

"Enough's enough. He's dead. Let's go."

Durant shook his head. "Evidence, Smiley. When are you going to learn?" He went to the tank marked ACETYLENE and turned the knob. It began to hiss. He opened the other one, the one marked OXYGEN. Another hiss.

Rick, done with his stomach, watched all this with growing

alarm. "Boss," he squeaked after a minute, "won't those things blow us sky-high along with the doc? Won't they?"

Durant smiled, shaking his head. "Not to worry at all. We will be long gone before any explosion occurs." He pulled his fancy electronic lighter out of a pocket, and moved the water dish from the toy bird, and put his lighter there instead. He positioned it, frowning with concentration. When his interior voice signaled bingo, he gave the bird a tiny flick with one finger. The bird began to bob in tiny little jerks. The acidic smell of the acetylene was getting thick. Durant got his cigar trimmer out and handed it to Martinez. "Get me one of the Jap's fingers," he said, and Martinez did. By the time he handed the trimmer back, everybody was coughing.

"Exit stage left," Durant said, and they went out.

The bird bobbed, its plastic beak dropping lower each time, aimed perfectly at the ignition button, thanks to Durant's diligence. Peyton was on the floor, stunned by so much pain so fast. He tried to stagger to his feet, but the world tilted out of control and he landed hard on the floor. He began to crawl, gagging on fumes, dimly knowing what was about to happen. In the corner of his vision he could see the bird, pretty little bird, a gift from Julie many years ago, about to touch off a spark and ruin everything for which he had worked for so long.

He made it to the table. He tried to grapple his way up, but his mangled fingers only slid across the polished steel. The bird bobbed. Peyton gave in to a sudden urge, and passed out.

After that there was only noise and fire.

8

Peyton

THE FORCE OF the explosion shot Peyton and most of his equipment skyward. The equipment, test tubes, glass beakers, petri dishes, a discarded pizza box, as well as the dead Yakky, were hurled nearly forty yards. The equipment chattered down on the foul-smelling river, sinking instantly. The pizza box became a distant kite, blowing in the breeze. Fire belched out of the laboratory, a giant mushroom made of orange and red.

Peyton landed in the river, just beyond the pier. So did Yakky, and a remarkable amount of glass and metal.

Yakky sank immediately. Peyton performed one of the world's biggest belly flops, smashing hard onto the brown surface of the river, tearing his clothes to shreds. He floated facedown, nearly dead, riding with the current. He came awake long enough to raise his head. There was not much to see: a burning building with no roof, a decaying pier, a tremendous fireball.

He groaned, then sank deep into the water.

9

Julie

PEYTON WAS OFFICIALY buried three days later, on an autumn afternoon. Multicolored leaves swirled down and a brisk breeze hinted at the winter to come. He was nestled inside the world's smallest coffin; all they could find was an ear. It was a bit ragged around the edges, but the coroner's report confirmed that yes, it had indeed belonged to Peyton Westlake. Of Yakitito Yanagita they could find nothing. The police decided that the explosion was a freak laboratory accident, and shut down their investigation. The laboratory was cordoned off, awaiting city demolition crews. The ear was given to Julie. She had it buried with full honors.

Pappas and Swain gave her two weeks off to do her grieving. It was not a good idea; too much painful time to endure. She phoned Peyton's mother in Indiana with the terrible news. Peyton's father had died some six years ago, and Mrs. Westlake was not well enough to fly out and participate in the funeral. She had cried on the phone, which sent Julie into an emotional tailspin. At the funeral it was Julie alone. The temporary marker at the head of the grave read simply, PEYTON WESTLAKE. The monument sculptor said it would take three weeks to get the real one done. He charged six hundred dollars.

While she waited, she cleaned out the catastrophe that was Peyton's apartment, and it went up for rent again. She cried as she lugged the boxes that were the remains of Peyton's earthly possessions to her own apartment; she cried as she sifted through the soggy black junk that had been his research equipment. Most of it was salvageable, but not many people were interested in buying unrecognizable burned machines that looked as if they had been to the moon and back.

Before she left the lab for the last time, she took the strip of carnival photos out of her purse, the ones they had paid a dollar for so long ago when the future was bright and there was still laughter in the world. She stared at them for a long time while hot tears coursed down her cheeks, the pictures of her and Peyton kissing and clowning around, the pictures of them in love. She shoved them into the crude slot Peyton had cut into the side of the computer.

She did not know why. It seemed fitting somehow. In a world full of senseless death and hideous surprises, it seemed somehow all right, the final act of a romance that had come close to being a marriage.

Yet perhaps, or perhaps not, for the simple reason that if there were computers in heaven, then Peyton would surely get the message.

10

Robinson

DR. PHILLIP ROBINSON was a very happy man on this Monday. The clouds in the sky were coalescing into black anvil shapes, promising rain. As chief resident of Whicock County Hospital, it was his pleasure to guide the four young interns new to the hospital as they began their careers. It did not bother Robinson that he had graduated from med school twenty years ago, or that medicine had made so many advances that his schooling had become archaic. He read the medical journals on a regular basis and considered himself up-to-date. He had even published an article or two in the *Journal of American Medicine*, articles that dealt with the treatment of radically burned patients. It was his specialty, his obsession. If two or three weeks passed without a single new patient in the burn ward, he became morose and irritable.

But three days before, a certain John Doe was admitted, a hideously burned man fished out of the river by a couple of teenage boys looking for crawdads. An ambulance had picked him up after the boys called, and he was put under Dr. Robinson's care as a ward of the state. To Dr. Robinson's way of thinking, it would have been better for the man to have drowned. He had not seen burns like this since Vietnam, where he had been in a MASH unit near Saigon. Back then it had been napalm. This time it was anybody's guess. Robinson suspected electrocution, judging by the condition of the man's hands (seventy percent exposed bone) and his face (now a charred skeleton head). This John Doe looked even worse than the crispy critters the soldiers occasionally dragged in from the field, victims of napalm, charred almost to the bone, weighing little more than a feather.

On this Monday, Robinson was making his rounds with the four interns following him like obedient ducklings. He could hardly wait to get to the burn ward, where John Doe was being dunked in a saline solution in preparation for the removal of the dead skin. Seeing this process for the first time, the interns would doubtless be shaken, perhaps ill. The screaming used to be the worst part, but this was a new age in burn treatment and the patients screamed no more; a new technique had been invented that prevented this: the Rangeveritz Process. Robinson had implemented this technique under orders from the chief of physicians, against his will. His mother had told him once that as a young boy he had loved matches. She had also told him that when he was seven, he'd doused a cat with gasoline from the lawn mower and set it afire. "Spanked you good," she had said. "You always were a firebug."

Robinson was paying his debt to cats, and society in general, by saving the lives of burn victims. The fact that his own mother burned to death in her bed did not alter his love of burns. Poor unfortunate lady.

"Burn ward," he crowed now to his four charges. "Hold your noses."

None of the four laughed. None even smiled. Robinson didn't care one iota. He pushed the double doors open and ushered them in, where the aroma of alcohol competed with the faint stench of burned things that Robinson so loved. Today John Doe was strapped to a huge metal plate, a hydraulically powered, multi-axled burn platform upon which the patient could be rotated and turned to any position the nurses and the doctor wanted. This eliminated the unbearable pain that accompanied movement of limbs gone stiff with incinerated skin and bleeding crust.

Robinson ushered his ducklings to Mr. Doe, who seemed to have passed out from the saline bath and the commotion.

His head was fully encased in gauze, nearly as large as a basketball, with slits for eyes. His hands had become white boxing gloves. The good doctor fished in a pocket and withdrew a small chrome wand. With a flick of a button it extended itself to eighteen inches. "Here we have a thirty- to thirty-five-year-old male, no ID, no medical history. Found the guy on the riverbank south of the city. There is a sizable number of homeless and indigents there. We get an average of three no-names like this every week or so. Nobody does anything about the homeless until they become human wreckage, like Mr. John Doe here. He has burns covering about forty percent of his body. The hands and face are the most severe."

A nurse sauntered over and worked the hydraulics, turning the hapless Mr. Doe upside down for a moment. The leather wrist and ankle restraints held him tight. She stuck an IV tube in his neck, adjusted it, then wandered away.

"Ten years ago," Robinson said, "pain from these burns would have been unbearable. This man would have spent many many years screaming in agony. Now we use the Rangeveritz Process. Simply put, we sever his nerves within the spino-thalamic tract."

He tapped his wand on Doe's head, just behind the spot where an ear should have been.

"The nerve cluster here transmits neural impulses of pain and vibratory sense to the brain, as you surely know. Because the brain can no longer receive impulses of pain, you can stick him with a pin . . ." He unwrapped a sterile hypodermic needle that he had been keeping for this, the fun part of the show. He jammed it deep into Doe's knee. ". . . and Mr. Doe feels nothing."

The interns gasped. Robinson worked the needle around, drawing blood but giving no pain. He plucked it out in one practiced motion. Doe slept on. "For better or for worse, however, there are some serious side effects from this procedure. When the body ceases to feel, when so much sensory input is lost, the mind grows hungry. Starved of its regular diet of input, it takes the only stimulation it has: the emotions. It amplifies them to a sometimes dangerous degree."

He pressed another button on his magic wand. It sucked

69

back in, now only four inches long. He hoped the interns were admiring his favorite toy.

"The result is alienation, loneliness, and uncontrolled rage," he went on. "Thus the patient must remain under supervision for the rest of his or her life, as the procedure is not reversible. This is sometimes difficult, because the procedure often causes increased activity of dopamine receptors in the brain, which in turn stimulates the adrenal gland, giving the patient extraordinary strength. For this reason we have John Doe, here, wearing leather restraints."

One of the interns raised a hand.

"Open for questions," Robinson said.

"Yes." The young man frowned. "Wouldn't it be preferable to endure the pain until the healing process takes place?"

Robinson smiled. The youngsters always asked this. "Doctor," Robinson said in a very grandfatherly way, "have you ever burned your finger?"

His head bobbed up and down. "Who hasn't?"

"Did you like it?"

"Not much." The others twittered, amused by this.

"In your case I would say the burns were first or second degree. Even a good sunburn is nearly excruciating. John Doe, here, has *third*-degree burns. If you could see his hands and face, you would recommend Rangeveritz immediately. I guarantee it."

That seemed to satisfy everyone. Robinson rested a hand on Doe's shoulder. "What we're encouraged to do here is remain optimistic. When he is able, we will discuss rehabilitation and plastic surgery, if feasible. Just between us, though, I rate the guy about nine or ten on the buzzard scale. He'll never look human again."

He stuck his fancy pointer in a pocket. "Now, on to the fourth floor, where we'll investigate the biological nature of mental illness, particularly depression and anxiety. Ever heard of imipramine?"

He led them into the corridor.

John Doe's eyes shot open, blue and keenly aware. He had heard it all. His head ached with almost senseless rage. A crazy urge to kill the ostentatious doctor surfaced in his mind, blotting out reason. With difficulty he reigned in his feelings.

70

The doctor was not the enemy. The enemy was the five or six gentlemen who had put him here.

He concentrated on snapping the leather restraints, one part of his mind swearing that it would be impossible, another part insisting that he was no longer Peyton Westlake and could do as he damn well pleased.

But if he wasn't Peyton Westlake, exactly who was he?

The restraints broke as if made of cardboard. There was a window nearby. Peyton crashed through it, leaving wires and tubes dangling. A nurse screamed and ran for an intercom. As Peyton recovered and hobbled across the hospital's lawn and parking area, a dark afternoon sky opened up and doused him with rain. Peyton would have hated that.

The creature he had become didn't mind at all.

11

Peyton

NIGHT.

A strong easterly wind was blowing through the city, flinging the curtain of rain into whipping sheets, an early-autumn downpour that was cold and miserable. Dead brown leaves flowed into the gutters with the rain, the rain carrying its load of dirt and paper and cigarette butts to a netherworld where light was alien and the air was poison. In a dark, filthy alley stood a battered blue dumpster with no lid on it, partially filled with stinking junk and week-old garbage. The rain splashed on the potholed pavement and spatted on the steel hide of the dumpster. Even the rats had deserted in favor of a dry place.

Something thumped inside. A bandaged hand, sopping wet and dirty now, clamped itself to the rim of the dumpster. Another hand popped up, this one clutching a shapeless black rag. A head followed, a modern mummy pushing garbage aside. The man who had been Peyton crawled out of the dumpster and thumped to the asphalt, where he lay breathing hard among the cans and rotting lettuce, the air pumping up and down in his scorched lungs, making them wheeze and groan asthmatically. In his fist he held the prize he had searched for in his delirium: a torn and ratty raincoat, a bit of dignity in a world that had suddenly become vile and cruel.

He clawed his way upright and sagged against the dirty

brick wall of an abandoned building that had once been a soap factory. This part of town, seedy and decaying, was, for the most part, deserted. Three- and five-story tenement buildings and factories squatted row upon row on either side of the street, built so close together that only a few ragged weeds had room to grow in the dead, trash-littered space between. Rusting fire escapes adorned sooty brick walls emblazoned with colorful graffiti; unused television antennas grew from roofs in skeletal disarray. Windows were mostly cardboard or waxed paper here; broken glass sparkled dirtily on the cracked sidewalks. Peyton pushed himself away from the wall, determined to walk and walk until this nightmare ended and reality began, but his tortured mind insisted with every step that no, this was no dream, and yes, he had been burned and a part of his brain had been carved out. Not only was he no longer Peyton Westlake, he was no one at all.

With difficulty he put on the raincoat and cinched it tight with the tattered remains of the built-in belt. The gauze that wrapped his legs and feet had slowly surrendered to gravity and was coming unwound, trailing sluggish, wet streamers five feet behind him. A look at his naked toes gave him a bit of reassurance, for though they were red and blistered from the explosion, they were still in one piece. Perhaps the doctor's slipshod remarks had been for the interns' benefit only.

He picked at the ball of gauze that enclosed his right hand, managing to split it wide enough to see a fingertip. His heart seemed to skip a beat, then race faster as he stared at the exposed thing that should have been a finger.

Yellowish bone, a slender twig. Crisped skin stuck to it, some of it sloughing off even now. A white string of tendon.

He jerked his hand away from his eyes with nausea crawling up his throat, his eyes squinching shut against reality and the horrible thing he had seen. Jesus, what had the doctor said, that his face and hands were the worst?

No. Dear God, no.

Against his will he began scraping and pawing at the gauze that covered his face. It was wet and heavy but not about to tear. He searched for a fastener or a loose end, growing frantic, a scream of desperation gathering strength in his throat. What did he look like? Skin bubbled and blackened, scar

73

tissue forming bizarre shapes beneath it? Hairless, scarred forever, a real-life Freddy Krueger?

He stopped, aware that he was breathing too fast, able to see dots and shadows swimming through his vision. Classic hyperventilation. He ducked into the nearest alley and forced himself to sit. With effort he slowed his breathing. His head sagged back against the wall. He was staring up at the sky, where clouds the color of soggy ashes trundled past on their endless journey to the east. Peyton was lost in a strange borderline state between panic and despair. Once again he lifted his hands and tried to strip the mask of gauze from his face and head, but his gauze mittens were too bulky.

He struggled to his feet, thinking deliriously that he must find a pair of scissors in order to free himself. His lab was not that far away, and Yakky would be there to . . .

Yakky?

He remembered with terrible clarity the look of terror on Yakky's face as he tried hard to breathe inside a plastic bag. He remembered some nervous young fellow with a bottle of whiskey in one hand and a pistol in the other. The back of Yakky's head had exploded, a fist-size chunk of brain and blood that the bag had captured and retained. Maybe, from the look of things, it was better for him to have died so swiftly.

That left Julie. Sweet, gentle Julie. She would cuddle him and protect him and make all the hurt and loneliness go away. He would find his way to her house and she would cut him free of this load of horror and gauze. She would weep over his blistered face and apply just the right amount of love and burn ointment. If he was to have scars, she would see to it that he got plastic surgery. Perhaps things weren't so terrible, after all.

But if only he could see himself, he would be more sure.

Julie had scissors. She had a mirror. She had a tender heart and would love him no matter how bad the scars were. And about that twig of bone where his fingertip should have been? No problem. They probably had had to amputate a little bit because of the severity of the burns. The bone had been left for the wound to heal around, and would be clipped in a few weeks. Make sense? Do you buy it, this little tale of how great things would be if only things weren't so lousy?

He swore to himself that he did, then aimed himself toward Julie's house, convincing himself of these things. He did not look at his finger again, and when he had convinced himself that everything was indeed okey-dokey, he tripped on an invisible crack in the sidewalk and fell heavily on his stomach, smacking his well-padded face on the cement. He pushed himself up on his hands, furious at his clumsiness, ready to scream with senseless rage. As if things weren't screwy enough already, he had to go and fall on his face. At least it didn't hurt, thanks to the Rangeveritz Process. His whole body seemed strangely numb. And the bastards hadn't even asked him for permission. Once again rage boiled through his veins. They hadn't even asked.

He stood up, toying with the idea of going back to the hospital and kicking some ass. Or maybe just hiding in an alley here and waiting for someone to happen by. Boom-pow-crunch. God, but would that feel good.

He shook his head to clear it. What was going on? He was no fighter, most certainly no killer. Where were these vile thoughts coming from?

He was about to take a step when something on the sidewalk caught his eye. He bent down and was able to scoop it up with his boxing-glove hands. It was a tooth. An incisor, to be exact.

Frowning at this mystery, he probed his mouth with his tongue. There was in fact a tooth missing, but he could not taste any blood. Worse than that, he could not find his gums. Just long, dry teeth anchored in bone.

He hurried on, too frightened to examine this hideous new catastrophe, afraid of its implications, because if he didn't have any gums in his mouth, he most certainly would not have any . . . any . . .

Any face.

He broke into a trot that quickly became a dead run, jumping puddles, falling and scrambling up again, his eyes full of rain, his gauze streamers flailing behind him and his borrowed raincoat flapping. He ran to escape this fresh burst of horror, which was threatening to extinguish his sanity. But the horror ran with him, ran inside him and on him and all around him, a horror with no name and no face.

* * *

Julie lived in a stylish brownstone in one of the more affluent parts of the city, where she paid an exorbitant amount of rent in exchange for a one-bedroom apartment in this safe and cozy neighborhood of doctors and lawyers and plumbers. On this rain-drenched night three days after Peyton's death, she had in mind to walk six blocks to the nearest Circle-K, not because she particularly needed to buy anything but because it gave her something to do other than sit in the house staring at a television she no longer heard, walls that seemed close and oppressive, a stereo that seemed to play only crashing heavy metal or funeral dirges.

She went down the stairway to the front door and the foyer, beige raincoat securely buttoned and belted, collar flipped up like Bogart, crazy-colored umbrella dangling from her wrist. She opened the door to a blast of wind and rain that seemed about to end this little voyage before it had a chance to start, made a decision, and stepped out, closing the door softly so that Mrs. Wiggins downstairs would not come out and hand out more condolences, which Julie was absolutely sick of. She let her umbrella spring open, gauged the wind direction and the slant of the rain, and went down the stone steps to the sidewalk. Streetlights glared off the street in white pools, and the maples that straddled the street danced and bowed, whispering their secrets to each other and casting leaves to the wind. Julie had a momentary vision of the wind hoisting her by the umbrella, Mary Poppins reborn, and depositing her in England. It was a goofy thought but it made her feel better, even made her smile to herself and into the dark. Anything was better than splashing around in a bottomless ocean of grief.

She turned at the corner and went right, her heels tapping steadily on the walk. For an instant she thought she saw something—a man, maybe—but the shadows shifted and there was nothing. Spooked a bit, she made herself move a little faster. Then she heard a strange swishing sound, the noise of wet cloth dragging on the wet street. She glanced over her shoulder nervously, where her apartment house stood safe and secure. Maybe this outing was a bad idea.

She went on, anyway, and when the hand crept out of nowhere behind her and pressed itself onto her shoulder, she uttered a squawk, instinctively ducking. The hand swung in front of her face as she bent, catching the streetlight and revealing, to her endless horror, a muddy flap of gauze with skeletal fingers sticking out like short white spokes. She screeched and spun around. A bedraggled mummy with black slits for eyes was there, making inhuman, piglike noises. The bandaged jaw worked up and down, squeezing out water that drooled down onto a threadbare black raincoat. The mummy reached out both hands to her, twiglike bones gleaming a loathsome dirty white in their bedding of soggy gauze. Her blood seemed to stop in her veins, instantly coagulated by shock and fear.

She screamed, a good, healthy scream of pure fright, and the mummy fell back, hiding its hands behind itself. Still it made the throaty gobbling noises.

Julie found herself suddenly running as fast as she ever had, to her building and her apartment and safety, her umbrella flipping inside out, the wind and rain making tatters of her hair. She got there in thirty seconds, hurled the door open, and disappeared inside.

Peyton batted a hand against his throat, shambling after her, trying to make his voice do more than squeal. As she vanished into her house he was able to croak out a sentence that was almost comprehensible.

"Julieeeee! It's meeeee!"

But by then, of course, she was gone, and all hope of ever seeing her or touching her was gone with her.

12

Darkman

IT WAS NEARING dawn when Peyton made it to the remains
of his laboratory. The eastern sky was an unhealthy shade of
pink and purple, and still the rain came down, came down
as if to wash away the world and the man whose name was a
memory, a man with no future and no past. Peyton found the
front door open and swaying back and forth in the wind,
while its hinges screeched as if in pain. He went inside and
tried to shut it, but the knob was gone as usual, this time
probably for good. He peered through the gloom while the
stink of old wet ashes stung his nose . . .

Nose? Have I got a nose?

Jesus H. Christ, of course you have a nose.

. . . and made his eyes water. The place was practically
gutted, the stairs a black shambles where fire had walked its
way down and nested in the old wood. Peyton tested the first
step, which shattered with a puff of ash and nearly spilled
him over. He took another step, not caring that sharp splinters were sticking out of the gauze around his right foot or
that the cloth was slowly staining red. He felt nothing. On
hands and knees he crawled up the stairs, nearly falling
through the missing fifth step. What had once been easy habit
was now forgotten, and when he did make it to the upper
story, his breathing was ragged and his mind was bordering
on rage again, rage at himself for being what he was and rage

at the human devils that had caused this. The roof was gone, blasted to powder, and the endless rain was making dirty puddles and piles of sludge on the floor. He stood up again and hobbled through the wreckage of his former world, stumping crazily because his foot was stuck full of splinters. With a groan he sat on the remains of a steel chair and pulled the splinters out. Blood dripped down into the ashes, nearly black in this ugly light. He did not care. Somehow his shoes were lying where the ThinkTank-PinkTank had been, curious casualties that had been ripped from his feet in the explosion. He unwrapped his dead feet and put them on.

A part of him that had not died in the fire urged him to get busy, to clean this place up and make it back into what it was. He stood and hoisted an overturned table, making it upright. He brushed the black putty of soot off it with both hands, turning the gauze an unlovely black, and stared at himself in the weak reflection of the polished steel.

He was a man made of dirty cloth, a bizarre Mr. Potato Head with no pipe and no hat and no hope. He scrabbled among the debris and found a charred scalpel, the one he had used to slice samples of Yakky's artificial face. He turned back to the table and carefully cut a small flap free from his right cheek, then peeled it back and looked at whatever mysteries might be inside.

It was . . .

Ah, God, no!

It was naked. . . .

Help me, somebody, help me!

It was naked bone and baked muscle, peeled and blistered like old paint, a hideous monster's face.

With shaking hands he cut another flap, this one on the forehead.

Bone.

And another over his nose.

Toasted bone with two skull-faced slots for nostrils.

The scalpel dropped from his fingers and clattered on the table. He mashed the flaps shut, almost too sickened to move. The bastards had not only stolen his future, but his face as well. And his hands, don't forget his hands, where dirty stalks of bone poked out of black gauze and cooked meat. Even a blind man would flee in terror from this monstrosity. And Julie? She already had.

He pounded his hands on the table, hoping to break the horrible white sticks where fingers should have been. Anger welled up, surging through his brain and body, pushing reason aside, turning him into the grotesque atrocity that he had so unwillingly become, turning him into a beast made of bone and scars and hate. He howled like an animal, beating his hands on his face now. He stuck his skeletal fingers through the gauze over his mouth and tried to bite them off. No such luck, but at least they didn't hurt. Nothing really hurt, thanks to Mr. Rangeveritz, may he rot in hell.

He stood up and hurled the table across the room, where it banged against the charred leftovers that had once been a wall. He threw the chair next, overcome with an insane rage more powerful than anything he had ever experienced. He stumbled backward and tripped over the black husk of his computer, a nice IBM job that had once held the secrets of his experiments, all those useless experiments. He pushed himself erect, seized the computer by its monitor, and hauled back to throw it, ready to scream with delight when it shattered. Something fluttered out of it, a thin strip of paper that pinwheeled to the ashen floor and landed faceup. Peyton looked at it and his rage dwindled to nothing.

Julie and Peyton, clowning around in a carnival photo booth, kissing, laughing, living.

He put the IBM gently on the floor. This was no accident, no freak occurrence. Julie had been here, standing among the wreckage of their dreams, and for reasons even God might never know, she had slipped the picture strip into the bowels of the computer. For the first time Peyton realized that he was considered dead, legally dead, and that Julie was stunned with grief.

So she still loved him. But could she love the gruesome creature he was now? Could she?

He looked around the lab. The force of the explosion had been vented upward when the roof blew. Maybe some of this junk could be made to work again.

He started sorting through the ashes while wild ideas sailed

through his mind, making his heart hammer. Could he do it?
Would it work?

Yeah. Ninety-nine minutes at a time, but time is what Peyton had by the handful. He was, after all, quite dead.

Something unusual caught his eye. He picked up a smashed amber prescription bottle, shards held together by a soggy label. He wiped it clean and held it to his eyes.

VALIUM 5 MG.
I TABLET 2 × A DAY
RICK ANDERSON 321 WESTERLY, APT #6

If he had lips, Peyton would have smiled. The man named Peyton Westlake was indeed very dead.

But the Darkman had just been born.

2

Revenge

13

The Party

WELL, THIS CERTAINLY stinks, Julie thought, feeling guilty and confused. Louis Strack had called with an invitation to attend a swank private party, where she could chitchat with the upper crust and possibly ingratiate herself with some old cad who held the keys to, say, the district attorney's office. "It never hurts to promote yourself," Louis had said, and with the reassurance that there was to be nothing remotely romantic between them, Julie had agreed to go.

And so she was here on this balmy Saturday evening eight days after Peyton had blown himself and Yakky to kingdom come, wearing a slinky black dress that gave new meaning to the world *curves*. She was in the powder room of the ultra-swank Condor Hotel's grand ballroom, practicing phony smiles in the gigantic mirror. It wasn't going very well. Her eyes seemed to have grown large purple bags in the last few days; in her mind her hair resembled a heap of straw, the dress a weary rag. She was tired and frazzled and sick of crying, because reluctantly she had acknowledged the simple fact that Peyton was never coming back, and that made it all the harder to bear.

There was a young woman seated beside her, smearing her lips with screaming red lipstick. Julie wished she would go away. Contact with other people, normal people, was an ir-ritation she could do without. It felt better just to sit at home and swim in a sea of grief. It seemed it was the best way to keep Peyton's memory alive. She had even sworn a private oath that she would remain celibate for the rest of her days.

"Super party, huh?" the young woman said, then clamped her lips over a piece of Kleenex. "Have you seen that movie-star guy yet?"

Julie shrugged.

"I can't remember his name, but he used to be on one of the soaps. I can't remember which one, but they told me he would be here. I haven't seen him, though. Have you?"

Julie shook her head. *Please go away,* she thought. *Just go away.*

"He's cool, I think. I think he's got blond hair like yours. Nifty hairdo you've got. I haven't seen one like it in years. Maybe his is brown. Who knows?"

You certainly don't, airhead.

"Well," the woman said sprightly as she shoveled the contents of her purse back inside, "gotta go!"

Do that. For God's sake, do that.

She left. Julie blew a small sigh of relief. The party sucked. She felt worse. She believed she was shrinking, fading away. Soon all they would find of her would be her shoes, and they would be full of tears. Peyton had left a gaping hole in her soul, stripped her clean of confidence and the illusion that both of them were immortal. The facts were cold and hard: You live and then you die. What fun.

Another woman breezed in, high heels clicking on the terra-cotta floor. She proceeded immediately to start yakking. She went into a booth, clicked the door shut, and went on talking.

Julie tiptoed out, knowing that the only way she would survive this evening would be to get loaded and stay that way. But she had tried that once before, alone at home slugging down straight vodka and waiting for the relief it would bring. But the bottle dipped down to the halfway mark and she wound up crying, like a derelict wino blubbering about some ancient hurt that had never healed. Did she have a hangover the next morning? Goddamn right she had a hangover. She chugged a quart of V-8 for breakfast and swore off booze forever.

Like most brash resolutions, this one faded in only a few days. Now she walked down the marble steps, hoping no one would look at this specter of ruin and death floating toward them and scream. No one did. She headed off toward the bar, leaving behind the party area and the dancing couples. The band was cranking out some old Guy Lombardo tune full of horns and muted saxophones. Men in tuxedos and women in their finest swirled and smiled and even laughed. It made Julie feel vaguely ill.

She parked herself at the bar and was immediately the center of attention. One bozo hopped up and planted himself beside her. His ruddy complexion showed he had indulged in too much liquor and had drunk it too fast. He breathed on her and she thanked God she wasn't smoking. The blast would demolish the building.

"How ya doon?" he said, leering at her.

"Doon fan," she said with enough sarcasm to make most mortals cringe.

"Drowning your sorrows, are you?"

Julie gave a little shrug, relenting. "Just giving them something to swim around in."

"Name's Jimbo, pretty lady. What's your pleasure?"

"I'm sure it wouldn't involve you."

He grinned. "Barkeep! Get the lady whatever she wants. Put it on my tab."

The bartender ambled over. "Vodka and lime," Julie told him, and he went away. Jimbo took the opportunity to put a warm hand on her thigh. Smooth devil, that Jimbo.

"Get your filthy paw off me," Julie said, beaming.

Jimbo opened his mouth to reply when a hand clamped down on his shoulder. He spun around in his seat, already snarling.

It was Louis. "You've had too much to drink. Get out."

Jimbo blanched. "Right away, Mr. Strack."

He hurried off and was enfolded by the crowd. Louis turned back to Julie. "Glad to see you," he said, smiling. In his well-fitted tux, Julie had to admit, the man looked like a million bucks. Maybe a billion.

"Thanks," she said.

He raised a finger. "No thanking allowed on your part. I'm very glad you came. Have you been . . . waiting long?"

"Just got here," she lied. In truth she had been in the powder room for almost forty-five minutes, unable to face this.

He seated himself as the bartender brought Julie's drink. She gulped it down as fast as decency would allow.

"I haven't bothered you over the last week or so because of what happened to Mr. Westlake," he said. "I know it's a tough period. But I have to know if you've come to a decision on the matter of the Bellasarious memo."

She nodded. "In fact, Louis, the decision has already been made for both of us. The memo disappeared in the explosion. But I—I really don't want to talk about it right now."

Want to know why, Louis, you million-dollar man, you? Because if I talk about anything remotely resembling an explosion or fire, I think of Peyton and start to cry because I am so lonely and I hurt and I want him back and . . . .

Louis touched her hand. "Julie, I am no stranger to the frustration and anguish that comes from the loss of a loved one. There's no cure for grief." He put her hand in his. "No cure, but there's something that eases the symptoms. It's called"—he swept her out onto the dance floor before she had time to react—"it's called dancing."

Her instincts told her it was absurd, but she had to smile at Louis's overpowering self-confidence and charm. She let herself be led, making the steps mechanically, gradually getting into the mood for real.

"Julie," he said, "I was quite impressed with your performance in the Von Hoffenstein negotiations. I want you to think about something, think about it hard. I don't need an answer right now. Just consider it."

Oh, God, she thought as a queer brand of terror stole through her veins, *the man is going to ask me to marry him.*

"I want you to think about becoming a permanent member of my staff."

She could breathe again. If he had proposed, she would have been shoved back into a past where Peyton handed out necklaces instead of rings and chased after her and begged her to marry him. And she would remember how crestfallen he looked, how puzzled and sad as the taxi drove away from Bowser's because she had needed time to think it over. Now he was dead and she had all the time in the world. She would give anything, anything at all, to be able to do it all over again.

"That's very flattering," she said, consciously forcing her thoughts to leave her alone. "But I have commitments to Pappas and Swain."

"I've already talked to Ed Pappas about it."

She jerked back, a kernel of anger seeding itself in her brain. He had no right. "I'll have you know I can deal with Pappas without help," she said, glaring at him.

"Don't be childish. I knew he didn't want to lose you. In fact, he swore he would fight tooth and nail to keep you at the firm. 'Good,' I told him. 'Good! I like a good scrap. If it's not worth fighting for, it's not worth having. Just consider that I won't be outbid.' "

She frowned, staring blankly at his black bow tie. Pappas and Swain would fight for her? She had had no idea. It had occurred to her more than once that she was a glorified gopher and little else. "Well," she said at last, "I'll consider it."

Louis gave her a fabulous, blindingly handsome smile. She felt herself wilting again, just as she had wilted at the Felix Heights Hunting Club so many lifetimes ago. This man had some kind of power inside, a tremendous magnetism.

"Say," he remarked casually, "did I ever tell you about the time when my father, may he rest comfortably, forced me to work high steel when I was eighteen? Forty stories in the sky?"

"I don't believe so," she said.

He told her all about it. And as he spoke, Julie knew something was passing between them, and she wished to God it would go away.

But Peyton was dead, still dead, dead until the stars winked out and the universe vanished. He was dead but she was alive. So was Louis.

Another brash resolution began to swirl slowly down the tubes, despite her efforts to hang on to it.

Lifelong celibacy no longer seemed so attractive.

14

Night Sweats

THREE A.M. JULIE in bed. Replays of the evening drifted through her dreams: Louis so handsome and suave, so rich and so powerful. Images of Peyton intruded, Peyton before he died, grinning his off-kilter grin, picking a bunch of dandelions and pretending they were a bouquet, posing in a carnival photo booth.

Louis lying on her bathed in sweat and lust. The man had been good at everything. She should have told him yes the minute he proposed. In her dreams Peyton and Louis stood face-to-face, measuring each other, ready to do battle. Who would win? Peyton because he was good at everything or Louis because he was equally good?

She wondered what it would be like to make love to him. The thought almost woke her up. Something stealthy and black moved by her bed. It pulled a box from under the bed and quietly rummaged through it. The box was slid back into place, another withdrawn. More subdued noises, papers rustling, glassware tapping against itself.

The dark thing pushed the box back.

It stood over Julie as she slept. One claw reached out and touched her hair. Julie mumbled and drew away, still asleep, unconsciously recoiling from the claw and the shadow.

It left her bedroom and her apartment much as it had come,

silently moving on shoes that were burned and twisted. It opened the door and went out.

In the morning she would discover that the front door was unlocked.

She would never notice that a small red plastic card was missing from one of the boxes under her bed. It was Peyton's Midwestern First bank card, his code to the automatic teller machine, and his life savings.

He would never go anywhere without it.

15

Bosco Delivers

Now BOSCO WAS not really named Bosco, and this Bosco business had nothing to do with a certain type of powder manufactured for the purpose of turning plain milk into chocolate milk. He was called Bosco by his fellow workers at Millings Business and Industrial Equipment Supply, where old Bosco had worked for the better part of thirty years, hauling every imaginable piece of business or industrial equipment known to man around the city and six Michigan counties. Once, in 1958, he had attempted to deliver forty barrels of live yeast broth to a huge bakery on the north side. The truck broke down. The refrigeration unit quit working. It was hot. This was his finest hour.

The yeast began to grow in its broth. One barrel blew its top with a noise like a bomb, then another, then all of them. The yeast began squirting out of every seam in the truck. Yeast has a tendency to smell bad; this load was no exception. As Bosco watched in alarm while holding his nose and hiding in a ditch, this Frankenstein batch hatched a diabolical plan. Because the seams in the truck bed were not sufficiently large to allow the overactive yeast a viable exit, it decided to explode, which would cause even the stoutest of men to quake and tremble.

When it exploded, Bosco quaked. Two thousand gallons of the Yeast from Hell rained down on him, a few passersby who had been getting quite a kick out of the show, and a tow-truck driver, who had been trying frantically to hitch the truck to his pickup and escape. A boiling mushroom cloud of yeast gas was loosed upon the city. People complained. Highway workers breathed through their gloves, griping. Passing traffic flipped on their windshield wipers and air-conditioning, honking furiously at poor Bosco, who had become a man made of yeast and was trembling indeed.

That had been a bad one. The trip today had been rather odd, but Bosco expected no trouble. It was only the peculiar nature of the equipment that had been ordered at the expense of Wayne State University, and the crazy address to which he was supposed to deliver it, that weighed so heavily upon him. It sure as heck wasn't the college, at least not as far as he knew it.

The address was 4519 Sequoia. Pretty name for a street located dead center in the city's most rotten area. Bums and derelicts hesitated to go there. The cops gave it a wide berth. Crime wasn't the problem. Poverty-level housing projects weren't bothersome. The area was just dead, eighteen blocks north and south on One Hundred Sixteenth Street, eleven blocks east and west on Birchwood. It was a blight and a sore, haunted by the ghosts of men long dead. It had been the scene of some of the city's worst union warfare back in the thirties, when the Depression had already entombed the world in a shroud of despair that would later give rise to Hitler, Stalin, Fascism, civil war, a world war, and fifty-two million dead. Peachy times, a peachy place. By 1945, the rest of the world had at last shrugged the Depression off; Sequoia street didn't get the news. All the businesses, factories, taverns, and hotels closed down—permanently. Bums came and went. Years came and went. Sequoia, along with one hundred and ninety-eight square blocks of city, was being allowed to degenerate into dust.

Bosco got the creeps while delivering this particular Monday morning load. He was at the wheel of a Millings Supply's step-van, tooling down Sequoia. Small truck, not much of a load. Weird stuff, but not much of it. It would take maybe five minutes to unload. Yet if memory served Bosco right, the address was an old soap factory where a hand soap called Fresh Splash had been manufactured. The name stank, and so did the soap. The factory died a much-deserved death. Died so fast, in fact, that most of the machinery was left behind because it was already antiquated. As a kid Bosco and the gang had spent some crazy times down there, rolling the winos, sneaking booze, puking out of windows ten stories high. In the soap factory they had smashed doors down and even set the place on fire. Tired old building, it had refused to burn. They found some other place to play.

Bosco checked the buildings now as he drove, looking for numbers. Not much luck. His skin was crawling; just being back there was a little too much. Nobody was there because there was nothing to be there for. So why had a college professor called in this goofy order and asked that it be delivered *there*? Crazy. Crazy, but the college had super-duper credit and never failed to pay. How Bosco got stuck with this delivery was anybody's guess. *He* sure as hell didn't make an extra dime, not one red cent. He figured they ought to pay time-and-a-half for hazardous duty.

He spotted a row of brass numbers on a door front, green with age. It read 4413. Fine, then. One more block. If this was some college prank, the bad boys who did it were good at their illicit trade. They even knew Wayne State's purchase code. Actually, though, Bosco wouldn't mind it. It would mean he didn't have to spend much time in this ghostly slum.

The soap factory loomed up on the right, looking as decayed and ramshackle as Bosco remembered it. There was a loading dock around the side on the alley, and that is where he stopped, backing up the truck professionally so that it was snug against the dock. He killed the motor and got out, ready to laugh this off when the kids said boo.

He climbed up the dock and stuck his head inside the dark mouth of the building. A search for a light switch proved useless. Anyway, Bosco didn't expect any juice in this old joint. A rat or a bat or two, but no juice.

He took a breath, not liking the looks of the place or the smell, which was a mixture of bone-dry dust and evaporated piss. As he recalled, he himself had pissed there one day many years ago, writing his name on the dirty cement while holding a bottle of Thunderbird wine, certified deadly poison. His name then had not been Bosco, of course, as it was now. He just wished he could figure out who had hung such a bizarre moniker on him. Frank Quail up in Shipping? Ralph

Barton? Nah. Most likely Jerry Kunz, forklift operator and the local funnyman. What a nerd.

"Hello?" Bosco called out in a voice that was remarkably dry and wheezy. "Yo there, anybody home?"

He waited, deliberating.

"Okay, kids. Enough's enough!"

More waiting.

"Okay, okay, good joke," he muttered, and turned to leave forever.

"Millings Supply?" a grating, whispered voice rattled out to him from the inside of the building. Bosco put on the brakes and turned back to look inside.

"Just set it by the door," the harsh voice said, and Bosco frowned a huge frown. Who the hell was in there? Jason? Freddy? Michael? Blackula? Holy hell, the joint was spooked.

"By the door," the voice demanded, and that was enough to set Bosco in motion. He opened the latch on the tail and shoved the accordion gate up. Inside were two small wooden crates, eight large boxes marked FRAGILE and IBM in several languages, smaller cardboard boxes heaped in a trash bag: light bulbs, electrical connections, two large insulators. There was even a big roll of banded-together heavy wire. Most unsettling of all, perhaps, was the aquarium. To this unusual request Mr. Millings, himself, had called a pet shop. "Go figure college eggheads," he had grumbled, and sent Bosco downtown to get it.

No problem, Bosco had assumed. The eggheads were going to dissect goldfish. Who was he to deny them this odd pastime?

So now he was unloading as fast as his fifty-six-year-old muscles would allow, really struggling with the crates, hoping to hell he didn't drop any of the IBM stuff and have to come back here with a new whatever-it-might-be. In two minutes he was sticky with sweat, but this was nothing new. It rained off his eyebrows and dripped in his ears. He could hear the monster inside breathing, hear the click of its teeth, the rattling of its bones. His eyes grew wide, his throat got dry. When he was done, he was almost ready to scream. He jumped off the dock and got back inside the truck, where the inventory/sales receipt and authorization were sitting on the dash. He got them and clambered back onto the dock, wishing he had brought a gun with a silver bullet in it. Silver

95

bullets were widely known to be the only defense against a monster; from the sound of its breathing, the dude must be the Creature from the Black Lagoon.

He stepped uncertainly into the shadowy maw of the factory, ready to bolt at the sight of anything even hinting at monsterdom. The papers rattled in his shaking fist.

"Need a signature," he squeaked, holding out a pen.

Something approached, some darker shadow against the shadows. It reached out a hand and took the pen. Bosco was sweating bullets. Bones rattled and clicked as the papers were signed. Bosco backed away.

"Yuh—you get a copy of each," he gurgled, backing now into the sunlight. Papers ripped. The tortured breathing went on and on. Bosco had just about decided to flee when a hand holding the pen and papers thrust into the sunlight. It wasn't very recognizable as a hand. It appeared to have spent a lot of time in the grave, all white bone and dead meat, and Bosco knew, as he snatched the papers away from those skeletal fingers with a supreme effort of will, that whoever possessed that hand was not someone you would invite to dinner. He backed away some more, his work boots thumping against boxes and things, his heart jackhammering away in the farthest recesses of his chest.

"Is that everything I ordered?" the thing with the hand croaked. *"Everything?"*

"Yuh yuh yuh," Bosco replied. "Yuh yuh yuh."

"Thank you very much. Have a dollar."

To Bosco's burgeoning horror the skeletal hand stuck itself out again, holding a crumpled dollar bill.

"Yipe!" Bosco informed the monster. "Yipe yipe yipe!"

He fell off the dock and landed hard on his elbows. He didn't mind. He got up and tripped over his own feet, falling again. This he minded. He got up and dived into the safety of the truck cab. The keys were there and he used them. He peeled out with his door flapping back and forth and the tailgate rattling up and down.

As soon as he got back, he filled out and submitted a request for voluntary retirement. He got it. They hated to see him go.

96

16

A Nervous Breakdown

RICK DESMOND HAD a problem on this dark and windblown Sunday night, a night when the trees groaned and rustled, ready to cast their leaves away and shut down for the winter. He had had this problem since the age of twenty, and it refused to go away, even though five years had passed. The doctors told him it was all in his head. The headshrinkers told him it was probably incurable. Nobody knew what caused it, but they all agreed that he must stop drinking and get his act together. One brave if slightly crooked physician gave him a prescription for Valium. They helped a little, but of course, by now he was hopelessly hooked on them and had two bad habits instead of one.

The problem was his nerves; better said, his nervousness. He trembled all the time. He had difficulty getting his breath. He sweated too much and as a result smelled like a dirty jockstrap most of the time. It was he who had pulled the trigger on Yakky and ended his short life. Rick was not a killer by nature but rather by sheer desperation. As skittish as he was, he could not hold down a real job. The slightest pressure to perform drilled through his brain like an arrow, incapacitating him, giving him the shakes. He usually went into the nearest rest room and threw up, then quit whichever measly job he had managed to land.

Working for Robert G. Durant, though, was not so unbearable. Durant absorbed the pressure and the problems and gave Rick only simple instructions for simple tasks, such as shooting this guy or that, torching a car, "arsonizing" a house. Rick didn't mind arsonizing, because one of Durant's talents lay in inventing new and clever words for banal and hackneyed crimes. *Arsonizing* was one. *Murderizing* was another, though Rick would privately admit that he had heard it before in an old Bowery Boys movie. The capper was probably *torchination*, which easily could be substituted for *arsonizing* without losing effect.

But Rick was about to discover a new crime that night. Durant might call it *torturization*, Rick would call it a one-way ticket to hell.

It was his bad luck on this lonely, windy night because he decided to leave his favorite tavern and go home. He stopped his car in the gravel drive and shut the engine and headlights off. Wind always made him jumpy; so did every other type of weather. That night was particularly alarming because the hissing wind and the billowing trees made so much noise, he would scarely be able to hear if some old aquaintance, a previous victim of robberization or arsonizing, decided to drop by for some revenge. Rick lived with the agonizing knowledge that he was forever being followed by someone who wanted to kill him; he knew, too, that the CIA had his phone tapped. His house, not exactly the Ritz in this crummy neighborhood, was full of video cameras hidden there by the FBI. Rick spent hours and hours trying to find them, but that bad old FBI was too slick. And to top it off, there was a monster under his bed.

Staggering under this tremendous burden, Rick bumbled through life in perpetual fear of being nabbed, shot, wire-tapped, burned alive, tortured, maimed, killed in an earthquake, or simply dropping dead from fright. The short trip from his car, a pitiful old Chevy Nova, to his front door was a journey of some twenty feet. This was a bad thing, because you never knew when something or someone would jump out of the bushes and scare you to death. The only weapon against such attack was booze, and of course the Valium. After Durant destroyed his prescription bottle Rick had gone screaming to his doctor for a new prescription. It was necessary to toss some greenery the doctor's way, about thirty or forty bucks per three-month prescription. Rick didn't mind. Durant paid him plenty.

For these reasons, and others even more horrifying, Rick sat in his car slugging down cheap bourbon, looking hard at the bushes, ready to dive under the seat if anything jumped out. Nothing did, and the wind blew alternately soft and hard, kicking up autumn leaves that looked soggy and black. Rick shivered in his lightweight jacket. God, but did those twenty feet look long, and God, did he have to take a leak!

His bladder finally convinced him to get out. Rick knew that it was essential to walk slowly while looking carefree; roving dog packs had less of a tendency to attack and kill. Rick had never seen a roving dog pack but knew they were out there somewhere. He capped his bottle and stuck it under the seat, then put his feet on the ground, already reaching for his new pill bottle. He shook two out and popped them under his tongue. They worked faster that way.

He took a step, then another. He reached back and eased the car door shut. The hinges made enough noise to wake the dead. He took another step, looking around with huge eyes. His muddy brown hair was tossed back and forth on his head, revealing a receding hairline. With all his worries he was amazed that his hair had not yet turned white.

The bushes were dancing and swaying. Leaves clattered down the street on their hasty journey to somebody else's lawn. Rick took another step, gathering the ruined remains of his courage. Then he heard the noise: a footstep on gravel.

Everything in his body froze up at once. If he fell over, he knew he would shatter into a million pieces. His terror was so complete that he wet his pants. Hot urine sprayed down his legs and soaked his slacks, adding to the fun. He began to cry.

A shadow zipped across the narrow strip of weeds he called a lawn. Rick whirled, his heart booming and filling his ears with noise. His body temperature sank below normal. He knew he was going to die.

He wasn't, but it was easier to move now that death had placed its cold bony hand upon his shoulder, waiting impatiently for him to surrender his life and his soul. Rick only wished that it be swift and merciful.

In this strange condition, he stumped to his front door, unlocked it with hands that no longer trembled, and went inside. He had left his television on to scare the ghosts and act as a night-light. It was full of electronic snow now. Its flickering blue light splashed on the walls, forming patterns and shadows.

"Who's in here?" he called out in a tiny voice.

Nobody answered. The cameras and wiretaps and monsters had not conspired to kill him, after all.

He breathed a huge sigh of relief. "Silly me," he said aloud, and took off his pants. One benefit of this catastrophe was that he no longer needed to use the bathroom, where spies lurked behind the shower curtain, where the Tidy-Bowl man rowed around in the toilet tank plotting mayhem and new leaks. Rick took his soggy Fruit of the Looms off and tossed them in a corner. His shirt went into the foul-smelling pile of old laundry. He got his jammies on and toddled into the bedroom, unable to believe he had survived another day on this terrifying planet. Foppishly proud of himself, he gave himself a mental handshake, turned on his Snoopy night-light, flopped onto the bed, and began to drift away toward sleep.

Four minutes later he awakened with new terror piping through his veins. In his agony he had forgotten to lock the front door. He flew out of bed and into the living room, locked the door, threw the dead bolt, snapped the padlock, hooked the chain, put the steel bar in place, locked it, too, stuck the wooden wedge under the door, and propped a chair against the knob. He dusted his hands, satisfied. But then—

A blast of wind came through the picture window—covered with cardboard to foil spies—and made the wooden shutters rattle.

He chewed his tongue, once again dying of fright.

He never opened his windows.

Someone had been here.

That someone might still be here. Lurking.

His brain turned into a whirlwind of hideous thoughts. He nearly passed out as new visions of destruction crossed the inner screen of his mind.

He raced to the bedroom and dived into bed. He covered

his head with the blanket. It came to him that he had left the window open, so he raced back and smashed it shut. Back to the bed. Pillow *and* blanket covering head. Knees knocking together, mouth dry as sand, sweat beading up all over his body. A quaking portrait of misery and terror.

No, he told himself. *You have been frightened to death every time something unexpected comes up, and the nightmares never come true. You are alive and well and nobody is in here, nobody at all. There are no dog packs or cameras or wiretaps or spies or monsters under the bed, so cool down and sleep.*

Almost convinced, he breathed a small sigh of relief.

A bony hand reached out from under the bed and caught his ankle.

"Wahooooo!" he screamed as he was dragged under the bed. *"Help Meeee!"*

Nobody was around to help. Rick thumped to the floor and was pulled underneath, shrieking and screaming, his well-chewed fingernails scratching across the tattered carpet as he tried to claw his way to safety. Snoopy watched all this from his safe perch in the wall socket, not seeming very interested, casting a light that now seemed far too dark.

With his last bit of reason Rick decided to beg for mercy, no matter what kind of arsonized monster this might be. He rolled over and discovered, without much joy, that he had been dragged under the bed by a mummy.

The mummy peeled back the section of dirty gauze that shielded its mouth. Rick saw a gaping maw of sooty bone and naked teeth.

"You always knew there was something like me under your bed," the mummy said raspily. Its breath was like burned hair and doom. Rick's eyes nearly blew out of his head, so large were they. The mummy stroked his cheek with what appeared to be a large white back scratcher.

"I believe," the mummy said, "that we have a lot to talk about."

Thus they chatted for a remarkably long time, cozy and close under Rick's smelly mattress, and all the while the remainder of Rick's sanity was steadily eroding, until none was left at all.

17

Lab and Light

ON THE FOLLOWING Monday morning the reborn apparition that had been Peyton Westlake was up by dawn. He had gotten barely an hour of sleep in the soap factory, the squat, dirty, two-story building that had seen the rise and fall of the Fresh Splash soap empire. Darkman had found a roll of ancient fiberglass wall insulation in the debris and had converted it into a bed of sorts. No one ought to be required to sleep in fiberglass, because every movement gives rise to dust clouds of itchy insulation. If Darkman had had sufficient feeling left in his body after the Rangeveritz process, he would have been scratching like a sufferer of the heartbreak of psoriasis while tiny red sores opened up all over his body. As it was, he could take a bath in the stuff and love every minute. If sores were there, then so be it. His body no longer transferred unnecessary information like that to his brain.

After spending most of the night with Rick, he had sneaked into the parking lot of an all-night grocery, found an abandoned shopping cart, and borrowed it forever. Pushing the ratty thing through the city, he was glad that no one was awake to see him, a bandaged cretin straight out of a Boris Karloff movie, a shambling thing too ruined to show its face. From the burned-out shell that had been his old laboratory he had brought several crucial items down the blackened stairs and put them in the cart. The Bio-Press was accustomed to extreme heat and had fared well. The microscope was missing entirely; no problem. The computer was obviously junk. The holographic plate where Yakky's nose had appeared in 3-D splendor was a bit warped but ought to work. The ThinkTank-PinkTank was a miserable pile of glass shards and burned goop. No problem again. Bosco had brought a new one, and a microscope and a new and even better computer as well.

Back home, if one could call a drafty, former soap factory home, he had found useful items. Old doors unpinned from their hinges were hooked horizontally to old chains, becoming irritably swaying lab tables. The skeleton of an old office chair with squeaky wheels became a lab stool. Out of raw computer cable he formed a crude interface, the link between the master computer and the burned-up, scavenged machinery from the old laboratory.

This was all quite nifty, but there was one crucial item missing.

Electricity. The transformer to the tank alone had to have at least two hundred forty volts so that it could build up its charge. Pink liquid was just pink liquid without a massive charge of two-thousand-volts, bullet-style. The computer and Bio-Press only needed one hundred twenty, but one twenty was one twenty more that he had. He had heavy electrical cable, thanks to Bosco—eighty yards of it. But where to hook it up?

He stood now in the dark guts of the factory with dawn providing feeble light through the broken-out windows, holding one end of the cable, wondering what to do with it. This whole area was dead. Redi Kilowatt had long since absconded. Darkman had found the power room that had once provided the juice for the machinery here, but under its inch-thick layer of dust the connectors and insulators were cracked and dead, the fuses long since stolen, the wrapping on the wires broken and crumbling. Even if it was still functioning, a man would have to be an idiot to try to use it. Death trap, just like the old lab's stairway had been.

He stood in the dim light, frowning under his bandages with eyebrows that were no longer there, a forehead that was only scarred bone; the memory of a frown, then.

Were any of the abandoned buildings here still wired to power?

Not a chance.

He stood and thought about this with his finger bones tapping idly on the thick wire. How the hell do you make electricity?

The solution hit him and he almost laughed. A generator, of course. There were dozens of brands on the market, even Honda generators, and you could bet they were good if the Yakkies of the world made them. Darkman grinned without facial muscles. Just find a phone and order one, he thought, just like you did with the other stuff. But that had been ordered at night, when no one was awake, in a phone booth clear over on Ackurd Street. Anyone could dial 1-800 anytime of the day or night.

He dropped the wire and thought it over. What was the risk of going out in daylight? Would people recoil in horror, scream, call the police? Well, they didn't do it when other human tragedies passed by in their wheelchairs or on their crutches. They didn't do it when paraplegics were wheeled around on hospital grounds for a bit of sunshine, their faces waxy and pale. They didn't call the cops when a flipped-out punk rocker ambled past with his hair all orange and sticking up, chains dangling from everywhere, three earrings in each ear. So why should they go berserk if Darkman happened by?

It struck him that he needed to make more than just one call. God, he had to buy wigs, makeup, maybe, something that might resemble eyebrows, some pale shade of lipstick for the illusion of lips. What else? Some cigars. A briefcase. A tape recorder. A camera with a telephoto lens. Some way to develop pictures. Who knew what else.

He dropped down in sudden misery and sat on the dirty cement floor, where old pigeon droppings were thick and rat droppings had long since lost their aroma. Everything was dust and bad light. How in the name of heaven was he supposed to get all this stuff? Even Millings Supply, that warehouse of wonderful everythings where Bosco no longer worked—even they couldn't handle this order.

He would have to go shopping. Encased in dirty bandages, he would have to go shopping.

Unless Julie did it for him.

He hung his head, aware that he was in the midst of a catch-22 with no way out. Julie couldn't see him until an artificial Peyton face, guaranteed to last ninety-nine minutes, was molded and set. For that he needed electricity, which he did not have. In order to get it he would have to use Julie as a mouthpiece.

He hung his head, assailed by new memories, new doubts. Why not just take a hike to the pier and plop himself into the river? It should have killed him last time. Why it hadn't was a fact too astounding to wonder about. His own memory of that day was sketchy. Suffice to say it was a bad day.

He sat in silent misery, the new king of a failed soap dynasty, thinking idly that if someone passed by, it would feel good to strangle that someone. He wondered briefly why he was having such homicidal thoughts, then remembered good old Dr. Robinson and his damn Rangeveritz procedure. Anger welled in his mind, sudden and startling, almost too powerful to reign in. He could see himself smashing the doctor's face in, strangling him, stabbing him with a knife, gouging out his eyes, shooting him. All manner of unusual tortures came to mind, clear visions too real to ignore.

He clutched his knees with the claws that had been his hands, shaking, ready to scream. But why the doctor? Why the doctor? It was that piece of human garbage named Durant he wanted. Robert G. Durant. Thank you very much, Rick, for the info. Too bad your brain shorted out.

He straightened, anger draining, departed eyebrows coming together in a huge but invisible frown. That Rick guy . . . what a basket case. There was little doubt that he was insane by now. Toward the end he had started flopping around like a beached trout, hyperventilating, crying, screaming. Sure he had shot Yakky, but the punishment was probably too excessive to fit the crime.

Ridiculous, his inner, angry voice shouted. *You let the murderer off too easy.*

Judge, he thought. *Judge and jury, Peyton Westlake. How nice to meet him. Got somebody you want trashed? No problemo, señor. Mr. Westlake is our judge and our jury in these parts. Not only that, he'll even become the executioner if the price is right. World, say hello to justice as it should be. No crime too big or too small.*

Darkman began to weep, making foul slobbering noises. Invisible tears flowed from destroyed tear ducts. He brought his claws up and wrapped his head with his arms. Why had this happened? Was he at fault in some way? Why hadn't he remembered from the start that he had had the memo in his pocket? *Here you go, Mr. Durant, here's your frigging memo. Don't thank me. Just use that door and remain a stranger.*

Too late now, though. Peyton's face was gone and his fingers were abominations. He was entombed in darkness now, Darkman was, and there he had to stay, hidden from the world. He even had to wait for sundown and its protective darkness before emerging from this hole.

He cried some more, then quit, knowing this wasn't getting him anywhere. He stood up, swaying with fatigue, knowing what he had to do.

He would brave the light and the humiliation, make his way to that phone on Ackurd Street and call Julie.

Because he trusted her. And more than that, he needed her.

She wouldn't be frightened by a simple phone call from the dead.

Would she?

The kids were the worst. With his hands buried deep inside the pockets of the raincoat and his head swathed in drooping bandages, Darkman forged his way through fear and nineteen blocks, not seeing a soul, if you discounted gutter winos who looked very dead. It was at the Martin Street crossing, block number twenty, that the first child screeched and pointed. The mother towing him by the hand looked over to Darkman with an apologetic expression, one that rapidly became a mask of shock and revulsion. Darkman wished he could suck his head inside his body, but since that wasn't possible, he decided to be casual and to whistle, as if everything were good indeed.

It was hard to whistle without lips. He wound up emitting a dry, catlike hiss, which sent the mother and boy hurrying to get away. Welcome to the world of the burned, you miserable bitch, Darkman thought.

No, no—no need to get angry. Plot your course by the sun and the stars and get yourself posthaste to a phone. Julie awaited, and with her the future of Peyton Westlake. He forced his numb feet and battered shoes to move faster, and left the frightened mother and the brat behind.

More trouble loomed as he was within a block of the phone booth. This time it was kids again, but they were older. Not wiser but older. Stupider, probably. They wore leather gloves with no fingers, sparkling chains, menacing hairstyles. Darkman's footsteps slowed as he approached them. The last thing he needed that morning was a brawl with three punks, one of them with green hair sticking out of his head like colored wires. Darkman's own sloppy, bandaged head was torment enough. He tried to cross the street but they had already seen him.

They nudged each other, grinning with inner secrets, not about to let this opportunity pass by. They smirked at Darkman, the tallest one flashing buckled teeth, the guy in the middle picking his nose and smirking, the smaller one smiling a cruel smile. Take the leather off them, Darkman thought, and you would have the three bears—Daddy, Mommy, and Baby, out for a walk in the cement-and-metal forest, ready to scratch and bite and kill.

He made himself move faster. The bears started after him, sauntering, looking casual. Darkman heard a click and knew it was a switchblade.

No, please, I'm just a college professor in a world of hurt. Give up on me and find some junkie to work over. Please? Pretty please?

He heard them coming closer, feeling like a scrawny kid in a strange school where the toughs ruled and the nerds crawled and begged. Was he a nerd? He probably was, not that he cared, but there was no more Peyton, only Darkman. And by no means was he a nerd. He had joined the ranks of the tough.

He stopped in place and turned around, hands still deep in his pockets, expression irrelevant because there was no face

107

to form it. The bears stopped and leered at him. Mama Bear flipped a booger his way.

"What the fuck are you?" the tall one with the switchblade said. "The invisible man? You look like a fucking stork with your pale-ass legs sticking out. Are you a stork, man? Or are you somebody just too fucking ugly to look at?"

Darkman's breathing speeded up. Adrenaline flowed into his system, making his stomach lurch as if he had jumped on a Ferris wheel going too fast. His vision swam momentarily, then solidified into one motionless picture.

He warned them, tried to; tried to warn them before it was too late: *"Run for your lives!"* Darkman hissed at them in his fire-ravaged voice.

"Oooh," Baby Bear said, being very casual on this jaunt through the cement jungle. "We're so fucking scared."

What happened next came as a surprise to everyone, even to Darkman. In unison the three lunged at him, intending to pin his arms behind his back and work him over from the front. The fastest one was Baby Bear, and he was the first to be surprised. As he charged, Darkman whipped one hand out of the raincoat, too fast to see, and caught Baby by the throat. The punk squawked. Darkman hoisted him off his feet and tossed him aside; he went end over end and smashed against a lamppost some fifteen yards away. Darkman blinked. How the hell had he done that?

"Fucking mummy man!" the tall one barked, and tried to stab Darkman in the stomach. Darkman's other hand flashed out and caught the cool steel blade in mid-swing. His finger bones crunched down on it. Papa Bear tried jerking it free, obviously appalled by the idea that a man could snag a knife blade and hold on without losing a few fingers and a lot of blood. Darkman gave a sharp pull on it, and then it was his, sliding out of the punk's greasy hand. His rage was huge, overpowering. He turned the knife around with the intention of stabbing Papa Bear to end his useless and miserable life, but as he drew back to do it he was overwhelmed with horror, seeing himself stab the kid again and again, gutting him like a fish. Disgusted with himself and this repulsive vision, he threw the knife away. It flew the entire length of the block and skittered into a sewer drain.

108

"Want to die?" Darkman hissed as his self-control began spiraling away, to be replaced by a whirlwind of insane anger. He reached for the punk's throat.

For a big bad bear Papa was getting very scared very fast. He looked at Darkman's reaching hands, his eyes growing large.

"What in the fuck *are* you?" he asked, falling back, seeming genuinely puzzled.

Darkman could have come up with a dozen handy answers. He lurched toward the boy, drunk with the desire to rip his throat out and see hot blood splashing, smell it, roll in it.

You are Peyton Westlake.

No way, man. I am the dark angel of death. I make the rules.

For God's sake, stop now!

Where was God when I was burned alive for no reason? Where is He when a mud slide in Chile kills twenty-five thousand people? There is no god left for me. I am the beginning and I am the end.

You are just the end, man. Just the end. No past and no future. Do yourself a favor and crawl in a hole with your cousins, the worms and the mites and the maggots. That is how low you will sink if you kill this boy.

"Shut up!" Darkman screamed aloud, scaring the punk even more. He turned and sprinted away before the bony claws had a chance to clamp over his throat. Darkman fought a lengthy mental duel with the voice of reason, the last remnant of the memory that was Peyton Westlake. Thou shalt not kill. It was no lie.

All that was left was the medium-sized guy, Mama Bear, the one with the green hair. He apparently didn't like the looks of this; his eyes were wild and frightened as he reconsidered things. He turned to run.

Let him go, Peyton Westlake commanded, and for a moment Darkman hated him more than he hated the punks, more than he hated himself and his new role. Lord, the chance to open a vein on the kid and watch his blood soil the street. And then gut him, gut him, gut him as if he were fresh and hanging in a slaughterhouse.

He jumped at the kid, who was ten feet away and moving

fast. For a moment Darkman was Superman, fifteen feet in the air with his arms outstretched and his hands hooked into claws and his raincoat flapping like a sorry black cape, performing the world's longest long jump. He landed behind the fleeing bear and spun him around. He hoisted the kid by the spikes of his hair. Leather squeaked and creaked as Mama Bear pedaled his legs frantically, uselessly.

Don't do it!

The voice was too strong to ignore. He kicked the bear in the crotch with one ragged shoe, wanting to do more, needing to do more.

The ghost of Peyton would not let him, but it was a voice that was growing weaker, becoming dim.

Darkman leaned his head back and shrieked with raw fright and interior pain. The Mr. Hyde inside him was becoming strange and frightening. He was one step away from mastery of his mind. He knew with a terrible and dreadful certainty that he was a man . . .

thing???

. . . on the verge of going insane.

By the time he found the phone booth on Ackurd, he was sick and shaking. He lurched into the booth and pushed the door shut, then slumped against the glass wall.

"What happened to me?" he whispered, full of doubt and a strange, drowsy kind of terror at what he was becoming. He stared at his hands, his criminal hands. "How could I think of doing that to those . . . boys?"

Simple. You redirected their miserable lives. You ought to be proud.

But—I . . . I wanted to *murder* them!

Law of the jungle, big boy. Ask Darwin.

Shut up. You don't even know who you are anymore.

We're Darkman, baby, and we can rock and roll. Julie's just a phone call away, and Durant can't be much farther. Revenge will taste even sweeter than tossing those boys around and trying to scare them to death. Dig it?

Darkman dug in his raincoat pockets, not digging anything but change. He dropped two dimes in the slot and dialed Julie's apartment.

It rang many times. Not there.

He dialed Pappas and Swain, and talked to the receptionist. "Miss Hastings is on temporary leave, sir," she told him, "but I can forward a message."

"Do you know where she might be?"

"Well, I probably shouldn't say, but I believe she is spending the day with Louis Strack."

"Who?"

"Louis Strack, of Strack Industries."

"Where can I find him?"

She gave him the address of the Strack family mansion.

And then he called Millings Supply for more equipment, racked with fear at what he was becoming, for what Julie might think of him when he came back from the dead.

The time, and this strange test, were not far away.

18

An Interlude at Millings Supply

JASON P. MILLINGS was the owner and president of that large company, and he had a standing policy that any unusual or exotic orders would have to be cleared through his office. On this early morning he had awakened with a pounding headache, thanks to last night's ingestion of a fifth and a half of Four Roses whiskey, normal fare for a man who stood five feet six and weighed nearly three hundred pounds. He was a man with a drinking problem so severe that he had to get drunk every day in order not to be frightened to death at the enormity of his addiction.

He was sleeping sitting up at his giant desk this Monday, his nose mashed against the blotter, his arms dangling to the floor, his ample ass spread across an executive chair manufactured especially for fat asses. The desktop intercom buzzed and he raised his head. His eyes were as red as spring tomatoes; his unshaved face a disaster area of Four Roses-ruptured capillaries and veins; his breath so bad, he could smell it himself. He slapped the intercom with one big hand and dropped his head back onto the desk.

"Yeah, what is it," he said with a moan.

"Another order that needs clearance from you. This one's wild." His secretary, Ms. Jackson, tittered loudly into the intercom. Millings flinched as these loud new hurts were pounded through his skull.

"Bring it on in, then."

She got there fast, holding a sheet of computer printout. Millings made himself sit up. She thrust the paper at him.

"Please," he grumbled unhappily. "Just read it to me."

She nodded. "Okay. One two-hundred-forty-volt generator, gasoline powered."

"We can get that."

"A Starling briefcase, brown with gold latches."

"We've already got a billion of those."

"A box of cigars seven inches long with one-inch diameter, dark brown in color, natural-leaf wrapping."

"What are we, a tobacco store? Tell whoever it is to get screwed."

"Fine. One dozen wigs for a size-eight head, no color specified."

"Screwed."

"Forty bottles of hair dye, every color."

Millings sighed. Why did some idiots think this was a department store?

"Five dress suits, long-sleeved shirts, and matching ties. Size forty-two."

"Help me, God."

She laughed. "There's a lot more. Four shades of lipstick. A tube of nontoxic mastic. A cassette recorder with microphone. An SLR camera with telephoto lens. Rolls of film. A package of men's underwear. Press-on fingernails. Eyebrow pencil. Colored contact lenses, nonprescription, in green, brown, hazel, slate. Two watches—one gold, another silver. A complete darkroom kit with chemicals. Tweezers. Pair of socks. Eleven things I can't even pronounce: protohydroemulsiactor, dillotantinantin, guar gum—what the hell is that for? Also, six other—"

Millings waved a hand to shut her up. "Get on the horn and tell whichever dipshit ordered that stuff that he can get his ass over to K Mart. The chemicals are no problem, but we aren't haberdashers."

She turned to leave. Millings made her stop.

"Who *did* order that, anyway?"

She looked at the paper. "Wayne State."

"Order code right?"

"Down to the last digit. Chemistry Department."

Millings frowned, puzzling over this. What was going on over at that college? It occurred to him that they might be building a robot or something. Either that or they had decided to put Millings to the test. By contract they had to buy all university-related equipment from Millings Supply, but that contract was due for renewal at the end of this fiscal year. Something was fishy here, and it smelled like a pullout.

"They're negotiating with another firm," he told Ms. Jackson. "Probably Willis Supply, the bastards. We're both being put to the test, I guarantee it. If we screw up, the deal is gone, and that sucker is worth over three mill a year."

She looked alarmed. "What should we do, then?"

He grinned, even though he hurt. "Give them everything they want. Everything that's in our power to get, and by God, if we can't get it, we'll invent it. Give them a ten-percent discount, just for the hell of it. No way am I going to let Willis steal my customers."

"Fill the order, then?"

He nodded. "Take the day off and hit the department stores if you have to. I want that order filled and delivered before noon. And Willis can sit on his thumb and rotate. We're the biggest, and we're gonna stay that way."

She nodded and left.

Millings sat around feeling very crafty, but his hangover got the best of him and he went to sleep again.

19

The First Move

BY LATE AFTERNOON Darkman was taking his first crack at developing film. The developing set, which arrived in the shipment from Millings around noon, came complete with bottles of developer, fixer, wetting agent, and enough pans to satisfy Betty Crocker. On his way back from the phone booth Darkman had scouted through several promising-looking dumpsters and trash cans, finding old clothing that stank worse than sour diapers, and even a huge, tattered black hat he could pull down past his ears. Feeling strangely proud of himself and his new wardrobe, he paraded back to the soap factory but didn't come across a soul. A pity, he had thought, and ducked into the cool darkness of home.

After the shipment came and was put into some semblance of order (the driver had not stuck around long to help, though), Darkman loaded up his brand-new Nikon XE-35X, unwound himself from his burden of bandages, and became a bagman. The smell of the ratty clothing he wore was revolting, but it would ensure that no one came very close. He tied a colored rag just below his eyes, a bandanna that was stiff with age but covered his absent face like a train-robbing outlaw. The hat went on top, the camera in his pocket, his hands safely buried there too.

It had been two o'clock, a hot and muggy afternoon, the sky a blank slate, when the sleaze bag named Pauly Reynolds arrived at Ernie's Best Deli, a place where Rick had said illegal transfers of money or dope took place almost daily. Pauly, Darkman remembered, was the tough guy who drank Maalox by the quart and enjoyed torturing innocent biochemists. Seeing him saunter to the deli with a smirk on his face and a blue bottle of Maalox in one hand, Darkman's rage had ballooned, threatening to split his skull and send him charging out of the alley where he had hidden himself. He could kill Pauly as easily as Pauly had killed him, and with greater effect on the man's future. *But,* he said to himself again and again, *I will not kill anymore. I will destroy.*

He raised his camera up and zoomed in on Pauly as he walked to the door. The Nikon was a professional model with auto-wind. He snapped eight pictures. Several moments later two other shady types approached, a Mexican fellow carrying a briefcase . . .

Martinez!

. . . and a man with a bad limp.

Skip!

Darkman got six clear shots, feeling absurdly as if he had known these unsavory chaps all his life. He watched through the big windows as they marched to a booth and sat down with Pauly. Though the fumes from his scavenged clothes were beginning to bother him, Darkman waited until they reemerged twenty minutes later. When they did, it was Pauly who had the briefcase. Darkman got three more shots, then pocketed the camera.

While on his way home, feeling safely disguised and smelling sickeningly of garbage, he stopped at a travel agency on McQueen Street and purchased two airline tickets. The fat lady he talked to was about to tell him to take a hike when he withdrew fifteen hundred dollars and handed it over.

After that she worked fast.

Developing the pictures now in near darkness, Darkman's heart was beating just a little too fast. The day was about to end outside, the sun giving up and sinking past the horizon, and if he wasn't able to do it tonight, he probably never would. In the planning stage it had seemed oh so plausible, so perfect and so fitting. Now that night was approaching, he was having an attack of nerves. His hands shook as he used tweezers to withdraw the photo from its bath. What if it was blank?

He carried it to the loading dock, finding the last of the day's light.

It was Pauly, all right. A little too fuzzy but Pauly nonetheless.

Satisfied, although still jittering inside, he developed the other photos and clipped them to a piece of old twine he had tied to the nearest mooring pillars. When they were done and sufficiently dry, he started the new generator (John Deere instead of Honda—oh, well), which purred to life and didn't make half the racket he had expected.

The connections had already been made while the prints were developing. For the first time in decades the dusty overhead lights came alive, filling the factory's lower level with a sick, feeble glow that made it seem even more haunted than when it was bathed in darkness. So? he thought defiantly. It's still home sweet home.

Almost trembling, he flipped the power switch on the big IBM computer. A green cursor began to flash on the screen while the hard drive whined, getting itself up to speed. Presently it announced that all was well and good.

He sat on the bones of his office chair and began to empty his scientific mind out into the computer. Peyton Westlake had been a genius.

The computer was even smarter.

By eleven his brain was frazzled and his ears were sore from the eerie and endless *tack-tacking* of his finger bones on the keyboard. The stench of his clothes was enough to fell a tree and he got out of them. Wearing only brand-new underwear that still smelled of its modern factory, his face exposed and his hands unwrapped, he loaded a floppy disk into the slot below the hard drive and clicked the lever shut. He typed two last commands, and the holographic plate began to sprout rainbows.

So far so good, he thought, and wished now that he could have salvaged the digitalizer from his old computer. The old way, you fed the picture in and the computer broke it down into vectors and angles. Now, holding the Pauly pictures like a deck of cards, he fed the information manually.

It took two hours. He was ready to collapse, but he was getting the hang of it again. He ran through the sequences that fed the Bio-Press. It signaled okay. He went to the ThinkTank-PinkTank transformer and started the charging process. Nervously gnawing on a finger bone, he checked everything over again, wishing he had skin on his face because he was hot there but unable to sweat. Just another annoyance.

When the bulletlike charge came, he hastily opened the pipette and watched the goop surf onto the hot Bio-Press. When it had filled all the crevices and was a shimmering, pancake-thin sheet, he turned the pipette off and waited. The smell of burned pork rose in the air as the hot pins of the Bio-Press adjusted upward to remake the picture Darkman had broken down into lines and vectors. In less than a minute it was done.

Darkman peeled it off the press with the tweezers and dropped the completed sheet into an aluminum tub. This he covered over with black plastic. In the dark it would be fine.

Growing excited, he manhandled the computer some more and made two new parts. They went into the tub. The hardest part came next, and while it was brewing, he used surgical scissors to cut the first two parts out of the remainder of the floppy sheet of artificial skin.

And then it was done. He turned the Bio-Press off with shaking fingers and picked up the tube of mastic. He painted his right hand with it, nostrils stinging against the turpentine smell. He uncovered the aluminum tub and fished out a piece. He placed it over the back of his hand and smoothed it out, looking for flaws. The computer had had a vectoring of his own mangled hand and had made the new one thick where it should be, thin where his own meat was still good. He fished the bottom of the right hand out of the tub and slipped it into place, carefully smoothing it.

He almost laughed. It was a hand! Pauly's hand, but as good as any other. It smelled a bit like chemical glue, and it didn't have fingernails yet, but it was damn good, and he knew it.

"Success," he whispered, smiling with no smile. "God-damn success."

If his face could have produced tears, they would have been falling now.

At last it was time for the Darkman to expose himself to the world.

He made it to Pauly's high-rise apartment before sunrise, never really feeling safe until the elevator had carried him to the seventeenth floor and he had successfully picked the apartment lock, which took far longer than was necessary. His face and hands were wrapped in fresh gauze. Mad at himself for not being a proficient lock picker, he pocketed the wire and the sliver of metal that comprised his crude locksmith's tools and slipped inside Pauly's place.

It was dark, of course, and it smelled of stale cigarette smoke and cheap cologne. Darkman went past the living room and eased the bedroom door open, the path to sleeping Pauly as clear in his mind as on the night Rick had described it. And Pauly was in there, flat on his back, snarking and snoring. An alarm clock on the stand beside the bed ticked loudly—no competition, though, for Pauly's slobbers. Darkman withdrew a large wad of cotton from one suit-coat pocket, a bottle from the other. This stuff was Nacoxidin liquid, light-years ahead of chloroform or ether, both of which wore off in several seconds. Two whiffs of Nacoxidin could knock out a rhino and keep him that way for hours.

He doused the cotton with it, holding his head to the side. The fumes were practically non-odorous and thus very dangerous. Darkman held his breath and advanced on Pauly's noisily sleeping form.

The alarm clock went off like a hurricane of bells. Darkman shoved the Nacoxidin in a pocket and fumbled for it. No snooze button in this little jewel; it was an old-fashioned job you had to wind up.

Pauly sat up in bed while Darkman fumbled with the clock. It thumped to the floor with a clang.

"Huh?" Pauly said.

Darkman whirled, seeing that his careful plans were headed

for the tubes, and mashed the cotton over Pauly's nose and mouth.

He went limp instantly. Darkman, still holding his breath, ran for the window, jerked it open, and threw the cotton outside, down seventeen floors to the sidewalk. He hung his head out and breathed for a while. No major problems yet. The rest should be easy.

He felt through Pauly's closet and found a suitcase. He stuffed it full of Pauly's clothes, carefully ransacking drawers, then snapped it shut. Out of his coat pocket he withdrew the two airline tickets the fat lady had sold him. He placed them atop the suitcase. Before he left, he found some of Pauly's cheap cologne in the bathroom and splashed himself with it. The medicine cabinet was stocked full of Maalox, and he took a bottle.

And then he did leave, hiding himself in an alley behind some garbage cans, because what happened next was up to Durant.

20

What a Ruckus

DARKMAN AWOKE WITH a jerk and didn't know where he was. He looked around, groggy and disoriented, and then everything packed itself into place, his connections with the past and the present fusing into something coherent, something real.

He was sitting in an alley with his back against a brick wall and his knees tucked under his chin. A pleasant breeze played across his face, gently flapping the bandages; this small noise had awakened him. A cat was scrabbling through one of the garbage cans that shielded him, making a clatter as it searched for a late breakfast: another possible explanation for why he had opened his weary eyes after only a few hours of sleep. The sun was high enough to cast long black shadows. With growing alarm Darkman looked at his new watch.

Almost ten-thirty. He pushed himself to his feet, becoming quietly frantic. His knees popped and his spine crunched, somewhat pleasant for the ordinary person but of little import to Darkman. He stood and unwrapped his face with shaking hands. Had Durant been there? Was the whole scheme going down in flames?

The white gauze formed a pile behind the trash cans. He went to work on his hands, these Pauly hands. The gauze unwound horribly slowly, but it did unwind. The fingernails looked good. There were bulges where veins should be. It lacked hair on the upper fingers and back, but who noticed that kind of stuff?

He felt his pockets. A bottle of Nacoxidin. He dropped it in the trash. His locksmith tools. They went into an inside pocket. A new stopwatch, courtesy of Millings Supply. This he kept. He patted his rear, almost satisfied, and realized he had forgotten Pauly's wallet.

New fear raged in his mind. *You dumb cluck! What if it's Pauly's turn to buy breakfast at the deli? What about lunch? You don't have a dime on you, you royal dullard! What if they realize that you are not you?*

He practically sprinted out of the alley. It came to him, too late, that he had not even started the stopwatch. How much time had passed since the skin had hit the light? Thirty seconds? Sixty?

He dug the watch out and clicked it on, then raced to Ernie's Best Deli, arriving in twenty minutes with sweat trickling down his back and the hot autumn sun shining on his sweatless face. Was there even to be a delivery today? Rick had said it was pretty constant. The money launderer handed the cash to Martinez and Skip of no-leg fame, and they passed it to Pauly. Pauly passed it to Durant, and God knew where it went from there.

He pushed the door open and peeked inside.

Martinez and Skip were already there—in the fifth booth, as usual. Martinez looked annoyed and was playing with a napkin, tearing it to small shreds. Skip's back was to Darkman. Both had plates smeared with egg yolk and toast crumbs on the table in front of them.

He made himself go in. The smell of morning bacon was in the air. Martinez looked up and narrowed his eyes.

"About fucking time," he croaked, and moved aside. Darkman slid into the booth.

"What's the big deal, Pauly?" Skip snapped. "You been messing with some woman till dawn again?"

Darkman formed a sneer, hoping to hell his remaining face muscles were pulling the mask in the right directions. It seemed they were, for no one reacted. Skip reached under the table and pulled out a briefcase.

"Durant wants to know where Rick is. He's really hot about

it—*really* hot. I don't know why, and I don't give a shit, either, but Durant likes that Nervous Norvis for some reason. Know where he is?"

Darkman shrugged.

"What's that fucking smell?" Martinez asked suddenly. "Smell it, too, Pauly?"

Darkman nodded. His stomach was a twisted rag, his nerves exposed and raw. He felt mildly dizzy. The goddamn mastic—maybe it was that. And maybe that was what Martinez was smelling.

"Anyway," Skip went on, flipping his head to get his long blond locks out of his eyes, "Durant seems to think we're all Rick's fucking baby-sitter. If you ask me, I think he's way too chicken for this line of work. One of these days he's going to step on his own foot, and we'll all take a tumble. If he's gone for good, I say good riddance. How about you, Pauly?"

Darkman nodded, beginning to feel like a mute sort of puppet, Howdy Doody's speechless brother.

Skip pushed the briefcase over, glancing left and right. The deli was almost empty; the owner, Ernie, seemed intent on cutting a roast into thin slices on a big noisy slicer on the counter.

Skip looked at Darkman and frowned. "Are you okay, Pauly? You look kind of . . . different. Where's the gold ring gone to?"

Thank God my face cannot sweat, Darkman thought, because at this moment he was feeling very much like a man who has stumbled into a trap that has no escape. He gave a shrug, then made a bye-bye motion with one hand.

"Lost it, eh?" Skip looked out the window. "We've got shit to do, man, or else Durant will be on us like white on rice." He checked his watch. "Damn, we have to meet him in twenty minutes."

He leaned back and waved at Ernie. The slicer shut down. "Mr. Moneybags is here," he sang out. "Pauly, pay the fucking check so we can get out of here."

Darkman felt like swooning. All his nightmares were coming true. He pretended to fumble in his pockets, of which there were many. That farce ended pretty quickly. In desperation he clicked open the latches on the briefcase.

There was money inside in neat little stacks. Darkman

guessed twenty thousand, at least. He stuck a casual hand inside and pulled one bill free from its stack and rubber band. He put it on the table and shut the briefcase.

Martinez scowled. "You're risking your life, man. Those bills are marked until the boss gets them laundered."

Skip was frowning again. "I still say you look funny."

Darkman's hand went into a pocket and pulled out the bottle of Maalox. He took three large swigs of it.

"Yeah, you're back to normal," Skip said, and they got up.

Martinez wagged a finger in his fake face. "Don't be late tomorrow, man, or I'll be telling Durant on your ass. Get me?"

He nodded. He got it quite well.

But the real Pauly would get it much worse.

And he got it, at eleven twenty-five, thirty seconds after the Nacoxidin had been sufficiently purged from his lungs and his veins, allowing him to come awake from his stupor.

He opened his eyes, eyes that refused to focus. There was a strange taste in his mouth and a funny odor to his breath. It smelled to him like a chemical factory. He sat up, grimacing, chewing his sleep-sticky tongue, groggy and confused.

He heard the front door smash open with a brittle crunch. Heavy feet tromped down the hallway. Three friends appeared at the bedroom door.

Martinez came in first. He hoisted Pauly under the armpits and thunked him into a wooden chair beside the dresser. Pauly looked up in wonder, aching in the ass, and saw the hard face of Durant towering over him.

"Ah, Pauly," Durant said, shaking his head in very convincing sympathy. "We've been mighty concerned about you. What have you done?"

"Done?" He shrugged, baffled by this. "What did I do?"

"That's for you to tell, and for us to find out," Durant said evenly.

Pauly sensed something very amiss in this situation. Martinez and Skip were frowning huge frowns at him. Durant exuded hostility with every expression of his greasy face, with every move of his lithe and muscular body. Even his pristine hair had suffered dislodgement; there were a few errant strands falling over his forehead. To Pauly's knowledge this had never happened before. The man was famed for his plastic hair.

"What did I do?" Pauly asked again, his eyes large and beseeching. "Just tell me and I'll make it up."

Durant's face grew stony. "Yeah, well, Pauly . . . Pauly, where is the money?"

"Money?" Pauly felt the blood drain from his face as his realization of the situation grew. "I didn't even make the pickup," he whined, hoping with every part of his being that he looked honest. "I swear it."

Durant stepped sideways and lifted two airline tickets off the suitcase standing by the bed. He flipped one open. "Ah, Rio. And first-class! How delightful!"

He opened the other ticket. "Here we have one for Rick," he announced to Martinez and Skip. "I guess this explains his disappearance." He aimed his eyes at Martinez, then at the suitcase. Martinez strode over and opened it. Piles of Pauly's clothing flopped out.

Durant shifted his gaze to Pauly, his eyes slitted with anger. "The money, Pauly. Now."

Pauly felt like blubbering. What was going on? He had overslept, overslept like a horse, and now this waking nightmare was being dumped on him just after his eyes had barely opened. What in the hell . . . ?

He slid down off the chair and landed on his knees. He clasped his hands together, racked with terror. "Boss! I swear! I didn't make the pickup—I overslept—I haven't been outside since last night. I swear to God!"

Durant slapped the tickets together and tucked them into the breast of Pauly's Road Runner pajamas. "Well, Pauly," he said, "I'd hate to see you miss your flight."

He flipped a hand at Martinez. Martinez clomped over and hoisted Pauly into the air once again. He carried him to the bedroom window, which was half open.

"So long, Pauly," Durant said, and Pauly began to scream and scream and scream. Martinez hoisted him higher. Scream scream scream. Martinez leaned backward, ready to toss him. Scream scream scream. Martinez smashed him through the window, utterly ruining the expensive glass. Pauly sailed out into the sunshine of a pleasant midday, glass splinters in his eyes and mouth, glass spears sticking from his pajamas like jagged diamonds, and scream scream screamed as he plummeted seventeen floors. In desperation he flapped his arms, much like the Road Runner imprinted on his pajamas. Gravity was not impressed; nor were Newton's laws. He reached a sickening velocity as he neared the tenth floor. His hair whipped in the wind. He flapped and flapped. His pajamas billowed in fantastic shapes as they whipped against his skin. He flapped and flapped, then screamed.

The last eighth of an inch was the toughest. Pauly was all over the place.

And Darkman, watching this from yet another alley, filled with glee and misery and doubt, turned away and went home, the taste of victory sour in his mouth and the knowledge of what the future would bring glowing in his mind like a cold and senseless fire.

There was no way to stop it, no way to stop him, though a tiny portion of his mind begged him to stop in a voice that was small and insignificant and just a shallow echo of Peyton the man.

Stop before it's too late.

21

Requiescat in Pace, *Rick*

POOR RICKY. HIS mind had roughly the intelligence of a baked potato now. His face was blank and stupid. After climbing out the window of his house (the locks were things of mystery now), he roved around in his pajamas for the better part of the morning, managing to propel himself to a shopping mall. He trundled in and window-shopped, seeing things and monsters and beasts no man had ever seen before. He was on the ultimate trip.

An escalator brought him to the second level. Another escalator brought him to the third. He wandered around, teenage kids laughing and tossing popcorn at him, old ladies avoiding him as one might avoid a rabid dog, children staring at him with their bright and mysterious gazes.

Sometime around three he stood at the low railing of the third level, looking down on a beautiful splashing fountain, his pajamas—no Road Runners here, thank God—slick with sweat, his face crumpled and insane.

"Wa-wa," he said, sounding quite terrified, quite lonesome. He tipped himself over the railing.

His flight was no more memorable than Pauly's. But he did make a big splash.

The papers carried a brief report about it the next morning.

Mall officials wanted it hushed up in a hurry.

And thus Rick died as he had lived, afraid of everything, unknown and unloved by his fellow man, a useless soul in a nondescript body.

Requiescat in pace.

22

First Kiss Foiled

NIGHT CAME, AS it tends to do, and on this night—shortly before one o'clock in the morning—Julie unlocked her apartment door and ushered Louis Strack in, both of them giggling at some joke they had pulled on the waitress at the club, deep in the new heart of the city, the South Side, where everybody that was anybody went. On the South Side, surrounded by new malls and boutiques and growing construction, the well-to-do of the city gathered to compare wealth and bank accounts and wives, hoping to come out on top and be the big fish of the day. Louis Strack had no time for such inanities, and Julie liked them even less. She was she and he was he. Enough said, to her way of thinking.

She was wearing a stunning green sequined outfit, a slinky emerald dress that Louis had bought for her two days ago. How he knew her size was a mystery to her. It would remain a mystery forever. He had handed her a large flat box and begged her to accept it. She did, with reservation. Pulling the dress out, she had almost laughed (and spoiled the mood) because a dress like this one seemed preposterous for a young lady lawyer trying to work herself up the ranks. If Louis hadn't been there, she might have tossed it out a window. But he was there, and at that time she only wanted to humor him.

As it turned out, the dress was just perfect. Especially for an evening like this. But the evening had ended, and the party was over.

"God," Louis said, slumping down onto her couch and hooking his hands behind his head. "This is one night I won't forget."

"Forget?" Julie smiled at him as she kicked off her shoes. They thunked against a wall. "Louis, you are the kindest man I've . . . ever met."

She supposed he saw, somehow, what she was thinking, and she was right. Peyton was still there, alive inside her. She was not yet ready to chase his memory away.

The silence grew too long between them. At the club—the High Rider, Louis's favorite hangout and a place that seemed reserved only for the rich and famous—they had danced and talked and delved hesitantly into each other's souls. Julie felt as if Louis were shouldering some of the burden that had weighed on her so much these last weeks: Peyton dead, servicing her clients; Peyton dead, Pappas and Swain to attend to; Peyton still dead, Louis's loving attention to ponder. Basically she knew that the man she had loved since high school was gone and never would be back. But he lived, in a way, in the memories she couldn't get rid of because they were so recent.

Sitting on the cushy recliner across from Louis, becoming embarrassed by their mutual silence, she opened her mouth to speak but discovered she had nothing to say. Louis was watching her, a well-built man with nice black hair, anybody's dream boy, every girl's secret boyfriend. Some kind of magnetism hung around him, an attraction that went beyond looks or money. He was invulnerable but he was also helpless. He was sweet enough to make honey sizzle but was able to command empires. He was, Julie had to admit, a very wonderful catch.

But Louis had a dark side, she had already concluded, and that dark side showed its strange face from time to time. A drunken businessman had stumbled over to their table at the High Rider while Julie and Louis were spilling out their souls to each other. The drunk quickly became a pest, a leering idiot with eyes that raked up and down Julie's new dress, a tongue that was hanging out and a conviction that he was Mr.

Cool. Louis had contained himself far longer than was necessary, but when the time was up, he grabbed the man's tie and thunked his head on the table. Mr. Businessman was ejected in a hurry. The manager hustled over with enough apologies to fill a wheelbarrow. Louis was kind, but there was a flickering in his eyes that said, *You just lost a customer.* She would swear that the manager went white before he was done shoveling out his apologies. She had just laughed. What kind of wonderful new world had Louis handed her? Scratching the depths of her checkbook in her old life with Peyton, handing out rubber promises that bounced and broke, she was now being catered to by a millionaire. Is this what she had wanted all along? Enough money to be an upper-crust, nose-in-the-air debutante, enough dough to toss power and weight around like confetti?

She didn't know, tried not to think about it. The whole thing was breathtaking and glorious, but it was dark and horrible too. What did she want out of life? The old stand-by-your-man routine, no matter what grievances the future might offer? Or let's-party-till-we-die, how about that? Louis Strack seemed to be a giver of both. He had enough cash to write his own ticket, and if she hung on to him, she would be a happy lady indeed.

So why did she feel so lost and afraid all the time, this after-Peyton time?

She shrugged inwardly. What was the use of pondering, anyway? That was yesterday and this is today. If life is a roller coaster, she was only along for the ride, no matter how scary it might be.

Now she felt, as the silence grew huge on this evening, that something ought to be said. She leaned forward in the recliner and softly rubbed her hands together. "Louis?" she said, almost a whisper.

He looked at her. "Still here, Julie. Still here."

She offered a smile that felt mechanical. Peyton was intruding. "I want to thank you for a wonderful evening. It's been a long time since I've really been able to enjoy myself."

Boy, but did this sound lame. Julie resisted the urge to run into the bedroom and drop dead. Instead she did the only thing left to do: "Can I offer you a drink?"

He smiled, nodding. "You bet. Whiskey neat, no fuss, no muss, no trouble. Want me to get it?"

He started to stand; she waved him down, glad to be on her feet and away from this awkward scene. What might Louis be thinking? Did he have thoughts of bedding her down or thoughts of being only a friend?

She snorted to herself as she made his drink. The man had more culture and breeding than your average French poodle. He did not jump a woman's bones simply to chalk up another one on his tote board. The persona that was Louis Strack screamed that delicious word *class* from head to toe.

She finished pouring the drink, and walked over to hand it to him. He frowned and stood up.

"Julie, could I use your telephone? Business call."

She nodded, and placed his drink on the coffee table. Apparently he felt as strange and wordless as she did. The attraction was there, and so was the memory of Peyton. Only the people were missing.

He finished dialing, and waited for an answer. Julie assumed he was about to raise the value of the peso in Mexico. The man was chock-full of surprises.

"Hello, Franz? What did gold close at in Zurich?"

He waited, listening.

"Sounds fine. Make a play for fifty-thousand Krugerrands when the market opens. I'll be in touch."

He hung up the phone, smiling a bit. "I haven't felt this good since the old days, when Dad would turn a catastrophic deal into a profitable deal. I guess I'm just an over-the-hill financier trying to recapture a few moments from his glory days."

Julie scowled good-naturedly. "Don't be childish, Louis. It's not nice to fish around for compliments."

He laughed. "You're right, damn your luck. You don't let me get away with anything." He sat back down and put his hands back behind his head. "You know what, Julie? Sometimes it's difficult being in a position of power. People defer to you, people tell you what they think you want to hear. But . . . they rob you of your humanity. I just want to be liked for what I am, not the power my millions have given me."

He sat up straighter, dropping his hands onto his knees. "Do you understand what I'm saying? Do you?"

He looked genuinely stricken, a portrait of confusion. Julie had a fleeting idea to go over and sit by him, stroke his hair, whisper good things into his ear. Poor Louis seemed dejected and upset, but she wasn't sure why.

"Were you ever married?" she asked, trying to turn the conversation around. "I know it's none of my business, but—"

He raised a finger and shook his head, indicating approval. "Damn right I was married," he said. "Married and in love. Deeply, deeply in love."

"What happened?" she asked, not wanting to open bad memories but curious all the same.

"She was killed," he said a little too easily, a little too fast. "Airplane crash over the Great Smoky Mountains. I almost went crazy. Ah, shit, Julie—I don't ever want to remember those days."

She nodded, feeling stupid. What a way to end an evening. The ghosts of the past were floating around both of them— his an old ghost, hers a new one. But both ghosts all the same. For a tiny moment she hated Peyton for dumping this catastrophe of grief on her.

Louis stood up, looking stricken. He patted his hair with the flat of one hand, a perfect crop of black hair with a troubled man beneath it. "I think I'll get some air," he said, and walked to the sliding glass door that opened on the balcony. "Join me?"

She did, trying to toss the image of Peyton aside but not quite succeeding. With time, she assumed, she would have trouble remembering his face. It was a fate he didn't deserve but a fate that was already prepared and handed out. Peyton Westlake, you no longer exist. May your ghost dwindle to nothing.

Unexpected tears formed in her eyes. Was it so easy to toss a loved one into the pot of memory and expurge it whenever it got to be a burden? Peyton had been alive two weeks ago. Did he mean that little to her?

She clutched her mouth with her hand. The tears spilled

down, hot against her fingers. She clenched her fists and begged this mental avalanche to draw back.

And it did, in less time than she thought was possible. Louis was out on the balcony, alive and breathing. The corpse of Peyton was all shattered life and inexplicable death.

She walked over to the door and stepped out. Louis had his hands on the railing and was searching the sky, where stars glimmered with a cold, strange precision. He turned to face her, putting on a limp smile. "Guess I'm getting morose," he said. "Thinking of the bad times."

Julie drew up beside him. "How long did it take you to . . . get over it?" she asked, immediately regretting it. What a depressing subject for the middle of the night.

"You never really get over it," he replied without hesitation. "The memory just dims. The pain becomes an ache, the ache becomes a permanent part of you. And sometimes it hits you so hard again, out of the blue, and you wonder why you're not insane from it all."

He inhaled deeply. The city lights were strung out below, orange and white and cold, forming rectangles. Louis put a small, tense little smile on his face. "You know," he said, "I can fight another man. I can fight the bigwigs who want to turn Strack Industries into dust. But I cannot fight death. Death is the only sure winner on this planet. More powerful than taxes, even."

He chuckled at this, but it sounded to Julie like a concocted laugh made of contempt and sorrow. She reached over and put her hand on his. "Louis, please . . . let's forget I opened this can of worms. We both have crosses to carry, and maybe together we can win in the end."

He turned his face, a face grim with memory and pain. No tears though, Julie noted. This is not a man who can cry.

He clutched her hand, squeezing it tight, almost too tight. Then suddenly he thrust his face at her, his hands coming up to draw her into an embrace, his shoes scraping across the balcony's cement floor as he drew near. It was too sudden, too quick. She was aware of his skin and the tiny stubble of his whiskers against her face, aware of his cologne and his breath. She jerked back with surprise, her thoughts scattering. What about Peyton?

134

"Oh, Julie," he whispered into her face. His breath was as sweet as his cologne. His lips were warm against her cheek and mouth.

She shoved him rudely backward, almost making him trip and fall against the railing. His face in the dim light was an expression of surprise and remorse.

"Julie," he said with a moan, finding his balance. "I'm so sorry."

She was ready to weep. It was screwy, everything was screwy. Peyton was dead, and no amount of denial would change that. For all practical purposes, his atomized corpse might as well be on Mars. The memory of him was nothing but failed hopes and pain. She realized this and started to apologize, but Louis was already through the door.

"Please don't leave," she said, going in, and he stopped.

"I understand your pain," he said to the front door, one hand on the knob. "I was there once myself. Good-bye, Julie. I'll call you sometime."

"Louis!" she blurted, but then he was gone, the door easing gently shut as she watched, for Louis was a gentleman who would never slam a door. Nothing could change that. Yet, above all, Peyton was still dead.

She wandered, almost in shock, almost ready to collapse, back onto the balcony. Her feelings dumped themselves on her in one great mental cataclysm, and she dropped to her knees and sobbed into her hands. The world was just too cruel.

And Darkman, standing across the street at the top of a minor skyscraper, watching everything without hearing, slunk away into the darkness, as puzzled as Julie was.

He still loved her.

But she wouldn't love him again until he became the man he once was. Right?

He found he did not know. Tomorrow still held many secrets.

Because tomorrow Peyton Westlake was going to come back from the dead.

23

A Ghost from the Recent Past

IT WASN'T UNTIL late afternoon the next day that Darkman was done with the manufacture of a new him. The hands, oddly hairless but very realistic, and the face, a little too tight around Darkman's naked cheekbones but passable, first struck daylight at four-fifteen. He clicked on the stopwatch and hurried to get himself into a suit. His hands were shaking and his throat was parched. For breakfast he had ordered a plain cheese pizza and a Coke. The delivery boy looked absolutely stricken as Darkman peeled dollar bills out of a large bundle, then recounted them, his claws chattering and clicking. The boy refused a tip and hurried out of the factory. A moment later he peeled out with a tornado of tire smoke, giving the aged red Pinto a good shaking as he fled for his life. Like Bosco, he, too, would hand over his keys and quit his job when he got back.

The pizza tasted like a hot piece of cardboard without its usual assortment of goodies on top, but Darkman had no desire for Peyton to have bad breath today. He ate it by rote, pizza sauce and red saliva dribbling down his skeletal chin, dripping on his trusty raincoat. Without lips, he had discovered with absolutely no glee at all, everything he ate tended to squirt out through his teeth. Just another benefit of being roasted alive.

It had taken six hours to complete the awkward digitization

by hand, a process the computer used to do in seconds with only a photograph and a lot of electricity. It had taken Peyton three months to invent it, back in the days when he was Peyton and the skies were blue. Next to the Bio-Press, it was the most important tool in skin production. But, like all of life's other disasters, Darkman was getting used to it. He smeared his head with mastic, just loving the odor, and assembled his new head in four parts: face, back, top, neck. He pressed the seams together and looked at himself in the chunk of mirror he had found in the dead and musty Fresh Splash rest room.

Not bad. The skin tone and texture were exactly like Peyton's, down to the small childhood scar on his chin. The lips were colorless, but a light application of lipstick would take care of that. The eyebrows had a hairlike texture to them. A little eyebrow pencil would make them passable. At this stage the most obvious flaws were the too-tight cheeks and the hairless head. Peyton reborn was a chrome-dome. Thus the wigs. He only hoped Julie would not run her fingers through his hair and dislodge the fake fur. Wouldn't that be a riot? The fun simply never ended in the wild and zany life of Darkman.

Millings Supply had furnished the after-shave he had requested. He dumped some onto his hands and splashed his face, hoping to trade the smell of the mastic for the manly smell of English Leather. That done, he used the makeup, not particularly liking it, and certainly not very good at applying it. But when he was done and checked his appearance in the mirror, he grunted with satisfaction. What a pretty face for a bald guy.

The hair went on next. Last night before going to bed on his mattress of fiberglass, Darkman had dyed the wig to the color he remembered, the medium-brown crop that formerly had resided on his head. A snip here, a snip there, and it looked great. Looking once again in the mirror now, Darkman was amazed to see Peyton Westlake staring back at him.

He had done it. He was back.

He smiled, and his new face, pulled by burned remnants of muscle and tendon, smiled with him, only slightly off-kilter. He frowned, and so did Peyton. He laughed at himself, holding up his hands, these strong man's hands where lines of veins showed and realistic knuckles stood out in bony perfection. He looked like a million bucks. Well, he was forced to admit, maybe just half a million, but that was more than he'd been worth five minutes ago.

Once dressed, tie in place, he ran a swift mental double check, looking for flaws or things forgotten. Everything was as it should be. The stopwatch registered eleven minutes.

He wended through the maze of his helter-skelter laboratory, opened the front door, and stepped out into the light of a glorious afternoon. Nothing could go wrong.

But of course something *did* go wrong, and it wasn't his fault. He arrived at Julie's apartment, barely able to chase a huge grin of triumph away from his face, nearly trembling with anticipation. There was a bouquet of red roses in one fist. The other hand was busy pushing Julie's doorbell.

His grin began to fade as the bell rang again and again. Wasn't this just keen? He makes a reappearance for the first time in two weeks and nobody's home. Why hadn't he called first, and why wasn't she home?

He knew the answer to these, for what it might be worth. Point number one, Julie would consider it a horrible practical joke if he had called, something a teenager would do out of raw meanness. Second, he realized now that she was probably held up at work. All of the hours spent constructing this facade had been wasted.

He dug the stopwatch out of his pocket and checked the elapsed time—a bit less than one hour. His heart went cold when he realized he had barely forty minutes left. He had had to hike some twenty blocks before he entered an area that was alive and had taxicabs. With the autumn sun burning on his face, the imitation skin should decay even faster. He shrugged to himself, full of bitterness that bordered on anger. Of all the screwball schemes in the world, this had to be one for the record. He had failed to perfect the artificial skin. He had gotten Yakky killed and himself cremated. He had failed as a scientist and as a man.

Slowly, not quite aware of it, Peyton crushed the roses between his hands, rolling them back and forth until the stems went limp. He looked down from the door that opened on nothing and saw what he was doing. His eyes narrowed.

"Son of a *bitch*!" he shrieked, hurling the flowers aside. He hammered the door with both fists, these perfect-looking but useless fists. He jumped back and was about to kick it down when the elevator at the end of the corridor slid open and Julie walked out.

He froze in place, anger forgotten, while his heart thumped loudly in his chest and throat. Julie was coming, barely thirty feet away, laden down with a green briefcase he had never seen before, a stack of manila folders, and a light fall coat draped over one arm. She was nearly staggering under the load.

He commanded his feet, in these wretched half-cooked shoes, to move. They did, agonizingly slowly, as if he had just yesterday learned to walk. When he turned, he stumbled away from the door and Julie's approach, filled with confusion and fright, knowing he could not see her now with these roses tossed all about and his skull baking under the stupid wig. Because of all the sunlight, his face and hands might begin to sizzle and smoke any minute now. He would have to try again tomorrow, maybe call her and suffer the agony of being hung up on as a cruel impostor.

He forced himself to keep moving, pretending to look at the apartment numbers, keeping his face away from her sight. Wearing real skin, his face would be red and broiling with embarrassment that was not entirely well founded. Why, he asked himself, was he running away from the woman he had come to see? Was he afraid of her, or of his own socially clumsy self? He felt much the way he had in elementary school the first day he'd worn glasses. Everyone then seemed to be looking, pointing, whispering. He was nearly dead with shame, trapped inside the strange confinement of a plastic frame and thick, heavy lenses, naked to the world, as exposed as a closeted four-eyes from the beginning.

He heard Julie rattle her keys. She slipped one into the doorknob. It turned soundlessly, and then he heard nothing.

Was she gone? Was she? He dared to look back.

She had tossed her things inside and was on her knees gathering together the junked roses. She looked misty-eyed and puzzled. Peyton felt a great surge of sorrow for her—and

139

the cold certainty that he had made her life pure hell these last weeks.

When she was done, she went inside and closed the door. The latch clicked softly, and their joyful reunion had changed from something wonderful to something strange and nearly sickening. Peyton came to the end of the corridor and stopped at the window there, looking out over the city without seeing. He propped his hands on the sill and leaned tiredly forward until his nose touched the glass. His breath fogged it immediately. Proof, at least, that though he was dead inside, he was still alive and kicking on the outside. The battle was not over, never would be.

He pushed away and started to walk to the elevator, defeated. Julie's door wafted open and she stepped out, no more briefcase, no more manila folders and coat. She had wrapped the stems of the roses together in tissue paper, salvaging them from what Peyton might have done to them, given enough time. Peyton flattened himself against a wall, thinking in desperation that he had almost walked into her, and what a neat surprise that would have been. They both would have screamed.

She went into the elevator. He saw her punch the control panel. The doors slid shut and she was gone.

He wiped a hand across his forehead in force of habit from the years when he had had real skin that could sweat. Feeling empty, he went to the elevator and tapped the down button, wanting only to get back to his crumbling hovel and get some sleep. Julie had been almost close enough to touch but he had turned chicken. To his inner list of physical and personality flaws he added a new crime: cowardice.

The elevator climbed back up and opened for him. He punched the *L* and began the trip to earth in this metal sepulcher made by Otis. The elevator stopped at the sixth floor and a fat lady got in. She gave him a glance and did not scream.

Whoop-de-doo, he thought tiredly. *The only monster here is inside me, and he is named Darkman.*

The elevator bottomed out and opened. The fat lady hustled away. Peyton strolled to the exit with his hands in his pockets, his face expressionless. Would he have more courage tomorrow? What if his anger ballooned out of control? Would he hurt her?

Please, no. He could not bear to hurt her.

He frowned as he went out onto the noisy street. Is that why he had not showed himself today? For fear of hurting her? What—mentally or physically?

Ah, stop asking yourself unanswerable questions. Get the hell home and curl up with some nice fiberglass.

He turned. Julie was at the curb, waiting for a slowpoke to pay the driver and free the cab for her. He did, and Peyton looked on, too stunned to move. She leaned inside and Peyton heard her tell the cabbie to take her to Eastlawn Cemetery.

And then she was gone, whisked away in a battered old Checker while Peyton stood with his mouth hanging open and his shoulders drooping.

Eastlawn Cemetery? Who was buried there whom she had known? Her folks were still alive, as far as he knew. Anyway, they lived in Chicago and had no business being buried here.

He puzzled for a few seconds while people surged past, most of them looking annoyed at this moody man who was blocking pedestrian traffic. Peyton jerked as the realization stung him. *He* was buried there. Probably Yakky, too, but Julie scarcely knew him.

A cab drew up and disgorged a passenger. The cabbie leaned over and looked up at Peyton quizzically.

Peyton got inside. "Where will it be?" the driver asked, looking at him in the mirror.

"Eastlawn Cemetery." He pointed. "Just follow that cab."

The cabbie snorted. "You ought to hire a new writer, bud. That stuff went out with Bogart." He chuckled, liking this.

Peyton didn't smile. "Just hit the road, will you?"

"Hit the road? Man, you are a scream."

He took off, laughing heartily. Peyton felt like strangling him.

The cemetery was on the north side, eleven dollars' worth of cab time. Peyton paid the happy fellow and hoped he would be in the middle of a ten-car pileup on the way back. Then he walked under the rusted steel arch and into the broad expanse of parched grass and leaning tombstones that was Eastlawn, a cemetery so unkempt and bedraggled that no one was dying to get in. Arf-arf, Peyton thought with dismal humor, and looked for Julie.

He saw her a distance ahead, stepping between the graves with the roses held high, obviously looking for something not easy to find. He ducked behind a dead tree and watched her until she disappeared over a rise. Slinking like a criminal, he made his way to the hilltop and hid behind a tall gravestone.

She had found her target and was on her knees. She laid the roses on the hump of dirt and tired sod that was capped only with a small stone marker. She ducked her head and he heard her sob.

He swallowed, not wanting to see her like this. *I did this,* he thought, not for the first time. *Why didn't I call her from the hospital? Why have I been hiding?*

It was too easy to answer. How do you come back into a loved one's life with your face burned off and your hands baked to cinders? One look at the real him and she would run in terror.

He checked the stopwatch. Nine minutes left. That wasn't enough time. He needed to go home and make a new batch, maybe make an appearance later tonight.

Okay, then. Tonight it is.

He turned to slink away when Julie tilted her head back and howled. The eerie sound made gooseflesh break out on his back. He turned again. She looked ready to collapse. It came to him what she had howled. A name, one name.

Peyton.

So it was his grave. What they had found to bury was something he would never know. He stood, in full view if she would turn around, his common sense battling with his desire that Julie's suffering be erased. It was when she pressed her face to the ground, doubled over with agony, that he made the decision.

He stepped away from the tombstone and walked toward her, his heart booming thunderously. He tried to say her name, but all traces of saliva had evaporated from his mouth and throat, leaving him speechless. He cleared his throat and tried again.

"Julie!"

She straightened, turned, and looked at him. The color

142

washed out of her face, which was puffy from crying. Her eyes grew huge. She lurched to her feet, shaking her head in silent denial. Peyton came close enough to touch her.

"You're . . . dead," she hissed, backing away. A wisp of hair was stuck to her wet cheek. Peyton moved to brush it aside, and she jumped like a cat, keeping her distance.

"Julie," Peyton said, "it's all right. It's me, really me."

She shook her head, seeming mesmerized. "No. You can't be."

"It was all a terrible mistake, sweetheart. I survived the explosion. I was in a coma. I was badly injured but not killed."

Her eyes became narrow and suspicious. This was not the reception he had envisioned. "You look the same," she said thickly. "You look fine."

"I *am* the same," he said, nearly pleading. "God, Julie, give me a hug!"

She came to him, moving slowly. He saw her nostrils flare slightly. "You smell like Peyton," she said dazedly, and pressed herself to him. He enfolded her in his arms, nearly weeping, wanting her to take him and protect him and make all the terror and misery go away.

"I needed to see you," he whispered as a breeze made her hair play against his face. He could not feel it. "I need to know if things could be the same between us. The same as before."

She hugged him fiercely. "Of course they can. But I don't really understand, Peyton. Where were you?"

He drew back slightly. "I'd like to tell you, tell you everything. But I need more time, a way to figure this thing out."

"What is there to figure out?" she said, smiling. "You're back and you're all right. What else matters?"

He drew fully away and looked at his feet. "There's some . . . things . . . you need to know. I'm not the same as I used to be."

"But you—"

He jerked suddenly. A blister had formed on his right cheek. He heard a thin snap as it ruptured. A tiny puff of smoke rose at the edge of his vision, and he slapped a hand over the blister, appalled. His hands were getting mushy, and starting to smell. Why couldn't the stupid skin last forever?

"Are you okay, Peyton? You look sick. What happened to your teeth?"

"Nothing," he lied, keeping his face turned. Blisters were beginning to pebble up on his left hand.

She hugged him again. "Hold me, darling, and never let go. I want you to hold me forever."

She raised her face, eyes drifting closed, awaiting a kiss. What if she smelled his lipstick? What if his lips fell off or stuck to her mouth? Peyton disentangled himself from her arms, nearly faint with horror. His hands and his face were about to self-destruct in full view of Julie. It would be too horrible for her to bear. He wildly looked around, needing a private place where Darkman could mutate unseen.

"Peyton?" she said, puzzled.

He turned and bolted for a field of scrub brush and thick trees some two hundred yards away. Julie screamed at him to come back. He kept a hand on his cheek. The skin was running like thick candle wax, emitting that terrible odor that was burned hair and rotting flesh. When he crossed the graveyard boundary and was safely in the dark shadows of the trees, he looked back to see what had become of Julie.

She had followed him a short distance. Now she was on her knees again, screaming for him. He watched her, torn with helpless despair.

She finally got up and left, staggering past gravestones gone blank with age, obviously crying, obviously bewildered. By the time she had disappeared behind the hill, Peyton's face had sloughed off and he was Darkman again, and none too happy about it. Getting angry, as a matter of fact. Very angry.

He let the rage take over, let it blot out reason, and for a very long time he howled and screeched while unearthing weeds in a frenzy of destruction.

And when it was dark, he went home, using back streets and alleys, his face bare and horrible. He only stayed there long enough to wrap himself with fresh gauze and pick up the cassette recorder Millings had supplied.

It was time for Darkman to take care of business.

24

Eavesdropper

DARKMAN WAS AT the point where it was getting necessary to purchase a car, that or walk his feet off. The house belonging to Mr. Robert G. Durant, local hood and graduate of a correspondence course in taxidermy from a dubious outfit called the Institute of Wildlife Restructure, was so far away that Darkman finally nabbed a taxi on the dark streets and had himself driven to within a block of the address Rick had said was Durant's street and number. The cabdriver had not said a word until it came time to pay, letting it suffice to stare at him in the mirror with huge eyes. Darkman tipped him two bucks. He was a softy for terrified people.

Durant lived in a very fashionable suburb that called itself Briar Wood Estates. His house had not been on this earth three years ago. In order to have it built he doubtless paid a very huge sum of money. For him it couldn't have been much of a financial burden. As the underworld king of the city he handled more money every day than most bankers.

When the taxi let him out, Darkman hurried away from the glow of the streetlight above him, needing shadow. He darted across someone's lawn, managing to wake up the family pooch, and set it yapping. The houses here were all dark. It was nearing three o'clock in the A.M., but Durant's house had a single window lighted. Darkman fought his way through a thick row of hedges to reach Durant's backyard.

A shadow was moving in the room. Darkman blessed the gods of fate for this bit of good news. He had been prepared to camp overnight and catch him in the morning. Right now was better. He flopped down on the cold, damp grass, and low-crawled military-style to the window and the rectangle of darkness beneath it. Already he could hear Durant speaking. Was he married, chatting with the wife? Perhaps enjoying a late-night brandy with a friend? It didn't matter one bit.

He put the tape recorder on the ground and tried to make sense of it in the dark. It had five square push-down buttons, no doubt eject, fast forward, rewind, play, and record. The cassette inside was a new Memorex, fully rewound. The player had both a built-in microphone and an external one. But which frigging button was record?

He cursed his stupidity for not having examined it before. A match would be handy now, or a penlight, but he had neither. The only light available was inside the house.

He thought that perhaps he should break in and simply kill Durant by turning his criminal head in a swift three-sixty, perhaps gouge out his eyes first and slice off his tongue. Hell, with a little lighter fluid he could be made to burn. Slowly. From the feet up, like Joan of Arc at the stake. Or electrocution, don't forget that. That would be even more fun to watch. He deserved it, yes?

Darkman's heart was already beating too fast as he envisioned Durant's upcoming destruction. Broken neck, no eyes left, no tongue, feet burning while he shrieked and whooped and his brain oozed out his eyeholes, jittering helplessly while a hundred and twenty volts baked him alive. He did indeed deserve whatever Darkman chose to give him.

The rage was there again suddenly, plodding through his brain like a trusted plow horse, digging up chunks of gray brain matter with its red-hot steel plow, furrowing his mind and leaving runners of blood and crescent hoofprints filled with the acid of slow insanity. Darkman saw himself performing these atrocities on Durant; screw the tape recorder, screw the methodical plan he had devised, just jump on in and make some blood flow.

His hands dug up clots of grass and moist dirt, turning his bandages there into strange paws. He pounded the ground,

146

barely able to suppress a bellow of white-hot rage while the toes of his shoes rattled out a furious drumroll on the lawn. Durant could not be killed enough; every method was too easy. Now he could see Durant strapped to a tree while the inhuman creature that was Darkman slowly carved his flesh with a straight razor and peeled it from his body like the husk from an ear of corn. Salt, then, a bucket of salt to throw on him and rub in with a wire brush while he drooled with pain, screamed in an agony more exquisite than anyone ever had experienced before. And then alcohol, don't leave that out of this satisfying little movie. Boiling hot alcohol, pails full of it to splash on the naked red muscle. More salt. More alcohol. Drāno in the eyes, gunpowder in the mouth, a ten-foot match through the nose to light the explosion.

Darkman got to his feet, his eyes burning with animal hate, his body trembling with the desire to kill—and kill again. He came fully into the light cast through the window and saw Durant at his desk, a phone held to one ear, a cigar idling in an ashtray while smoke rose up in silver strings.

The rage dimmed a bit. Darkman dropped back down, breathing hard, his real skin pasty with sweat. *Adhere to the plan,* he told himself with a demanding mental voice. *You are a scientist, you are in control, you have plotted and planned for too long to ruin it now. Durant will meet his end but only when the time is right.*

The pounding of blood in his ears lessened. He forced himself to breathe easier. No rush to kill, promises to keep. After the incident with the three punks he had sworn he would not go berserk again. But that morning seemed faded and old now, ready to be forgotten. The rage he had felt then was nothing compared to today's.

So it was getting worse, this disease of the mind. Somehow it seemed oddly sexual, a desire that needed to be fulfilled and was only under minimal control. He imagined it must be the way a rapist feels as he cruises the street looking for victims. It was a lust, an inner hunger, a desire too powerful to ignore.

He needed blood, guts, screams, terror. He was a hollow shell without it. He desired it as much as he was revolted by it.

Darkman was becoming a monster. Peyton Westlake was about to sign off the air forever.

No, it won't happen, I can control it, I am master of it. I am a stronger and better man than any other currently alive. Durant did not kill me. He invented me. He was Viktor Frankenstein, and Darkman was the monster he had created.

A tiny voice informed him that he was going loony. He pounded his head with his padded fists, needing to scream.

Durant chatted on, his voice muffled and serene. Darkman stopped hitting himself and listened.

"Okay, Rudy . . ."

Martinez!

". . . go ahead and plan to meet me tomorrow. Are you certain Mr. Fong won't change his mind?"

Darkman thumbed the buttons of the recorder. One clicked down and sprang back. Had to be record. Only one button worked now, and that was play, so he pressed both buttons at once and let it play, even though it wasn't playing at all but recording. He hoped his knowledge of eavesdropping was adequate. He held the remote mike against the window ledge.

Durant was sighing. "All right, then, we'll just have to see him tomorrow and convince him of the error of his ways. After losing that bundle to Rick and Pauly I don't feel like getting fleeced again. If Mr. Fong doesn't like it, he gets to be number seventeen in my collection."

Darkman imitated a frown. Collection?

"I'll meet you at nine. Yeah, Fong's place. We'll give him a fortune cookie he won't forget."

He was silent for a moment. Then: "That would be . . . just fine."

He hung up. Darkman raised himself slowly, interested in this collection business but doubting that it mattered.

Durant was still sitting at his desk, turning lazily back and forth on his office chair. He picked up a rolled-up white cloth from the blotter and unfurled it, revealing some kind of short, pale cigar. He began brushing it with something from a small can on his desk, using a minuscule paintbrush.

Darkman squinted. The can's label read TrueLife. TrueLife? What the hell was that?

It sunk in, at last, and he could tell exactly what the cigar really was.

It was a finger in the process of being mummified with taxidermist's solution.

Nausea slithered up Darkman's throat like sour heartburn. This Durant guy was a real sweetie. What a hobby.

Durant picked up a box from his desk and opened it. It was lined with purple velvet. He carefully put the finger inside. Darkman had no need to look. Sixteen fingers were in that box, one of them Yakky's own.

He clicked off the recorder and headed for home. It was a long walk but he had plenty to think about, most of it visions of Durant being killed in various ways.

The trip back seemed much shorter than the trip out had been. Darkman was home by dawn, bent with fatigue, but with no time to spare on useless sleep.

He sat at the computer and began to work, a picture of Durant hanging from twine in front of him, listening to the tape over and over again, imitating the voice badly at first, then better.

By the time Durant's face and hands were done and Darkman was able to imitate his posture and voice, it was close to eight o'clock.

He put himself together, Durant's twin brother, pocketed a handful of cigars, and gave his new voice one last test.

"That would be . . . just fine."

And it was just fine.

Time for phase two.

25

A Brazen Robbery and
Happy Times at Chin Fong's

THE NEAREST 7-ELEVEN happened to be a monstrous distance away, and once more Darkman wished he could buy a car, but this Darkman routine was draining his bank account at a tremendous rate. He doubted that he had two thousand dollars left. Pauly's marked bills were too risky to use. And when he was broke? Your basic slow starvation.

But today he was Robert G. Durant and not ashamed to announce it to the world. He came to the 7-Eleven and breezed inside, the sole customer at this early hour. With satisfaction he noted that the store had four security cameras peering down, every corner covered. He went to the frozen-food case and withdrew eight boxes of frozen pizzas, then went to the checkout.

The young man looked sleepy and uninterested. There was an ashtray piled full of butts by the cash register, and he was smoking a fresh one. Darkman slapped the pile of pizzas down and waited for service.

The clerk took his own sweet time. The cash register made noises. Presently the man informed him of the total. "Twenty-nine oh-four," he said tiredly.

"Fuck you," Durant's crafty twin told him.

He frowned. "What's your beef, buddy?"

"The name isn't Buddy." This Durant said with a snarl.
"It's Durant. Robert G. Durant." He turned to the nearest
camera and waited until it had swiveled his way. He grinned
at it. "Get that? R. G. Durant. I have a concealed weapon
and am about to use it on this pimple-faced shit head."

The clerk went pale, making his pimples stand out like
infected bee stings on his white skin. He swayed on his feet.

"Boo," Darkman said, and the young man ducked out of
sight. The brazen, yet petty, crook bearing the false name of
Durant ambled out with the pizzas. Outside, he threw them
in the gutter. A passerby stopped and frowned down at them.

"Old?" he asked. "Moldy?"

Darkman shook his head. "Stolen."

The pedestrian scooped them up and scrambled away,
shouting out a belated thank-you. He rounded a corner and
was gone.

Darkman leaned back inside the store, grinning. The poor
clerk was dialing a phone with shaking fingers. He looked up
and saw Darkman. The phone clattered to the floor.

"Nine-one-one," Darkman said, and left, actually laughing for the first time in ages. Durant was headed for a ton of
trouble. Far less than he deserved, but enough to keep him
occupied while Darkman began the process of destroying his
empire and ruining his reputation as a good crook.

He got to Chin Fong's restaurant shortly after nine, cursing
the world and the nonexistent taxicabs for forcing him to walk
so much in his dilapidated shoes. He stopped at the entry,
breathing hard, and checked the stopwatch.

Ninety minutes. Great. Nine minutes left in which to do
this dastardly deed. And this one would be tough—yes, it
would. He was not famed for being a good impostor, but it
was either this or nothing at all.

An old green Chrysler drew up beside the curb and stopped
with a short squeal of tires. Martinez, failed boxer and no
beauty-contest winner, stepped out. On the other side the
chap named Skip climbed out and stomped to the sidewalk,
walking in the peculiar, swaying way amputees tend to. The
morning sun slanted down from a flawless blue sky, an autumn beauty of a day. Darkman felt his insides tighten up.
Was this going to work at all?

151

"Your leg loaded?" he asked Skip in the best Durant voice he could muster.

Skip grinned. "You betcha. We gonna see fireworks today?"

"Chinese fireworks," Darkman said, and all three of them laughed. But meanwhile . . .

. . . the real and actual Robert G. Durant was walking angrily down the marble steps of the courthouse, ablaze with rage. His attorney, Myron Katz, was beside him, hurrying to keep up.

"Idiots!" Durant was screaming. "Restitution for the pizzas! Forty hours of community service! Seven-hundred-dollar fine! That's what will happen if I get convicted, and I wasn't even *there*!"

"Count yourself lucky they let us post bail," Myron said. "They have the whole thing on video. Are you sure you weren't sleepwalking? It's a lousy defense, but it's all we've got."

"Get screwed," Durant snapped. "Where's that goddamn taxi you called?"

As if on command, the taxi appeared. Durant jumped in. "Chin Fong Restaurant. Fast."

It took off, fast as ordered, leaving Myron Katz behind to flag down his own transportation. And at the restaurant . . .

. . . Darkman, Martinez, and Skip went inside, clanging an overhead bell. Darkman was shivering within, aware of the slipping time, the unhappy position he was in, and the smell of Chinese food, which filled the place like a pleasant fog. At least it was semidark inside, good news for his disguise.

A short, middle-aged Chinese man in a white suit passed through the colorful bead curtain that blocked the kitchen from the dining area. He looked at Darkman and smiled apprehensively. "Wahbuht Dewant! So good of you to favor me with your venerated pwesence. Pwease honor me by sitting in my shabby chair."

Darkman stared at him, not moving.

Chin Fong bowed. "Or do me the greater honor of remaining on your feet."

"Tell him," Darkman said to Martinez.

Martinez blinked. "Huh?"

"Tell him why we're here."

He shrugged. "Okay, boss. Hey, Fong! Where's the fucking money?"

Fong looked surprised. "Money?"

"Yeah, the dough I was supposed to collect yesterday."

Fong brightened. "The money! Yes! Wahbuht, how I tremble with shame. How I hide my face."

He did so, looking absurd. Darkman kept quiet, wishing he knew what the hell this might all be about. Probably a payoff of some sort. Protection money? Let's make a dope deal? There was no way to know right now, but Martinez and Skip were staring at him, obviously uncertain. What was wrong with Wahbuht today? Going soft in his old age?

Martinez spoke up, frowning. "Quit the crap, Fong. We're here for the money and we ain't leaving until we get it."

Fong bowed again, looking genuinely sad. "How I regret having to burden you with my miserable difficulties. You see, I have no money."

Darkman stared at him, suddenly at a loss. How would Durant be handling this?

Chin Fong stared back, curious. He seemed to be waiting for a reaction, some tough-guy stuff. "The white powder no longer flows in its former volume, Wahbuht. All of the members of Tong languish in poverty."

Tong? Oh, yeah. The Chinese Mafia in these parts. And the white powder that no longer flowed? Take a guess.

Fong covered his face again. "And of all your unworthy servants, Chin Fong is certainly the most destitute. I do not have a dollar, much less fifty thousand!"

"You're making us cry," Skip barked, glancing at Darkman with the same puzzled expression Martinez wore. "Make him pay, boss."

Fong raised a hand and snapped his fingers. Four very large and very mean-looking men the size of sumo wrestlers came through the bead curtain and ranked themselves into a forbidding line. Darkman grinned to himself, knowing exactly what to do. This was exactly the development the doctor had ordered.

"Even my own miserable friends sometimes ignore my

wishes," Fong said tenderly, "and they tend to upset those whom I cherish most deeply. Wahbuht, they know nothing of our golden fwendship and are likely to injure someone!"

Darkman looked at them, glad that just because he looked like Durant he was not supposed to *act* like him. In fact, he realized with amazement, this was developing even better than the original plan. Durant would soon be laughed out of business with the tough boys who ran the crime scene. About now the real Robert G. would doubtless whip out a pistol or some such, instruct Skip over there to take his leg off, tell Martinez to get it and spray these ass wipes with hot lead, and all kinds of other nasty crook-type things. The phony Durant was going to make a scene no one would forget.

"W-well," he said, stammering, "I d-don't want anybody to get hurt, Mr. Fong. What's fifty thousand when you stack it up against a friendship like ours?"

Fong nearly fell over. His associates' jaws dropped open. Martinez and Skip gaped at him, amazed.

"In fact," Darkman went on in a high, whining Durant-voice, "if any other men of Tong have debts to me, well, tell them to forget repayment. I know times are tough for the Chinese-American community."

"Boss!" Martinez hissed out of the side of his mouth. *"We net over five mill a year from the chinks!"*

"Please," Darkman said daintily. "No racist remarks. We dare not offend others."

"What?"

Darkman turned back to Fong. "My friend, this opens a new avenue for understanding between our two peoples. By setting an example we can ease the tensions between us." He went to Fong, picked up his limp hand and shook it. Fong seemed to be in shock. Darkman stifled a chuckle.

"Skip, go start the car, please," he said. Skip was rooted to the floor, blinking in astonishment. Darkman got out a cigar and handed it to Fong, who was mute with surprise. "I hope the brand is acceptable."

"Eh?" Fong stared at it. "Uh, sure. No problem, Bob." In his state of confusion he forgot to use the accent. Now Darkman did chuckle. He handed cigars to the other Chinese, as joyful as a man with a new baby to celebrate.

154

"Good-bye, old friend. Rudy, my boy, shall we go?"

Martinez looked like someone attempting to solve a difficult math problem. He stared hard at Darkman. "You're kidding, right? I mean, you're just softening them up for the real stuff, right?" He flipped his T-shirt up and jerked a black pistol out of his belt. "Who gets wasted first?"

"Stick that thing back in your drawers," Darkman snapped. "The time for killing is over. Skip, I thought I told you to go start the car."

Skip flinched, looking about ready to faint. "But the fifty grand . . ." he mumbled, and Darkman waved him away. He lurched outside, clanging the bell above the door.

"Well, then," Darkman said warmly, "I guess it's time to go. So long, men. Rudy, lead the way."

Martinez turned like a slow robot and went outside. Clang clang. Darkman cast a last sweet smile to his new friends and started to follow him.

He had the door halfway open when a taxi squealed to a stop in front of the restaurant and Robert G. Durant jumped out.

The nine minutes were up. And so, it seemed, was the short career of Darkman.

26

A Confusing Situation

ROBERT DURANT SKIRTED Skip's aged green Chrysler, stopping long enough to bend down and snarl at him. "Where the fuck is Martinez?"

Skip pointed over his head. "Right behind you. But I thought you were still inside."

"*Still* inside? What kind of dope you been smoking?" He straightened and turned. Martinez was most certainly behind him, and behind him, halfway through the door, was Robert Geoffrey Durant in the flesh, dressed in nearly identical clothes, his face taut behind the glass, his jaw hanging open in surprise.

"Who the fuck is that?" the real Durant screamed into Martinez's face, in such a frenzy that spit flew from his lips, making Martinez blink and rub his eyes.

"It's you, boss," he said.

"You dumb fucking spick! I'm right here!"

Martinez eyed him. "I guess you are. How'd you pass me up? And what's with the racist remark, asshole?"

Durant shoved him aside, screeching with rage. He went to the door and tried to pull it open.

His twin held it shut. They stared at each other through the glass, one livid with hate, the other pale and unchanging. But pale or not, he was still healthy enough to hold the door shut. Durant began kicking it, hoping to break the thick glass, but

156

it was reinforced with wire mesh and too stubborn to give in easily. Durant tried to punch a fist through it, needing to smash the imposter's face in, but the topside glass was just as stubborn as the bottom, and all he got was a case of sprained knuckles and more fuel for the fire burning inside him, Hate Central Station flaming red-hot and out of control.

He tried to bite the glass, an inner, surviving part of his sanity asking quite calmly if he really hoped to accomplish anything by this. He decided not and whirled around.

"Martinez! Shoot the fucker! Through the glass!"

Martinez whipped his pistol out fast, through force of habit. He aimed at the man behind the glass, then became confused, his eyes snapping from one Durant to the other. He lowered the pistol. "Have you got a twin or something?"

A knot of morning pedestrians hurried by. A woman saw his gun and screamed. They scattered like dandelion seeds in a storm, heading for safety should the ugly brown man decide to use the gun he had been waving around. Durant's face was taking on a decidedly purple hue. *"Shoot him!"* he bellowed.

Martinez aimed, but once again that twinge of doubt stopped his trigger finger. What was going on here, anyway? How could there be two identical bosses? Was this a practical joke, something to test his loyalty? If so, the man in the mask (whichever one that might be) was taking one hell of a chance, and so was the real Durant. Unless, of course, they had loaded his gun with blanks.

He stared down the barrel while the Durants wrestled the door back and forth. Nope, there was a bullet waiting down there at the bottom, where the pretty spiral dead-ended. So just what was the deal?

The Durant inside the building let the door go. It flipped open, sending the other one crashing down on his butt. The inside Durant became an outside Durant, and the outside Durant became the Durant on the sidewalk. Martinez began to sweat, not used to posers like this one. He looked helplessly at Skip. Skip shrugged.

"Shoot him!" the new outside Durant commanded, and Martinez aimed the pistol at the man on the ground. The Durant on the ground wobbled to his feet and pointed at the outside Durant. But they were both outside now, and there weren't any handy labels to differentiate the two. But then, one Durant was red-faced and sputtering mad while the other seemed just as mad but still looked okay.

"Shoot him!" one of them said, but it was getting hard to tell now. Martinez fought the urge to point the gun at his own head and end this confusion. Both Durants were pointing at each other, shouting. From nowhere a puff of yellow smoke rose in the air, smelling funny. Now one Durant had a hand clapped to his cheek.

Shoot him!
Shoot him!
Shoot him!
Shoot him!
Shoot him!
Shoot him!

Martinez almost wept. That stinking yellow smoke had drifted his way, and it smelled like burned hair. It occurred to him that the red-faced Durant was hot enough that his hair might catch fire, so he aimed at him. But no, it was still impossible to tell. Unfortunately, as far as mental prowess went, Martinez was not Mensa material. More puffs of yellow smoke were drifting up, along with strange popping noises. The white-faced Durant lunged at him, screaming "Shoot! Shoot! Shoot!" He swung a hand and slapped Martinez across the face.

Now that was more like the boss. He aimed at Red Face.

"You fucking idiot!" Red Face screamed, and lunged at Martinez as well. He began to throttle him. Also unfortunately for Martinez, this was more like the boss too. On the verge of nervous collapse, he threw the gun at the door, managing to explode the glass and make four huge Chinese fellows charge out. Twinkling glass crunched under their shoes and sluiced across the sidewalk like glistening pebbles. Martinez was relieved when two of them pulled Red Face away, who was most certainly the boss, because the other Durant had sprinted away with his hands over his face, trailing smoke as he high tailed it from the scene of the botched crime.

Durant wrestled himself away from the Chinese men. He snatched Martinez's gun from the place it had landed and charged after the impostor. Happy once again, Martinez bent and yanked a small backup pistol from his ankle holster. To-gether he and Durant, followed lamely by Skip, gave chase.

The impostor turned a corner, ducking out of sight. Durant and his employees thundered around the same corner thirty seconds later. Durant stepped on a smoking pile of slop on the sidewalk and fell down hard, hurting his knees and el-bows. He jumped up, enraged, and looked down the street for the other Durant.

Pedestrians, dozens of them. He had melded with the crowd.

Durant shook his fists. What the hell was this bullshit all about?

"Hey," Martinez said behind him. "Hey, boss."

Durant spun around. Martinez had picked the puddle of slop up with two fingers. It was sizzling, producing foul yel-low smoke. As Durant watched with endless disgust it fell into three revolting pieces, two of them plopping to the ce-ment. They looked like melting latex gloves. Martinez slung the last piece against a building. It stuck on the bricks there, dripping and burping, Durant's own footprint marring the features, but Durant could still tell what it had been.

His face.

It looked like the crime game was becoming a little too technical, a lot too strange.

27

Later That Same Day . . .

DARKMAN MADE HIMSELF into Peyton once again, doing it much faster now that the digitization procedure was on hard disk inside his new computer. He could become Durant anytime he felt like it, become Pauly if he needed to come back from the dead, which wasn't likely. Durant's other goon, that Smiley fellow—well, there were no photos of him yet. It didn't matter much, he was not a pivotal part of the plot. He would die, as would the others, when the time came. It reminded Darkman of that old board game called Mousetrap, where a touch of one part of the Rube Goldberg apparatus set the trap in motion and eventually caught the toy mouse. Darkman was not an assassin. He was Rube, and if his traps got set in motion by blundering goons, well, tough luck. There would be no blood on his hands.

Copping out?

No. Shut up.

What kills? The gun, the bullet, or the man holding the gun?

Do shut up.

Building the gallows does not obviate you from guilt when the trapdoor opens.

Yeah? Sez who?

Never mind. I'll shut up.

Thanks so much.

It took an age to leave the dead part of town behind and find a taxi, and Peyton swore to God and his angels that he would buy a car or die trying. He made it to Julie's apartment with only thirty-three minutes left on the stopwatch. They went to Baker's Square, where a carnival had been set up for the upcoming Oktoberfest, and strolled between the rides and gyp joints and food stands, hand in hand, listening to the barkers and the thundering diesel engines and the terrified screams of kids eighty feet in the air and having fun.

He had called Julie after the desperate escape from Durant and his boys, shaking, knowing he had nearly bought the farm, needing to see her. It was Saturday and she was free. He promised to be at her place by four and he did not lie. She assailed him with a flurry of questions, both on the phone and when he picked her up, and he tried to handle these fastballs and tricky curveballs without sounding defensive. Uppermost on her list was why he had run away at the graveyard. He stuttered something about needing medication, and she had frowned and let the matter drop. Good move on her part; Peyton did not want to lie to her, merely keep a lid on the truth until either the skin was perfected or she was ready to accept Darkman as her lover.

Hardy-har on that one. He could barely stand to look in a mirror—what would she find attractive in him?

The answer was, most surely, nothing at all. Thus the lie must live and prosper.

It was at the carnival, where a mellow afternoon sun beamed down on the whirling rides and the smell of sawdust and pony manure was thick yet somehow exhilarating, that Peyton almost blew the whole thing. Never one to try the booth where crooked BB guns were waiting for a sucker to dump quarters into the barker's pouch, he let himself pass every rip-off game without a qualm. There were ringtoss and coin tosses, plastic ducklings floating with secret numbers on their undersides, the Wheel of Fortune, the Alligator Lady, the Incredible Two-headed Baby soaking in his jug of form-aldehyde, another plastic fraud. He laughed at them, and Julie laughed with him. The air was mildly cool, speaking of winter but not demanding it, and good fun was only a ticket away. It was when they passed the throw-a-softball-at-the-milk-bottles game that Peyton's descent into horror began.

It started with Julie suddenly squealing and pointing. Peyton had an arm slung over her shoulders as they walked. She was pointing at a large pink elephant hanging on Peg-Board in the softball booth, an elephant surrounded by other stuffed animals and looking very new and expensive. Peyton shook his head good-naturedly, knowing that once you started, it was hard to quit. Besides, it was just a big rip-off.

Barely two minutes ago, as they were passing the noisy double Ferris wheel, Julie had made an attempt to close the gulf of silence that had existed during his absence. "Peyton," she had said, "I've been trying to sort out a few things. Things about us. All that time you were gone, when I thought you were dead, I kept thinking about that day of the fire, when you vanished. Do you remember proposing to me?"

He smiled. "Awkward situation, wasn't it?"

"Uh-huh. I tried to call you that afternoon, but no one answered. I wanted to tell you that I had decided about the marriage. I was going to say yes."

She looked faintly embarrassed. Peyton caught her chin with a gentle hand and guided her into a kiss.

When she pulled back, she rubbed her lips, frowning. She looked at her fingers. "What's this?" she asked, and Peyton's chest felt suddenly hollow. It was lipstick.

"Medicine," he said. "Burn ointment."

She frowned, looking puzzled, rubbing her fingers together, then bringing them up to her nose. "Lipstick," she murmured.

He forced a laugh. "Next you're going to say I'm gay."

"Don't be silly. But why do you need burn ointment? You look fine."

He searched his mind for new and better lies. Something clicked, and he had it. "I inhaled a lot of superheated air. It burned my entire respiratory system, including my mouth and lips."

"Is that why you smell a bit odd? Does the medicine have mineral spirits in it?"

He almost panicked. It was the mastic she was smelling, that dumb, stinky glue that held his lie together. "Must have,'' he said, growing nervous. He pulled the stopwatch out and furtively checked it. Eight more minutes and he would have to ditch her. How long could she go on with a man who ran away so often? He ground his teeth, feeling helpless and ashamed. Goddamn Durant . . .

"When do you want to get married?" she was asking.

He ducked his head. "Springtime would be nice."

"All right, then. April first it is."

"April Fools' Day? Heavens."

She laughed and changed the date to April second. They walked on a bit, barkers shouting at them, and then he stopped. "I have a question, Julie. A delicate one that I shouldn't even ask."

"Ask away," she said sprightfully.

"Sure. Um, while I was gone, did you happen to, ah, find someone else?"

"Find someone else? Hardly. I did meet a nice man who helped me through the grief as best he could. I respect him for his kindness but he's only a friend. You'll meet him, I'm sure."

"Okay."

They walked on toward the softball booth—and the catastrophe that was waiting. He checked the stopwatch again, trying to dredge up a decent excuse for leaving abruptly.

She saw him do it. "Will you please stop looking at that watch, Peyton? To hell with the time. Let's spend the whole day together, the whole night. The whole week, maybe."

He grunted a temporary answer as apprehension slithered up his spine and oozed fear into his brain. What now, Mr. Bright Guy? Spill the beans? Let the cat out of the bag? Open a can of worms? Pandora's box?

"Julie," he said, almost breathless, "the fire . . . it changed me. Both physically and, well, mentally. I—"

A shout interrupted him. Ahead, a greasy-looking barker was loudly inviting people to come into his show of nature's freaks for only a dollar. Beside him was a man in a rubber lizard suit, snarling and hissing. Though it was fake, it turned Peyton's stomach. Why wasn't *he* up there, a living freak with no face?

He decided that Julie must never know.

And at this moment, sure that his secret would die with him, they crossed in front of the softball booth and Julie saw the pink elephant and pointed. Glad for the change in subject, he decided to try for it, hoping Julie was done with her questions. He looked at his watch.

Three minutes left. Would the elephant help placate her when he traipsed off to nowhere? Better than nothing, maybe.

He laid down a dollar, which the barker snatched up. He was the perfect gyp-joint operator: dirty blond hair, blackheads all over his face like blown pepper, no shirt, a filthy baseball cap on his moron's head. He thumped three softballs onto the dirty counter.

"Pink elephant if I nail it?" Peyton asked.

The kid made a noise. "Good luck, Pops."

Pops? Did he look that old?

He threw the first ball, ignoring the taunt, missing the stack of wooden bottles entirely. He gave Julie a grin and threw the second one. It hit the stack at the base, where the ones weighted with lead shot were. The softball bounced off. The kid barked a short laugh.

Peyton picked up the last ball, growing angry. Sure it was a rip-off, sure it was rigged. But he wanted that pink elephant because Julie did.

He threw the ball hard, the adrenaline of anger pumping through his veins and making his ears ring. The ball hit the lower tier, the weighted bottles. They exploded off the stand and thumped against the canvas behind.

Peyton breathed easier, glad that he had kept control. He grinned at the kid. "The pink elephant, please."

The kid stuck a cigarette between his lips, looking bored. "It don't count if you're not behind the line," he said.

Peyton looked down at the dust between his feet. "There is no line."

"Pity, huh?" The kid's eyes twinkled, showing that, at the very least, he was actually alive.

"Do you see this woman?" Peyton asked, feeling the adrenaline again. He touched Julie's face. "This is my fiancée, and she wants the pink elephant."

"Tell her to buy a bottle of booze. Pink elephants guaranteed." He laughed again and lit his cigarette.

A dark pall seemed to descend over Peyton, a billowing red shroud called anger. With tremendous effort he reined in the feeling. "The pink elephant, if you please!"

Julie tugged at his sleeve. He jerked away.

"Peyton, it doesn't matter," she said, putting a hand on his arm.

He jerked away again. "It does *too* matter. I won a pink elephant for you. For my fiancée."

"Buzz off," the dirty kid said, and flipped ashes at him. "I got other customers."

"The elephant!"

He sighed and prodded Peyton's chest with two dirty fingers. "Get out of my face, asshole, or I'll knock you upside the head with your own fucking leg. Scram."

The shroud became complete. Peyton's right hand swooped to his chest. It wrapped itself around the two prodding fingers there. The kid's eyes became larger.

Peyton bent his fingers until they touched the back of his hand. There was a short, damp snap as one of them broke. He twisted tighter. Another snap. The kid uttered a hoarse, breathy moan. Peyton hoisted him by the hand, tossed him up as easily as he might toss a balloon, and caught him by the neck and crotch. He hurled him through the other standing bottles. They clattered like loud bowling pins. The kid flopped through the canvas back of the booth and was gone. A moment later he ran out onto the fairway, hands clamped together, leaving a trail of drops of blood in the dust.

Peyton leaned over the counter and unhooked the elephant. He jerked it away and thrust it at Julie.

She took a step backward, shaking her head slowly, eyes wide with terror.

"Take it!" Peyton said in a voice hoarse with rage. His hands were shaking and his face was twisted into something obscene. A blister formed on the back of his neck where the sunlight had played longest. It popped. Yellow smoke rose in a tiny cloud.

"Peyton, please," she said, her eyes jerking to the people who were beginning to stop and stare at the spectacle of a man about to clobber his date with a stuffed elephant. "Please," she said again.

165

He bared his teeth while more smoke bubbled from the back of his neck. *"Take the fucking elephant!"* he screamed.

Julie blanched, frozen, staring at him with incredulous eyes. Boils were forming on his cheeks and nose. One popped with a puff of yellow smoke. He covered his face with a hand, but the hand was alive with rising blisters.

He turned and ran, the elephant tucked under one arm, forgotten. Julie broke out of her shock and ran after him. The trail was easy to follow. She only had to follow the wispy smoke and the smell of Peyton as his face and hands disintegrated into mush.

3

Unmasked

28

Julie

HE SHOULD HAVE bought a car.

Julie, not quite thirty yet, was occasionally known to go insane and get up before dawn, slip into her Jordache jogging sweats, and put in two miles before sunrise. She didn't do it regularly or often, but it proved to her that she still had the strength, if not the willpower. And unfortunately for Darkman the man named Peyton was a notorious couch potato whose only passion was research. He didn't have a potbelly yet, and his years prevented any possible heart disease, so he was, Julie had sometimes thought, a guy who would wake up one morning and find himself forty going on dead. Then he would go insane, as she did, and he would jog and play racquetball and tennis, and he would begin to eat bran flakes because he couldn't stand the thought of wearing a colostomy bag as he cruised toward fifty and the health-horrors that waited there.

So it was not all that surprising that Julie could keep up with him as he ran, smoking and blistering, back to the only refuge he knew now. Julie stayed about a block away, slinking into alleys and shadows when she thought he might turn around, flattening herself against dirty brick walls when her instinct told her he was about to glance over his shoulder. As soon as he left the lively part of town he slowed, seeming to feel more at peace in the ravaged section where nobody went, and his pell-mell run became an easy, fast walk.

Julie was wondering about many things as she followed. Uppermost on the roster, though, were what was wrong with his skin and what was wrong with his temper. She had never seen him so enraged. Her Peyton shuffled along with his head full of formulas and his feet stuffed into Hush Puppies, the world's kindest man, if a bit eccentric. When he wasn't deep into a research project, he was as nice as you please. Behind the hard blue of his eyes was a brain that never stopped, always running in high gear on an eternal speed trip to the farthest reaches of human knowledge. Julie wondered if this was why she loved him—for his brain and the places it could carry him.

What had happened to him? What was he hiding?

It struck her that she should not ask and never know. The baloney about superheated air cooking his lips was barely plausible, if at all. That stuff on her fingers had been lipstick. And when he held her face to be kissed, his hand had been as cool as a corpse, his lips as cold and unyielding as ice in the sunlight. And that other smell, the turpentine. What was it?

Go back.

No, not quite yet. First we must discover what has become of Peyton Westlake.

You don't want to know, Julie. He is kind and good and is hiding a dark and terrible secret. Let him work things out by himself.

A block ahead, he slowed and turned his head.

Julie shrank back, in time to miss his gaze but with enough time to see one side of his face.

He had a halloween mask on, some plastic device that looked like running tallow and bare bone. She dived into the protective shadow of an alley, panting, her face red and slick with sweat. *Okay, Julie,* she said to herself, *you're a lawyer. Put this case together. Assemble the facts and damn the torpedoes.*

Fine. Something was wrong with Peyton's face. Something was wrong with one of Peyton's hands, maybe both. He had mentioned a coma and severe burns.

But . . . he didn't *have* any burns.

She frowned. Still frowning, she peeked around the corner.

He had veered left, crossing the street. Ancient factories and high rises bulked to the sky around him, buildings black with coal soot and decay. He looked over his shoulder once more, pulled the elephant free from its position under his arm, looked at it, then banged open the door of a squat two-story building and vanished inside.

Huh?

No problem here, she thought in an attempt to remain cool. Peyton has become a fan of dreary darkness, slum dwellings, and half-starved pigeons. The guy always had one strange quirk after another, as genius scientists tended to. And if he wanted Julie here, he would have asked her to come.

She walked to the building, pulling her sweater tighter against the windy gusts of the oncoming season, determined to follow him until she knew everything, and then she would help him. No matter how strange his affliction might be, she would help him.

She came to the door and touched it gently. It did not open. She pushed harder and the hinges squealed a metallic protest. Pulling her hand away, the door still open a crack, she was still debating, still unsure.

A noise from inside caught her ear. Something—cloth?— was being torn in there. Someone—something?—was shouting and grunting, the echoes in the abandoned building rebounding off the walls two times before evaporating. It was as dark as a cave inside, vaguely damp and cool. A breeze wafted out of the crack in the doorway and reeked of dust and rotten meat.

She gathered her nerve and pushed the door fully open.

Something large and whitish was hanging just above eye level, hard to see in this light. Under a cloak of dead varnish and dust was a sign proclaiming this place to be

REYTON SOAP COMPANY
HOME OF FRESH SPLASH SOAP
AND OTHER HOUSEHOLD PRODUCTS.

How nice, she thought. Peyton has purchased a soap franchise. Time to go now, Julie, old pal, and on April second we shall be wed.

She stepped inside, wrinkling her nose at the smell. The place was dimly lighted by old lamps hanging on chains from the ceiling. She stayed motionless, waiting for her eyes to adjust, seeing big blotches of purple and silver where the sun had shined in her eyes. In thirty seconds she was less blind.

The tearing sound went on, somewhere back in the shadowy corners, and so did the inhuman slobbers and grunts. She went forward cautiously, expecting only pleasant surprises, too scared to envision anything but Peyton playing a huge practical joke at her unwilling expense. She opened her mouth, about to make a funny remark for Peyton's benefit, but she realized that nothing was funny here. There were no jokes at all left in this miserable ruin of a factory, and whoever was in that corner making horrible noises had to be Peyton and no one else.

Her feet gritted over dirty cement as she walked to where the light was better, down a short flight of steps and into the heart of the building. Her hand slipped up to cover her mouth, and her wide eyes took in everything.

It was a lab, a sordid copy of the laboratory where Peyton had slaved so long, this one nothing but splintered doors hung from chains, crates for tables, a dead office chair parked in front of a computer. Empty Pizza Hut boxes were in a ragged pile nearly five feet tall against the far wall. She shook her head in disbelief. From the look of things he had been here quite a while. But why?

The grunting and ripping noises stopped abruptly. Something—some black and furry thing—sailed out of nowhere, flipping end over end, and flopped against the computer. Two black-button eyes glittered from its face as it fell and rolled across the floor.

Julie had almost screamed, thinking of giant bats, but this was no bat, this twisted rag.

She walked resolutely to the thing on the floor. She picked it up.

A stuffed elephant. In better light it would be pink. No matter now. It had been torn and smashed, the stuffing gutted, the arms and legs perforated with bite-size chunks still damp with warm saliva.

She let it drop to the floor. The computer screen to her right was pulsing, casting a sick green glow across the rusty frame of the office chair. She bent to look, pushing the chair aside. The wheels squeaked briefly. The screen read,

PEYTON DIGITIZATION COMPLETE.

She frowned again. That sounded familiar, that odd word, that digitization thing. She had pet names for almost every piece of Peyton's research equipment, having spent many hours with him, serving as timekeeper. Everything had a name, from the Camera-Slamera, the ThinkTank-PinkTank and the Bio-Mess, to the Digitization and Masturbation machine. It had been kind of cutesy, back in the days when Peyton was so sure he would be successful, before his dreams and his artificial skin disintegrated into flames and failed hopes.

So he was trying again. She was still not sure why.

Burns.

He isn't burned.

Artificial skin for burn victims.

HE ISN'T BURNED!

A hideously mangled victim of explosion, flame, super-heated air.

Superheated air?

She could hear someone breathing, now that the tearing noise of the elephant being ripped to shreds was gone. She thought she heard deep, almost piglike moans and slobbers, but they came from a dark corner of the factory, where the lights were burned out and a broad wedge of shadow masked what might be inside. She stepped toward the strange sounds, tight inside with fear and a timid sort of curiosity. *Madame,* she thought with a sick and bloated kind of bad humor. *Madame, the lady, or the tiger. The door behind you is no longer a mystery. The dark ahead is a door of another kind, something that may be revealed as light and hope, something that may be horror and death. Enter at your own risk.*

She was about to ease into the shadow when something

flipped through the air over her head. It plopped against the lid of the Bio-Mess and lay there hissing and bubbling, giving off a loathsome smoke that smelled of decay and putrefaction.

She pressed a hand over her nose, breathing through the cracks between her fingers, wanting to see what Peyton had worn over his face.

She went over and picked it up with two fingers. It was hot, a melted mask with drooping slits for eyes, two holes for a nose, and a long horizontal slit for a mouth. Dripping lipstick ran from the soft bulges that had been lips. Even in this stage of cellular destruction she knew what it was. She had seen masks like this hundreds of times, when Peyton had been working on his doomed project. But the remnants of this bubbling sample even *looked* like Peyton.

Two more flapping objects sailed a short distance into the light and flopped across the dusty floor, leaving wet smears that exuded thin yellow smoke. One was a ball of mush, unrecognizable. The other was a sticky rubber glove, its deflated fingers crossed over each other and tucked under the palm in disarray, the whole hand going rapidly flat, smoky.

It took her the space of four seconds to add two and two. The sum she came up with was as four as four ever got.

Peyton was burned—had been burned. His . . . face was destroyed. His hands were disfigured.

She whirled to face the blackness of the corner where Peyton had hidden himself, where he had murdered the elephant, and where he had hidden when he'd hurled his disturbing costume across the room.

"Peyton!" she snapped, actually angry now. "Why didn't you tell me? If you loved me, why didn't you tell me?"

Better accustomed now to the dark, she could perceive his shadow and a small outline of his face. In this dismal light he looked very fine, and she wondered if her two and two might equal five.

He raised his arms and covered his face. This did not change Julie's attitude. Why was this new Peyton so strange, anyway? There were thousands and thousands of burn victims in the world, maybe millions. Did they shuffle off to an empty rat hole like this? Did they avoid contact, run away, hide in corners? She thought not.

"Peyton," she demanded. "You come out here *now*!"

He didn't move. For no particular reason Julie could think of, she began to cry. God, the hurts she had endured, the grief and agony, the desperate wish to die and be with him, the hours spent at his graveside seeking peace. And all along, here he was in this rent-free dump, putting his laboratory back together, making himself a new life, a masked marvel.

Julie stared at the black apparition named Peyton Westlake, sobbing with anger because he had put her through a special sort of hell while he schemed and chemistried and slunk in darkness like a rat.

Her teeth were clenched tight, her fingernails digging into the heels of her hands, burning tears slipping down her cheeks, ruining her mascara. "Talk to me!" she screamed, and the man in the corner stepped forward hesitantly. A bar of yellow lamplight struck a portion of his face momentarily, and Julie saw crispy black skin at the edges of his face, a chunk of dirty white bone, twin holes the shape of apple seeds where his nose should be.

She shook her head, her eyes full of reproach and pity. "You really thought it would make a difference to me, didn't you? Did you also think that I was in love with your face and nothing else? Your hands? How little do you think of me?"

His head dipped with obvious remorse.

"Peyton," she said firmly, "you will come to me now and we will plan our future together. I do not care what you look like."

The shape moved. Feet scraped over filthy cement.

Julie waited, tense, a reservoir of pity and helpfulness that was held in place by a solid dam of love, the dam ready to crumble and engulf this wretched man in the balmy waters of unquestioned acceptance.

And she waited, ready to raise her arms and engulf him, absolutely not caring how mangled he might be.

The footsteps faded. They quit abruptly.

"Peyton!" she screamed.

Nothing

"Peyton!"

Nothing.

"Peyton?"

175

Nothing.

And then, very far away, maybe on the second floor, a raspy whisper: *Julieeeee* . . .

But she had already had enough and was finding her way out. The path was dim, her eyes swimming with tears, the floor littered with lines of cable. She stumbled once, falling to one knee and tearing her pants open. Finally the back of the Fresh Splash sign was overhead. She had found,the door.

29

Louis and Julie

THE NEXT MORNING found Louis Strack in high spirits. His investment counselor in Austria, Franz, a wonderful businessman who never dressed like an Austrian—no feathered cap, no lederhosen—was working miracles for Louis. Louis's original investment of fifty thousand South African Krugerrands two weeks ago had witnessed a gain of nearly eight points on the international monetary exchange, and Franz, true to his word, waited for a slump and then bought at the bottom. Louis Strack became twelve thousand dollars richer in thirteen days.

Only twelve grand. Louis was not satisfied. That morning he was prepared to celebrate, but with only a twelve-grand profit he decided not to invite anybody to the celebration but himself. Guests of Louis's caliber did not assemble to congratulate a piddly fortune of such a shoddy magnitude; they wanted to see molten gold flow from fountains, silver from water faucets, platinum and uranium from backyard sprinklers. The local crème de la crème would hardly stand for rejoicing bum's wages.

But Louis was pleased enough with his own prosperity to refuse to invite a bunch of octogenarians and their decrepit spouses to his house, anyway. It was this attitude, then, that ruined the idea of a party. Sure it was a meager profit for a multimillionaire to make, but the old geezer, Strack, who had run the company for so many years, never had experienced such fast money. His drab old real-estate purchases were usually in the discussion stage for two years, the closing set for two additional years later, the parties involved paying lawyers hefty fees to rake the other parties over the coals and find a flaw. It was a business that was conservative to the bone. Louis would continue in his father's footsteps, but first he would do something he had dreamed about for years.

At exactly quarter after eight in the morning, when he was normally up and stuffing four poached eggs down his throat with toast and coffee, Louis was doing something quite strange. He was taking a bath in Krugerrands. Strange even for Louis, who was not prone to such peculiarities.

He had told Franz to ship him a strongbox of fifty thousand Krugerrands via Federal Express, damn the expense and damn the fear of getting embroiled in an international money scandal. The Krugerrands had to pass through Britain, which was a problem, because England refused to do business with anything even remotely connected with South Africa. Thus the loot had to be disguised. That left good old Franz of Austria in a bit of a bind, so he marked the incredibly heavy crate MACHINE PARTS, and off it went. Louis received it one day later, not a scratch on the old-looking crate, a box of machine parts if ever there was one.

It was in the bedroom of his mansion now, carted there the previous day by two Federal Express teenagers in blue-white-and-red outfits. Louis had tipped them a gold Krugerrand each. Young, baffled, they had asked if it was a Spanish doubloon. Better than that, Louis had replied. They went away, smiling uneasily, studying their booty, wondering if they had gotten the shaft.

You dumb little jerks, Louis had thought, and slammed the door on them.

Now, however, he was fulfilling a fantasy.

The strongbox had been heavier than a crate of anvils. Dragging it this sunny morning by one rope handle, naked to the bone, he tugged the crate across the floor to the bed, then paused there, panting. With more effort he upended the crate and let the strongbox fall open on the unmade bed.

178

They sluiced out, bright gold tiddledywinks surging across the mattress, clattering change that could make a monk swear off poverty forever. The box got lighter as it emptied. Many of the golden coins slid off the mattress and tinkled to the floor as Louis shook out the last few of them, probably a million dollars' worth of 99.99 percent pure African gold.

He dropped the empty box beside the bed, his eyes large with love. The gold coins winked at him as the morning sun played through the windows, the breeze ruffling his chiffon window drapes, strong sunlight filling the room with yellow beams and making these odd coins the size of silver dollars sparkle happily. Louis took three steps backward, pressed his hands together as if to pray, and launched himself onto the bed and its coating of gold. Having dreamed of this moment for years while his late father doddered around in a dark age of stupidity, Louis was sure it would be the best roll in the hay of his life. Sure the Rockefellers were rich, and the Kennedys, the Morgans and the heirs of Howard Hughes—if they were finally sorted out—the Capusteins and the Fords. But Louis had a need for money they could never understand. The Stracks had never had a silver spoon shoved into their infant mouths, had never been handed the family fortune and the keys to an empire without working for it. Louis had worked high steel for two years, just to get the feel of real sweat. Old Man Strack had been a self-starter, rich because he'd made himself that way, and this fact put his many financial rivals on the offensive. Had to work to get rich, eh, old boy? How perfectly shoddy.

Not much of this was on Louis's mind as he breezed through the air of his bedroom like a pink dolphin and landed facedown on golden coins. The landing was unexpectedly abrupt, even painful, but it didn't matter. At last, at last, he was actually swimming in gold. He crowed a laugh into the pillow, turned over, and backstroked through the coins while making sea-gull noises. His sexual feelings had switched to high gear, shifted there by feelings full of power and gold. He flopped over again, grinding his hips into the mattress and its cool blanket of money. He would have been content to lie there all day, his head thumping with desire and his body determined to get satisfaction, even if he had to order another fifty thousand Krugerrands to make the penetration complete.

But the phone rang. He sat up, his face growing angry under his tousled cap of black hair. He raised a hand and brushed his fingers through his hair, with little effect.

It rang again. *"Jenkins!"* he shouted, knowing that the old geezer was toddling around with a feather duster, stupidly intent on his current task, deaf and dumb to the world like dear departed Father had been.

"Jenkins!"

Ring. Ring.

Louis jumped out of bed, ready to hire a hit man to take care of Jenkins, and pounced on the phone. His teeth were bared as he answered it. "What!"

The lines of his face quickly smoothed out. He smiled. "Of course, Julie, of course. Don't worry about this being Sunday, and no, I don't go to church. At the office in one hour? Damn right I'll be there. In an hour. No problem."

He hung up and looked sourly over his shoulder to the bed, where a ton of money sat waiting to be spent. Or hoarded. Or melted down to form the world's largest ingot. Hmm. At any rate, it was here.

He dressed quickly, tailored suit as always, impeccable shoes and shine, a tie that was brother to the suit. Before he left his bedroom he checked himself in the mirror on the wall.

"Hairbrush," he said, and went out.

She got there five minutes after Louis arrived, stepping out of the elevator on the third floor with the Strack suite just ahead to her left. She walked to the door, then hesitated, summoning her courage, nervously touching her hair as if her appearance really mattered at this stage of their doomed relationship. She did not know what to expect from Louis when she dropped this particular bombshell, but he was a gentleman and would probably bow out with no hard feelings. Anyway, he seemed permanently in love with his dead wife, and now that Julie was no longer a victim of tragedy like Louis, they no longer orbited in the same sphere.

She tried the doorknob. Unlocked. So Louis was already

there. She swung the door and stepped inside, where the aroma of newly cleaned carpet and filtered air was light and refreshing. Past the secretary's large desk, the door of Louis's office was open a bit, a trace of cigar smoke drifting out to be snatched up by the air ventilators. She could hear him speaking and wondered if someone else was here. Timidly Julie went to the door and knocked softly.

A phone was hung up in a hurry, plastic banging against plastic. Julie hesitated again, feeling like a snoop. She flicked the door with her fingernails, not knowing what to expect.

"Julie? Come on in."

She pushed the door fully open and saw Louis standing behind his desk, his clothing flawless, his desk utterly clean save for the intercom/telephone, a closed brown briefcase, and an ashtray in which a dead cigar sat looking glum. There was a large velvet drapery on the wall to his right, something Julie couldn't recall having been there. But then again, maybe it had been. She was always so fascinated by Louis that she failed to take in what her eyes offered, nearly hypnotized by his presence and the authority he exuded. "Hi, Louis," she said, and went to one of the two chairs that faced his desk. "Sit?"

He rolled his eyes, grinning. "Nah, don't dare sit in front of me, woman. I am Lord Strack of Strack Industries, and of gold investments."

She returned his smile, nearly overwhelmed again by his personality, and sat down before her knees could unhinge and dump her on the floor. "Louis," she said before her nerve had a chance to leave her dumbstruck and speechless, "we have to talk."

He rubbed his hands together, never losing his smile. "Sure thing, doll. I love to talk. Brandy before we start?"

She shook her head, determined to see this through without false courage.

"Up to you. I think I'll have one, though." He rolled a drawer open and pulled out a bottle and a snifter. He blew into the snifter and wiped the rim on his sleeve. "Ancient things, these," he said by way of apology, and turned to the window to let the morning sun travel through the glass, inspecting it for traces of dust. "I must warn you, Julie, that this is a very fine Napoleon you have just passed up. Chances like this don't come often. Share?"

She shook her head again, inner resolve spiking up her courage, goading her on before this got smarmy and she professed her undying love. "Louis," she said, "I can't see you anymore."

Okay, fine, now it was out. He turned. She glanced into his eyes, expecting anything between a laugh and an atomic explosion. She got neither.

"Settle down," he said jokingly as he poured his brandy. "Don't rush yourself or me. As you said, let's talk."

Julie stammered a few unintelligible words, her mind cruising in useless circles, desperate to pick up a thought that was relevant. She loved—still loved—Peyton. He was back and needing help in a hurry. When he had asked her if she had found someone else in his absence, she had mentioned Louis as a personal friend, feeling strangely that she was lying. For Louis her desires stopped at the friendship stage. But for Louis Strack himself, well . . . he had been making his desires more and more obvious. Yes, Louis, was a man on the move.

Sure, the evening a few days ago had been a catastrophe, that evening he tried to kiss her. The next evening had been far better, and under the pressure of his hands and fingers she reluctantly had given in. But as her mother would have secretly asked when Julie was a teenager, "For God's sake, did you go all the way?"

To be honest, no. After the incident on the balcony Louis had become the wounded lover, bereft of pride, ego-battered, love-tested to the extreme. And when he did rub her thigh a night or two ago, she had not protested. When his fingers crawled up her skirt on a mission very important for him, she had not thumped him with an ashtray. Expecting the night to end as it should have, she had been startled when he stood up and announced that he must go home and to bed.

Strange character, Louis. In forty-eight hours he had turned Julie's unintentional victory on the balcony into a success for himself. The lady was primed, the night was soft and full of promise, the liquor flowed by the bucket. Somewhere in that process she forgot her place and caved in to his mastery, fully expecting a night full of secrets and dark passion.

None of that happened. When he announced his departure and walked out, she felt betrayed and was almost angry. Call her nutty. The man who meant nothing to her had made her mad by not demanding a tumble in the sack.

But she still loved Peyton, didn't she?

There was a black curtain hanging between her and her own past—the shadows behind the curtain a memory of Peyton, the light before a more recent memory of Louis, the fellow griever and comforter. But Peyton was back. Damaged and different now, he was back. Peyton's first appearance in the cemetery was now a vague memory of something that never had happened, something that had transpired in her fevered mind and nowhere else. Thus she could pass it off as wishful thinking. But yesterday afternoon, when she chased him into the deserted ghetto and cornered him in a soap factory—that was not easy to pass off as hallucination. Peyton was alive, and he needed her.

Louis was staring at her as she took this trip down memory lane, puzzled, his head cocked and his eyes bright. She came to herself with a jerk.

"Need sleep?" he asked when her eyes were clear. "I could rustle up a cot somewhere."

She touched her temples, driving the daydreams and memories away. "Sorry," she whispered.

His smile became very fatherly. "You said something about never seeing me again. What's up?"

She ground her knuckles into her eyes. Just what was up? She felt like a jittery woman at a job interview. How silly. She made her face stern and went on. "Louis, you know that I was engaged to Peyton Westlake before he . . . vanished."

He nodded, then leaned forward and placed his elbows on the desk, idly shoving the briefcase aside. A brass latch popped apart, and the briefcase split open awkwardly, crammed full of industrial secrets. "Engaged? You never told me that."

She dropped her head, ashamed. "He asked me before he died. I mean, he asked me before the . . . fire."

"And?"

"And I finally told him yes."

Louis laughed without much humor. "Julie, is that what brought us down here on a Sunday? Is this what you wanted to talk about?"

"Partly," she said.

"Fine, then. It does not disturb me that you were engaged to the late Peyton Westfrazzle, or whatever his name was. Ooops, sorry. I don't mean to belittle the man."

"Forgiven," she said mechanically, needing to say more but not wanting to.

He flashed that big smile again. "Darling, don't worry yourself about the niceties of a new relationship like ours. You and I are lost, both of us, trudging around on a parched desert of pain and grief. No one I've ever met before has given me the space to acknowledge my feelings without seeming moody. All I offer you is equal treatment for your malady." He paused, drawing a breath. "Pals now?"

She wished she had checked her purse before coming, for inside, nestled among makeup and nameless useful odds and ends, might be a small pack of tissues. The tears were coming on fast, a floodgate waiting to be opened. She rummaged through her purse and found nothing but hard junk.

"Louis," she squeaked, fighting those tears, "Peyton is still alive. He was burned in the fire, horribly burned. I don't quite understand what happened, but I know he needs me. I know it."

Louis stared at her for a moment, expressionless, then looked down at his desktop. He set the snifter of brandy aside and wormed his fingers together. "Oh, Julie," he said softly. "Your news has a bittersweet flavor. Of course I am very happy for you and wish the best for Peyton. If there's anything I can do—medical care, money for him to live on, even a job when he's ready, it's his. I, uh, I just wonder . . . how badly was he . . . injured?"

Julie mashed her purse to her face, a purse smelling of leather and time and the day Peyton had given it to her for no reason at all; just like the necklace, which had been his queer way of asking for her hand in marriage. Her sobs were enormous, sobs for Peyton and his peculiar suffering, sobs for Louis and the love affair that had been star-crossed from the start.

Louis's telephone began ringing like an unwelcome stranger to this party of grief, and Louis snatched it up, covering the receiver as he walked to a far corner. Julie's breakdown was nothing that a business client should have to hear about. He said hello, then talked into the telephone, his voice low and impossible to understand. Not that she really cared. The tragedies that life was intent on heaping on her shoulders were becoming too much to bear.

She looked up, her face wet with tears smeared into crazy shapes by the angles of the purse, and looked the desk over, wishing to God Louis had some Kleenex someplace.

Something caught her eye, and she forgot about tears and Kleenex for a long time.

The briefcase had one latch undone. Packed paperwork spilled out of the narrow gap in the brown leather while the other latch held on for dear life. Two or three sheets of paper were now visible. The only thing that was extraordinary here was the topmost paper, the one with the ring of spilled coffee on its face, the one Peyton had set a cup of coffee on so long ago.

The Bellasarious memorandum.

Her throat clenched up, trying to strangle her. The office seemed incredibly hot all of a sudden. The form of Louis in the corner was abruptly menacing, skulking through secrets, plotting crimes. Even the smell of his after-shave was repulsive.

He hung up the phone and carted it back to his desk. "Ten thousand more Krugerrands, Julie. The sky's the limit, huh? God, how I love . . ." He glanced down to the desk and the paper she was staring at.

There was a long silence then.

"You," she said at last, a word spat out with the acid of anger, the steam of raw hate. "You did it all."

He put on a lopsided grin. "Yes, the Bellasarious memo. Too bad you had to see it, and all my fault. This may be a serious strain on our relationship."

"You burned Peyton's lab," she hissed.

"Not me personally," he said, looking wounded. "I have

an employee who does certain things for me. Things I would rather . . . not do myself."

She stared at his face, trying to find a motive there for having turned her life and Peyton's upside down, a reason for his goodness and his badness. His face was a blank stone.

"Now I guess you have to kill me," she said coldly, full of ice and dread inside.

He smiled ingratiatingly, as if tutoring a small child about the ways of the world. "Hardly, Julie. You have nothing solid on me, and I believe you would find a very unsympathetic police department should you report this. Much of Strack Industries money goes to beneficial causes, including the bribery of police officials, the best charity of all. So before you get into your head an idea of conquering the nasty capitalist and its uniformed henchmen, please consider this." His face went soft. "I love you," he whispered. "I really, really do."

He walked to the velvet curtain before Julie could get her thoughts together, and slung it apart, revealing a large square table. He snapped on a light and waved to her.

"This will be the riverfront in two years, Julie. Office buildings, shopping malls, clean sidewalks, and safe condominiums. No crime, no filth, no poverty. A new city within this dying city, a new start."

She went reluctantly to the large scale model on the table. Someone had put a great deal of time into constructing it, with its buildings and its exotic landscape and its miniature cars parked in tiny lots. There were even tiny trees with leaves made of green foil and miniature pedestrians strolling about, frozen in time. All in all, Julie was impressed, but only by the architect who had designed this and nothing else.

"You and I," Louis said, and Julie glanced at him. "You and I, together, building a new city. We cannot let anything get in the way of that goal."

She glared at him, hoping her eyes were boring twin holes through his expensive suit *and* expensive hide.

He winked at her, mocking. "Despite the way things might appear, you can't pretend that moments haven't passed between us, Julie. We shared something, and we can still have it."

186

Her eyes became narrow. "If you're not going to kill me, I have better things to do."

He waved a hand. "I'll be in touch."

She went to the door, filled with rage and betrayal and the righteous desire to snap something obscene in his face.

Instead she went out and never came back.

But she would see him again, on different turf, in a different way, a way that would be very deadly.

Louis snatched the phone up the second Julie was through the door and out of sight. He dialed a number he knew very well, the number of a man who did not mind working on Sundays.

It rang once. "Yes?" Robert G. Durant said.

"Do you want the bad news or the good news?"

"I like bad the best, Mr. Strack. Hit me with it."

Louis sat down. "Do you recall the little difficulty I had with my father, and how you resolved it? I must say, even I was surprised."

Durant chuckled. "Call me lightning, Mr. Strack. I strike when you least expect it."

"That's what I pay you for, Robert. Now I have a similar problem with a certain Julie Hastings. Know her?"

"Yep. She was that dingleberry Westlake's main squeeze. So?"

"She is our key to Mr. Westlake."

Durant drew a quick breath. "Boss, he blew up with his chink pal! I swear it!"

Louis propped his feet on his desk beside the briefcase. "It seems that when you retrieved the Bellasarious memorandum, you failed to expunge the good professor."

Durant sounded weak. "Please say you're kidding."

"No joke, Robert, and I don't put up with shoddy tactics. I want him dead."

Durant gulped into the phone, sounding much like Elmer Fudd. "But—but—but—"

"Do not have a nervous collapse like your friend Rick did, or I will have you eaten by crocodiles. Got it?"

There was a pause. Then, timidly, "You mean real crocodiles, Mr. Strack?"

"I never lie. I want Westlake eliminated forever."

Durant sounded very childlike now. "How can I find him, boss?"

Louis smiled. "I believe we have a little girl who will guide us there."

They talked for a while and then hung up. Louis went home and swam in gold the entire afternoon, then called his favorite prostitute to join him on his mattress of money.

He tipped her ten Krugerrands beyond the normal fee. No one would ever call Louis a skinflint, just like no one would ever call Louis a crook.

It was a grand life, after all.

30

Durant

ROBERT G. DURANT hung up the phone after Mr. Strack had clicked off, his face creased with confusion, his lips pursed in a mystified frown. Westlake not dead? Preposterous. That egghead scientist had been blown to bits, along with his chink buddy. Plus, he had been electrocuted and gotten his face fried off. But why, oh why, Durant wondered, hadn't he told Martinez or even that jitterbug Rick to invest a few bullets toward the good doctor's future? Who could have foreseen that he would survive that kind of treatment?

Durant stood in the den of his expensive house in Briar Wood Estates, surrounded by potted plants and a regal bookcase that took up two walls. There were Thoreau and Twain and Joyce, massively thick volumes of every kind of book. To top it off, Durant even owned a rare collector's edition of a Jack London novel.

Of course he had not read any of these rare editions. His head was too full of thoughts about crime and money ever to let him concentrate on the written word. But when business acquaintances dropped by, this luxurious combination of den, greenhouse, and library was most impressive. If there was one truth about him that should never be exposed, it was the fact that he was borderline stupid and a social cripple. Most of his talents lay in the area of being a cutthroat and a bully. Those were roles he played quite well. Let others think of him as a self-made rich man, a gentleman and a scholar. Very few would think of him as the coldhearted sleaze he really was.

Standing amid this luxury, staring blankly at the telephone, he tried to dredge up some decent reason for Westlake to be alive. At the same time he wondered how to extricate himself from this monstrous blunder. Mr. Strack had not sounded very angry on the phone, but he hadn't sounded all that overjoyed, either.

Durant slumped into his expensive leather desk chair, eyebrows drawn together, frown deepening. He picked up a pencil and began to tap it on the desk. In another room a stereo was playing some unpronouncable German opera, for Durant had quite a collection of classical works. He tried to spend at least twenty minutes every day listening to the crap, figuring that eventually someone might mention opera at a stuffy party and he didn't want to sound dumb. If there was one thing he hated more than almost everything else he hated, it was looking like a dope and feeling like the brainless crook he was.

The pencil tapped. The stereo blared Wagner. The frown hung on. He was feeling like a dope. One little shit named Westlake had managed to put his position with Strack in jeopardy, and that position was the only thing keeping him from poverty and bread lines. Strack was considered Mr. Nice Guy to the bone. His charitable donations kept the police away from Durant, freeing him to perform every dirty trick in the book.

Durant gave his padded shoulders a little shrug. Today he was wearing a black pin-striped suit and an Indiana Jones hat. On his feet were patent-leather shoes with tips as pointy as spears. In about two hours Dana was supposed to come over and screw his brains out, and he had hoped to surprise her today by actually dressing up before they got down to business. Even better, since the old whip was worn out, he had bought a new one. God, but did that Dana scream loud. He couldn't ask for a better partner in S and M, his favorite sport next to killing people.

Yeah, that again. While musing, he had almost forgotten about Westlake and the sorry mess he had landed him in. Bad enough that this Sunday's weekly screw was, well, screwed. Strack wanted Westlake dead in a hurry. Sure, no problem, boss. We'll follow his girlfriend and find out where Mr. Genius scientist lives. Then we shall plug him and watch him die.

Really think so?

Well, yeah. So he survived electrocution. Who wouldn't? That boiling pink shit in the tank had toasted him, made him bald, burned off his face. Big deal.

What about the explosion?

Ahem. Yes. Ahem.

He's one tough sumbitch. Maybe wears bulletproof long johns. Why bother, though, when your whole head is one burned marshmallow? Jeez . . . no hair, no scalp, no face, no . . .

No face.

No face!

Durant felt himself suddenly trembling as various mental tornadoes churned up new thoughts from the depths of his limited brain. That disgusting thing in the alley beside Chin Fong's joint, that was a melting mask. The smoking gloves, fake hands? Why? To avoid leaving fingerprints? No. Because Westlake's hands were black and burned clear down to the bone.

He was a master of disguises, obviously. A genius, a survivor, a terrifying menace. What if he did wear bulletproof long johns, like those metal suits skin divers do when they're in shark territory? How do you get around that?

He sat there and thought, still frowning, his forehead beginning to ache from it. If Westlake was smart enough to look like anybody he wanted to, maybe Pauly hadn't been lying. Westlake made the pickup, not Pauly. Rick would drop dead on the spot if he saw Westlake, and maybe he had. And just maybe Westlake was Mr. Strack now. Maybe.

Durant realized he was on the brink of panic. Why would Westlake pretend to be Strack? Why would he tell Durant to kill Westlake if Westlake was really Strack, and could he be Strack and then Westlake at the same . . . ?

He dropped his head into his hands, wallowing in confusion and misery. New Wave crime, techno crime, seemed to be the rage now. What had happened to the Capones and Dillingers? God, but it had been easier in those days. Not that Durant had been alive back then—he was only thirty-seven now—but the old black-and-white movies he had watched made those years seem fun.

He decided to give this matter a lot of thought, even though his head was aching already from the mental gymnastics. The murder of Westlake would not be an ordinary hit, you could bet your buns on that. This particular job demanded courage, intelligence, and a better weapon than the standard Ruger .22 pistol at close range, the choice of both the CIA and R. G. Durant. A silenced .22 made less noise than a door being slammed, but it wouldn't be any good if Westlake was wearing body armor or some kind of bulletproof mask.

Damn. That melting thing in the alley by Fong's place—had it been bulletproof? Hadn't looked like it. But still . . .

An idea jumped into his mind. You can bulletproof yourself all you want, but a .50-caliber machine gun will penetrate many inches of solid steel. Even if it didn't punch through the armor, the force alone would shatter Westlake's insides, like getting tossed off a building and landing hard on a steel rod. Shooting Westlake with a .50 would be very satisfying indeed. But therein lay a small problem.

A .50-caliber machine gun weighed about a zillion pounds, despite the comic books that show Sergeant Rock carrying one in each fist. It would be possible, with some metalwork, to anchor one to the roof of a car; however, the cops, bribed or not, would hardly stand for carting a gun that big and that illegal around town.

Well, damn, Durant thought wearily. It wouldn't be all that hard to get one: Notify the supplier, who gets his wares from Colombia, that you would like to buy one, and pretty soon a van comes over and the supplier's boys haul it out in two crates. Cost? Maybe five grand. Pocket change for Mr. Strack.

So, how to mount the thing? Forget a car. Truck? Nah. Airplane?

Durant emitted a cheerless chuckle. Airplane. Har-har. Why not just buy a helicopter? They only run about three hundred thousand. No, it seemed . . .

Wait. Durant's eyes were growing larger. *Helicopter!* Two

years ago he had done a large favor for a man who piloted an air-ferry service from the shore of Lake St. Clair. It seemed the man's ferry business was about to fall apart, and he needed a million dollars in a hurry, twenty-five percent going to Durant if he would make the wife's death look quite natural. "No problem," Durant had said. "Go ahead and buy that million-dollar insurance policy. In two weeks she will be very dead. You just make sure you have a solid alibi every moment of the next fourteen days."

Fourteen days later the poor man's wife was kidnapped. The police found out about the insurance policy that was so new, the ink still smelled funny. The husband was arrested, but not for long. His alibi was rock solid.

It was three days later that they found her nude body in a ditch not far from home. She had been raped, and stabbed forty-seven times. There was a strange fingerprint on her purse latch, and a check showed it belonged to Roddy "King Killer" Dorado, a minor crime figure who had been murdered years before.

The APB went out: He ain't dead. Find Roddy.

The coroner had the body exhumed. It didn't smell all that great, so his team worked with unusual haste. The only strange thing they found was that one of Roddy's fingers was missing.

The case was never solved. The pilot got his million. Instead of getting a quarter of a million dollars, Durant settled for two hundred grand.

"I don't get it," the man had said, and Durant grinned at him.

"The stabbing wasn't all that fun," Durant had said, "but I loved the part where I got to rape her."

They enjoyed a hearty laugh, and Durant showed him his collection of fingers, proudly pointing to the one that had been Roddy's before Durant had killed him those long years ago.

Musing over those happy times, Durant lit a cigar and dialed the phone. It took thirty seconds to place the gun order. It took a full minute to get hold of that pilot guy, but he agreed it would be a lot of fun, and do you mind if I land in your front yard?

"No problem," Durant said, then hung up and called Martinez and Smiley and Skip.

When it was over, Durant leaned back in his chair and smiled. Mission almost accomplished. Westlake was about to be dead again.

31

Smiley

"I CAN'T BELIEVE this shit," the man nicknamed Smiley said as he drove. His real name was Sam Rogers, but few people knew that, because he did not know many people. If by chance he did meet someone, the someone would usually see to it that their paths never crossed again. Below the grimy tangle of his mud-brown hair was a dull and flattened face, a small potato for a nose, a mouth welded into a permanent loony grin. In other words, your basic crazy man.

When Sam was thirteen years old, he was notoriously famous as the cruelest kid on the block. Dogs, puppies, cats, kittens—any sort of pet let outside the house in his crummy little town, Wabash Heights—usually wound up dead. His favorite kick was to bury a cat head down in a hole that, shoveled full again, left only the cat's tail poking up like a bizarre twitching weed. That, or tie the kitties' tails together with twine and drape them across a clothesline, where they would hang and spit and attack each other in a frenzy of fear. The loser got tossed into the woods to rot. The winner got its skull smashed in with a shovel, then made a similar trip to the woods.

And it was in the woods behind his parents' ramshackle house that Sam Rogers—Smiley—did his most dastardly deed. He had seven or eight brothers, a few sisters, and when the newest addition to the family was born, little Sarah, he decided enough was just enough. He would spend hours staring at her in her battered crib, this tiny white thing with its egg-shaped bald head and black eyes that did not focus, tiny imitations of hands and feet flexing and waving without direction. Mom was sick of having kids, but Pop was one extra horny drunkard, and he took what he wanted. The new baby was just one more miserable soul in an Indiana life that had no meaning.

So one afternoon when Mom was watching *Days of Our Lives* in the front room, Sam had picked up the baby and carried her out the back door. On the way to the woods he got a shovel out of the garage and went into the shadows of trees and weeds. He buried the baby head down and left one leg sticking out.

Not much time had to roll by until there were search parties hiking through the woods, most of them convinced this was a kidnapping, but because the Rogerses didn't have any money, it was probably the work of a sex fiend. In short order they found the leg sticking up, a small pale foot, bright in the sunlight leaking through the trees. When they pulled her out, one searcher keeled over, overwhelmed by the sight of a newborn baby with a broken leg and skin gone the color of dirty motor oil.

Sam couldn't understand all the commotion. It was around this time that he began to develop the permanent idiot's smile that would later get him nicknamed Smiley. It also was around this time that he pleaded guilty of murder and was shipped to the state hospital for the criminally insane until the age of twenty-one.

Then they let him go, and he wound up in Detroit driving a midnight-blue Lincoln Continental, cautiously following a woman named Julie Hastings as she worked her way into the dead heart of the city, a shopping bag parked on one arm. Beside Smiley was Rudy Martinez, who could have been a contender if only he knew how to box.

"Can't believe what shit?" Martinez grunted.

Smiley's smile was almost a frown; he was only half happy. "The boss letting me drive his car. And for what? Following that lady? We've been at it since four, and it's almost five. Where is she going?"

"Taking us to that Westlake guy. You know that."

"But shit, Rudy—nobody lives down here. She must be wise to us, and's leading us in circles while Westlake takes it easy."

Martinez slouched down and propped his knees on the dashboard. "Who gives a shit? We're getting paid. Quit bellyaching and drive."

"Fucking crazy," Smiley muttered, feeling useless. At this moment they were the only car on these deserted streets, and all Julie had to do was turn around a few times to know she was being tailed. He dropped back even farther, trying to look nonchalant—tough job for a guy as "chalant" as he was. Presently Rudy began to snore. Smiley jerked his arm, and he sat up.

"Qué?"

"Yeah, and elemenopee too. No sleeping on the job. Remember what happened to Pauly."

Martinez nodded, rubbed his face. Between the seats were a pair of military walkie-talkies, the bulky green Army-surplus kind most often seen in Central America. Each man was carrying the weapon of his own choosing: Martinez had a double-stacked 9-mm pistol, a Smith and Wesson that held fourteen rounds. Smiley was not so particular: He carried a simple sawed-off shotgun of dubious origin. But it fired, and he had some extra shells, so he was happy.

The walkie-talkies hissed in unison. A moment later Skip was playing Army with the airwaves, and not for the first time. "Mobile unit two to mobile one. Come in, one."

Smiley grabbed one of them up, mashed it to his ear, and thumbed the talk button. "What now, Major Asshole? Another radio check?"

"Roger, one. Do you read me?"

Martinez snatched up his walkie-talkie. "I'll be reading your goddamn obituary if you don't stop playing with your radio. If there's—"

Suddenly Smiley was pointing. Martinez followed his finger.

The Hastings lady had stopped at the large rusty door of a building that had once been a soap factory. A faded sign on the roof said something about FR SH SP ASH, the letters obscured by decades worth of pigeon droppings. Julie had put her shopping bag down and was trying to break open an ancient padlock the size of a hubcap. Smiley stopped and eyed a faded street sign.

"Corner of Beech and One Sixteenth, I think," he said, and talked to Skip again. "Get your ass here fast. Where the hell are you, anyway?"

"Fuck if I know," Skip said, and laughed. "Go ahead and grab her. I'll cruise until I find your location. Shouldn't be long."

Smiley was about to bark something unkind when Durant's voice boomed through the walkie-talkie. "I'm gonna have your balls if you aren't there in one minute!" he shouted to Skip. There was a lot of noise behind him, the sound of a huge engine and rotors beating the air. How Durant had rounded up such hardware was a mystery to his employees.

"Smiley," Durant barked over the noise, "give me some smoke. We're flying in circles."

"Okay, boss." Smiley pointed to the backseat with a thumb. There were several old-looking grenades there. One of them had the word SMOKE printed on it in fading yellow. Martinez leaned over the seat and picked it up.

"What now?"

"Wait till I get closer, then pitch that fucker out the window."

Martinez waited. When Skip stopped the car across from the factory and the woman beating on the door there, Martinez pulled the pin and let the elderly grenade fly. It hit the sidewalk near Julie's feet, rolled to the curb, and instantly began to squirt thick yellow smoke. Smiley's grin got bigger as he saw her hold her mouth and start to cough. The smoke grenades were fun, but the real fun was in the helicopter with Durant. He had a huge machine gun and about a billion shiny belts of bullets for it, and some kind of black tube on a rack, that fired grenades. Before they left to begin this operation, he had called it his special bonus from Garcia, though Smiley had never heard of a Garcia. It didn't matter. Durant had assembled the equivalent of a small army, complete with a helicopter and a machine gun and a grenade launcher. But

. . . why? That Julie Hastings didn't pose any threat. And Westlake was just one man. So why all the artillery?

"I see it!" Durant shouted, his voice sounding tinny through the walkie-talkies. "We'll be there in one minute."

"Okay," Smiley said.

"Unit two to unit one," Skip blared. "Unit two to unit one. Come in, unit one."

It was Martinez's turn to talk. "You dumb, one-legged, bony-eyed asshole!" he shouted. "Stop fucking around!"

Skip sounded wounded. "I just wanted to tell you I can see the smoke and I'll be there in just a little while. Do you copy?"

Martinez eyed Smiley, shaking his head. "He's watched one too many Vietnam shows." Then, into the walkie-talkie, "Roger Ramjet, Skip. We'll wait."

"Ten four," Skip replied.

"Up yours," Martinez answered.

So they waited. The smoke was a drifting fog now, Julie a lighter shadow inside it. She was banging on the door in a frenzy, coughing and crying. Smiley happened to look up, and saw a figure behind a shattered window, a man whose head was a ball of white bandages, whose hands were white clubs. He was staring down at Julie, shouting across the distance for her to get away before it was too late.

"Check it out," Smiley said, and leaned back to let Martinez have a look.

He smiled. "Westlake?"

Smiley nodded. "Gotta be. Groove on those bandages for a while, Rudy. Who else would be wrapped up like that?"

Martinez nodded and picked up his walkie-talkie. "Boss," he said, "we've spotted Westlake through a window. What now?"

Durant's reply sounded almost rabid. *"Shoot!"*

He clicked off, and the two men shrugged at each other. It was too damn easy. They got out, Martinez pulling his pistol out of its hidden holster, Smiley reaching to the backseat for his shotgun. They looked up through the haze of smoke.

Westlake was still there, still screaming down orders to the lady on the ground, the gist of which Smiley could understand quite well. He wanted her to run before the fireworks started.

Unfortunately for Smiley, the distance was a bit too far for his shotgun to be effective, though it wouldn't be hard to bag Julie. She turned and looked through the billowing smoke, tears flowing down her cheeks, her eyes bright with fear and sorrow. Kind of cute, Smiley thought, and wished it was him, and not that idiot Skip, who would get the drop on her. A little tussle in the backseat would be just fine. Perhaps she would bear his children.

He looked back up at Westlake. He was no longer shouting, no longer waving his arms. He looked like a statue.

Smiley nodded to Martinez, who brought his pistol up and steadied it on the roof of the car. He squeezed one eye shut. *Pop!*

A chunk of Westlake's face burst away in an explosion of tattered gauze. He toppled over backward.

Martinex frowned at Smiley, who could only shrug. Westlake was dead. What a fool Durant must be. Smiley leaned inside the car and got the walkie-talkie out. "Boss?"

"Yeah?" He sounded closer now.

"Uh, Westlake's dead. Martinez nailed him right through the head. Any, uh, other instructions?"

A long pause. Then: "What about the girl?"

Smiley looked. She had sunk to her knees on the crumbling sidewalk and was crying into her grocery bag, looking absolutely miserable. He keyed the walkie-talkie again. "On the ground crying. Should I shoot her?"

"Not yet. Find Westlake's body and make damn sure he's dead. The fucker has nine lives."

"Roger. Out."

Christ, he was starting to get as goofy as Skip. He motioned to Martinez just as Skip roared up in his junk pile of a car, a 1969 Javelin. His bald tires screeched, and he jumped out. By now the smoke was thinning, along with the smell of burned sulfur. Skip stomped over, his wooden foot slapping on the street inside his Reebok high-tops. "Done already?" he asked, panting, his face glowing with expectation.

"All over," Martinez said, and Skip's face drooped. "Only thing left to do is find the bastard's body. I imagine Durant will want a finger, like always. Skip, put the lady in your car until the boss can figure out what to do with her. She's a witness to all of this—and he won't want her alive for long, I imagine. Smiley, what say we go inside and pay our respects to the newly departed?''

They went across the street to the door. Skip hauled Julie upright and kicked the grocery bag away. Forty dollars' worth of food tumbled out as the bag split open. Mindless with grief and fear, she tore away from Skip and went on her knees to pick the groceries up, sobbing. Skip put his hands under her shoulders and dragged her to the car. She screamed and spit, trying to claw him. He opened the trunk and dumped her inside. ''Serves you right!'' he snarled after he slammed shut the trunk, then massaged his leg where flesh ended and wood began.

Smiley exploded the old padlock with one close shotgun blast. Most of the pieces clattered down to the cement, very old and very rusty, yet worn to the smooth metal in spots, as if someone had been using it quite often lately. He freed the remains from the hasp, tossed them away, and looked inside.

Dark.

He started in, shotgun ready, Martinez skulking close behind.

32

Martinez

HE COULD TRAIL Smiley in the dark because Smiley happened to have more B.O. emanating from his body than a road-killed skunk under a broiling sun. Competing with this un-pleasant aroma was the smell of age and dust and decay, a ghost factory where the machines were silently rusting to nothing, walls collapsing, rats inbreeding, mutating. It gave him the spooks, and he wished he had cat eyes to penetrate the musty gloom. All he could see was the back of Smiley's Scooby-Doo T-shirt, where Scooby was imprinted holding a bowl of dog food in one paw, a kerchief around his neck, tongue hanging out and dripping. Never one for goofy T-shirts, Martinez was wearing his usual Western shirt, Levi's 501s, and real snakeskin boots. The high heels clicked and gritted on the black cement floor. As he walked behind Smiley he pulled out a comb and ran it through his greasy hair.

Smiley was walking in large circles. Martinez tapped his shoulder.

"Wuh?" Smiley whirled around, banging his shotgun on a rusty pipe that climbed from the floor to the ceiling, slowly dripping foul water. It hummed like a huge tuning fork.

"He's upstairs," Martinez whispered. "Find the stair-way."

Smiley slapped at his chest, indicating a heart attack.

"Don't ever do that again, man. And I don't know where the goddamn stairs are."

"Find a light switch, then."

"What do you think I am? The meter reader?"

They walked, grumbling, stumbling over dark things, side-stepping shadows, barking their shins on old cable spools and giant discarded cogs. Weak spears of light shone down the cracks in the ceiling, proving that there was a second floor full of window light. So how did Westlake get up there?

Smiley stopped. "Here's a cable hanging down. Climb up it."

Martinez looked up. The cable was anchored somewhere in the ceiling, with no sign of a trapdoor or anything remotely resembling one. He turned on Smiley. "You numskull—what good would that do?"

They walked, getting mad and getting scared. Finally they passed a spot where sunlight beamed through cracks in the wall. Martinez tapped the wall with his foot, and it rattled like an old steel garage door, which it practically was. They had found the loading dock where Bosco's replacement, and various pizza-delivery boys, feared to tread. Martinez found a handle and pulled the massive door up. Bright sunlight washed in, making them squint.

"What is this?" Smiley breathed.

Martinez turned. His jaw dropped.

It was a gigantic science laboratory, something out of Frankenstein's era when mad scientists concocted terrible things and made the dead walk. Martinez's skin tightened into gooseflesh from his ankles to his scalp as he saw what Westlake had done.

Lab tables made from doors and crates, loaded with beakers and petri dishes. Pizza boxes. Exotic things looking much like Julius Kelp's fabulous machinery in that Jerry Lewis classic, *The Nutty Professor*. Spirals of glass tubing full of green-and-pink fluid. Pizza boxes. Bunsen burners flickering away beneath tall glass beakers in metal stands. Test tubes whirling in a centrifuge, full of pretty colored liquids. Pizza boxes, crushed paper Coke cups. Lengths of twine stretched overhead, some bearing large pictures on clothespins, others draped with some kind of pink, drippy blobs. Pizza boxes.

A large computer with a blank screen. Scattered boxes marked IBM. Two tall green tanks labeled OXYGEN and ACETYLENE.

"Jesus," Smiley whispered. "What *is* all this?"

"Looks like Frankenstein's dungeon. Let's go."

"Huh? And tell the boss Westlake's dead, even though we can't be sure? I don't know about you, but I plan to postpone dying as long as possible."

Martinez frowned. What was he scared of? He had shot a 9-mm bullet almost dead center in Westlake's face. White gauze had tattered and flapped before he dipped out of sight. There could be no doubt that he was dead.

But what if Durant wanted a finger? Lately he always did. An immense amount of shit would hit the fan if Durant were lied to and then came in wanting to see the body. What to do? "Golly gee, boss, we couldn't find the stairs. So sorry."

"Search for stairs," he told Smiley, and they split off in two directions, passing around corners, avoiding crumbling pillars, climbing over piles of crates and soggy cardboard. Huge dark rafters spanned the ceiling overhead, but now they were swaybacked and bent, wooden spines holding too much weight too long. Martinez figured the place could collapse at any time, and was probably held together by the tons of cob-webs in its corners. He stepped on something round and nearly lost his balance, his boots tapping out a beat as he fought to remain upright. He bent and picked up the round thing. It was heavy. He brought it to the light.

A fat piece of pipe.

Martinez threw it out the loading dock door, not under-standing why his heart was hammering so hard. Hadn't he thought—just for a moment—that he had stepped on an arm or a leg? Crazy. No one was here but the bugs and rats.

He looked around some more. The smell of moldy wet cardboard was nauseating. Water was dripping somewhere, ghost splashes in the poor light. He threw damp wooden crates aside, which splintered into mush in his hands. His stomach was trying to get bad.

He stepped on something else, and had to do the boogie-woogie once more or fall into the debris and maybe get a stick in the back. When he had his balance, he picked up the piece of debris and was about to . . .

debris?

. . . throw it when he glanced at it and saw that it was an old skull, one that was crumbling in his hand, wet gray bone-meal making his fingers feel sandy. As he looked, horrified, a small rat wormed out of one eyehole and looked at him with shiny black eyes, its whiskers twitching.

He screamed and dropped it. It made a wet plopping sound on the cement. The rat squealed. Martinez danced his way out of the garbage pile and made it to the safe light of the dock. He leaned against the wall, panting.

"Over here," Smiley brayed from somewhere in the darkness. "Come on!"

He made himself go. The boss's punishment would make that little face-to-face with a rat seem mild in comparison to the tortures Durant could dream up. He had once poked white-hot nails into a man's eyes while Martinez held him down. This did not amuse Martinez, nor the man he was holding captive.

So, yeah, you bet I'm coming, Smiley. I wouldn't miss this for the world. I could have been a contender, but I don't want to be a corpse, so I very much want a ringside seat at the Westlake funeral.

He found Smiley, who was already on the stairs. They looked mushy and rotten, the railing long since fallen off, rusty nails poking up here and there to snag incautious feet. Martinez waited until Smiley was up, then made his own way, ready to abandon ship if this soggy staircase decided to sink. But he made it to the top and it was much better here. There was a breeze and light and not much debris.

"I think it was that window," Smiley said, pointing left.

They walked that way, spooks and creeps and crawling flesh forgotten. They came to Westlake's body, the thickly wrapped head as good as exploded, the gauze hands splayed out beside the body, which was cut off at the waist and spilling what looked like wet newspaper onto the floor.

Martinez and Smiley exchanged incredulous glances. Smiley kicked the thing and it flew a bit before landing a few feet away. The head fell off and rolled in its direction of choice, light as a puff of cotton.

"Oh, shit," Smiley muttered. "Oh, damn. Oh, hell."

Martinez was silent. The spooks and creeps and crawling flesh were coming back, stronger than ever.

"What do we do now?" Smiley asked, whining, as if Martinez were the mastermind of this little troupe.

"Call the fucking boss," Martinez snapped. "Where's your radio?"

"Mine?" Smiley's smile was a thin bloodless slash. "In the car. Where's yours?"

"Same."

"Well then, what?"

"I want out of this place."

"Ditto."

They scrambled to the dark rectangle that opened on the stairway. Smiley jumped down first, rattling down the rotted steps two at a time, and Martinez had a foot out and was ready to follow when Smiley screamed. There was a huge flash of light, a burst as fast as a thunderbolt. Martinez shrank away from it, reaching for his pistol.

Silence. Martinez clicked the safety off the pistol while sweat beaded up on his forehead. *"Smiley!"* he hissed into the blackness, the hairs on the back of his neck spiking up as his fear grew. *"Goddammit, Smiley, what happened?"*

"Shit," Smiley replied. "Rudy, come down here and help me out of this stupid mess."

"What happened?"

"Stair broke. Scared me half to death. I thought something had grabbed my foot."

Martinez blew a long, gratified sigh. No death here, no danger. Just rotten wood. He put his pistol away and, stepping lightly, went down, then grabbed Smiley under the shoulders and hoisted him while Smiley kicked free of the splintered wood.

"I wonder what the deal is," Smiley said with a grunt. "This Westlake must love dangerous stairs. Remember his old lab, the one we blew up?"

"Yeah. Fifth step missing."

"How many steps are behind us?"

Martinez walked his hands back up the stairs. "Five."

"Coincidence?"

"Don't know." Martinez edged down past Smiley, a puz-

206

zling thought rising in his mind. He stepped past the ruined step, stuck his hand down into blackness, and felt around.

Shards of soggy wood, some with nails hanging out. A length of twine, stretched taut.

He backed down to the floor and went under the stairwell, found the twine again, and followed it through eyebolts and hooks set in the wall to a spot twelve feet away. His hands found a tripod. He followed its slick aluminum legs to a camera screwed on top. He caressed it, frowning, blind. The twine was hooked to the camera's shutter button with some kind of gizmo. The flash unit on top was still warm.

"We got trouble," Martinez said. "But I don't know what kind."

Smiley came down, his B.O. following in a cloud. He gave the camera a similar feel-over. "Took our picture, seems like. What for?"

"I swear I don't know."

"I'll tell you what," Smiley said grimly. "I happen to be camera-shy because of all the damn police photos I've had to stand for. So when some civilian ass wipe snaps my photo, I usually grab the damn camera and rip the film out."

"So?"

"So this."

Martinez waited. Smiley fumbled with the camera. The back opened with a tiny "boing," and the fine, clean smell of a Japanese camera factory wafted out. Pretty new, then.

"Bingo," Smiley said, and dug for the film.

The camera was empty.

"It's time," he said gravely, "to get the fuck out of here."

Martinez could not agree more.

33

Darkman

HUNCHED OVER THE computer keyboard, his heart hammering, finger bones chattering against the keys, invisible sweat cascading down his face.

A freshly developed photograph hanging in front of him, still wet and dripping. Smiley's face, frozen in time, eyes wide with surprise, mouth open, foot beginning its crash through the step Darkman had cut almost in two.

The thin, twisted face of Martinez, one cowboy boot slung over the first step, hands on each side of the door frame as if preparing to parachute out of a plane.

The loading-dock door, still open, the generator putting out a gentle purr as it kept all the lab equipment running, but not the lights.

Distantly the flapping noises of a helicopter.

And time running out.

34

Martinez

THE HELICOPTER DURANT had managed to obtain for this
tremendous undertaking landed a few minutes later on the
street between the junk heap that Skip dared call a car, and
the car Smiley had been driving, Durant's own Continental.
The helicopter's noisy tornado of wind swept away the last
remnants of smoke, and rolled a large amount of paper and
similar debris out of the gutters to tumble against the deserted
buildings. Skip rolled his window up against the wind and
the noise, even though the sun was beating down as if it
thought this were still balmy summer, Indian summer. In the
back Julie pounded on the walls of the Javelin's pitifully small
trunk. Skip wondered idly if she might suffocate back there.
He found that he didn't care one bit. Hauling that banshee
around had made his stump sore where it met the prosthesis,
the fabled machine-gun leg, so to hell with her.

The wind died a bit as the motor wound down to idle, and
Robert G. Durant, in his finest blue polyester suit, hurried
over. Skip rolled his window down again.

"Where's Westlake's body?" Durant snarled in his face,
but Skip could only shrug. He didn't have a clue.

"Where's Martinez? Where's Smiley?"

The two men in question came charging through the door
of the building just then, as if chased by wolves. The large

steel door behind them clanged open and shut, thunking against its frame. Both men looked somewhat pale and shaky.

"Where is it?" Durant barked at them. "Where's the goddamn corpse?"

They skidded to a stop and began inspecting their shoes, fidgeting. Both wore a bright coating of sweat on their arms and faces.

"Talk to me!" Durant shouted.

Martinez spoke up first. "Well," he said, "well, boss, it seems that I, um, I . . ."

"Shot a dummy instead of Westlake," Smiley finished, doing his best to make Martinez the whipping boy in this little scene.

Durant frowned wickedly, his eyes snapping back and forth between the two. "What dummy?" he asked softly.

Smiley smiled as always. "Westlake made it, I bet. He stuck it in a window for us to shoot at."

"Must have thought you two were really dumb, huh?" Durant said very quietly.

"Guess so," Smiley said. He eyed Durant hopefully. "So it's no big deal, huh? One little mistake. And how were we supposed to know he was gonna take our picture?"

Martinez helplessly ground his teeth.

Durant's eyes eased shut. His face shifted into a gentle smile. "You shot a dummy and then posed for a picture. That is really something. Yeah, something."

Smiley giggled. "He had a trap set up for us, and I stepped right into it. You shoulda seen it. Foof! Like that old show *Candid Camera*, a little. I hope I was smiling!"

Durant nodded. "Of course you were smiling, Smiley. And I bet Martinez was holding two fingers behind your head to make you look like a rabbit."

"Nah." He turned to Martinez. "You didn't, did you? I'd hate to look stupid in my picture."

"You fucking idiots!" Durant screamed, turning purple. Martinez flinched back. Smiley frowned for the first time in six years. Durant seemed well down the road to insanity, skin mottled, eyes bulging, a barrage of spit misting past his lips, his hands waving too fast to follow. *"You stupid brainless wonders! Get back in there and waste him!"*

210

"But, boss," Martinez whined, "it's darker than midnight in there, and so full of junk, we can't move around. Westlake's got some kind of laboratory set up. And traps like you wouldn't believe. It's like the Vietnam jungle inside."

"Do tell," Durant screeched. He yanked a huge black pistol out of a holster nested below his back, right at his belt line. The odd-looking gun, a modified KG-99—currently in great favor with mobsters and drug runners—caught on his belt and he had to wiggle it a little to pull it free. He raked the cocking lever back, putting thirty rounds of major ammo behind his trigger finger, and waved it at Martinez and Smiley.

"Vietnam was a picnic compared to what I have in mind, if you two don't go in there and kill Westlake," he growled, angered into a new and higher frenzy in which they had ever seen him before. "I give you ten minutes. No Westlake, no pay. No pay, no life. Do my village idiots comprehend?"

What the hell is a village idiot? Smiley started to say, but Martinez rammed an elbow into his ribs. Christ, Martinez thought, numb with dread, is this man a moron or what? What a buffoon, this psychotic man-boy named Smiley. Martinez forgot about him and lifted his chin, arranging his face into a Mussolini-style sneer, a sneer of pure bravado with no brains behind the vacuous brown eyes.

"Give us ten minutes, boss. His fingers will become yours."

Durant took a step toward him, eyes slitted down to microscopic slots, teeth bared. "I don't want his fingers," he roared into Martinez's face, "I want his fucking head!"

"Head it is," Martinez said briskly, and turned to Smiley, who was smiling no more. If he happened to live long enough, they would soon call him something else. His hair was glued to his forehead with sweat. His dull brown eyebrows twitched up and down a little. His lips had repositioned themselves into an ugly frown, which he would wear to the end of time. As far as the modern world went, Smiley was dead. In his stead, Grouchy was born.

"Chase the fucker up to the roof, if there's an exit," Durant said, already edging toward the helicopter. "Force Westlake up there. I'll take care of him like he won't believe.

211

Skip, take the bitch to Strack's place. He wants to talk to her in person.''

He ran to the copter, swung one of its small white doors open, and climbed in. Martinez saw him clamber between the bucket seats and disappear into the belly of the craft. Soon a door slid open sideways, like the side cargo door of a van. Durant had positioned himself behind the huge machine gun, legs crossed, sunlight beaming off his perfect teeth, eyes bright with hate. The brass cartridges gleamed golden and evil under the dying sun, bandoliers of .50-caliber ammo made for the express service of blowing giant chunks out of scared soldiers and making blood flow in the mud. He motioned the copter up, and the pilot didn't hesitate.

Durant was shouting as he rose in the air, chunks of syllables and verbs tangling with one another as the helicopter wound up tight and whisked the sentences away. Durant was fifty feet in the air before he decided it was useless and quit hollering.

"Land on the roof," he shouted to the pilot, his former business associate. The man was more than happy to oblige.

And on the ground, not much bigger than toy soldiers from Durant's viewpoint, Smiley and Martinez were contemplating their dismal futures.

"God, I'd hate to die today," Smiley said, groaning. "If it ain't Westlake doing us in, it'll be Durant. How the fuck did I ever get associated with this screwball outfit?"

"Shut up," Martinez hissed. "For once in your life just shut the fuck up."

"What'd I say?"

"It's not so much what you say," Martinez growled. "It's more how you smell."

"Smell?" Smiley raised an arm to expose one poisoned armpit, where a sweat spot the size of a fairly hefty pancake was spreading. He stuck his nose in the mess and inhaled deeply, frowning. "Sweeter than a rose," he said, and Martinez wished he could produce a rose so that Smiley could watch it wilt under the steamroller of his B.O. But then, it didn't matter. They were doomed to die, one way or the other. Westlake was just too tricky, being a college egghead and all, and Durant was just too mean.

"Let's go back in," he said, squaring his shoulders and checking the pearl buttons on his shirt to make sure he wouldn't make a slovenly corpse. "It's just one guy against you and me, and a helicopter full of guns waiting topside. And quit aiming that goddamn shotgun in my face!"

Smiley pointed it skyward, where the first tinges of dusk were painting the puffball clouds pink and orange. The air was growing cool, still tainted by the helicopter's jet-fuel exhaust as the craft landed on the roof and shut down.

"In," Martinez said, and they went to the steel door that had quit flapping and banging, and stepped inside once more. Behind them, Skip drove away, the girl in the trunk pounding and screaming. He was grinning and seemed glad he did not have to chase shadows in the dark. Martinez snorted and wondered what he had done to deserve such luck.

"Wish I had a flashlight," Smiley muttered as the dark interior turned his idiotic Scooby-Doo T-shirt a pale shade of gray.

"Put it in the suggestion box," Martinez snapped, almost gagging on the man's hideous odor. "Let's split up. You go left, I go right. Got it?"

"Yeah, sure. Do you have your peashooter out?"

"It's out, smelly. Turn left."

He did, and Martinez had time to find a space of clean air and actually breathe again. Already sweat was rolling into his eyes, making him squint as he walked under the dusty sign that said this or that about Fresh Splash Soap and other banal items that didn't concern him one way or the other. He just wanted Westlake in his sight, a 9-mm bullet that would fly straight and true, a gun that would not jam up at the critical moment, as automatic pistols tended to do. All in all, he just wanted to be done and at home swilling cold Miller beer down by the case, forgetting everything.

He walked into a door with a loud clump, his twisted nose taking the brunt of it. His fear tempered by anger, he tried the knob, but because the door seemed locked, he kicked it open just to show who was really boss around here. The door ripped off its upper hinge and groaned as it slumped downward, its edge to the floor. Martinez kicked the useless thing aside and went in, daring the impotent dark to frighten him again. He was Rudy Martinez—a tall, strong man, if a bit ugly—and he could have been even *better* than a contender, he could have been champ.

Something thumped to the floor, something hollow and hard, and rolled to a gritty stop at his feet. He bent over and felt it, discovered it was only a Coke bottle, and almost threw it away before realizing that most Coke bottles do not hit the floor and roll to your feet unless thrown that way.

"Westlake," he said evenly, searching the dark with blind eyes, his left hand clutching this baffling prize. "Nobody gets hurt if you do what I say."

He waited. Seconds ticked past.

"Westlake!"

Nothing.

Martinez turned in a circle, boots clumping. Only the faintest bit of light penetrated the small corridor, and it wasn't enough. His bravado shrank, replaced by new fear. What kind of trap was this?

A minor notion came into his head. Two could play the same game, right? He tossed the bottle back from where it had come, waiting for the glassy *ping* as it hit the floor, or the explosive noise of a large glass bottle smashing against cement. Instead he got . . .

Nothing.

???

"Where are you?" he screeched, heart thundering, his pulse pounding thickly in his ears. "Westlake, come out here like a man!"

Nada.

What was left of his self-control took a hike into the deeper recesses of his brain. What it left behind was a crazy, frantic kind of terror.

He fired his pistol into the dark, pointing at everything, pointing at nothing. Sweat drizzled off his face. With each shot the walls were illuminated with bright bursts of orange, exposing spiderwebbed tools and shelves mantled with ancient dust. And Westlake?

No sign. Martinez fired in a blind panic, spinning in circles, momentarily forgetting that his pistol held only fourteen rounds. Some dim part of his mind must have remembered, though, because his spastic finger stopped pulling the trigger on round number fourteen, leaving it, and it alone, between him and the horrors of this ghastly, dead factory and the creature that lurked there.

He waited, trying to be silent, lungs screaming for breath, sweat soaking into the collar of his Western shirt as if it were a sponge.

Something scraped on the floor. Ahead? Behind? He tried to look both ways at once, gun held ready in his slick fist, his greasy hair stuck to his forehead in strange zigzags. *"Westlake!"* he screamed in terror and desperation, *"where the fuck are you?"*

Silence. Then . . . a strangled voice.

"Closer than you know."

Martinez, all courage gone, whirled around to the place from which the voice had spoken. He heard thumps there, like someone walking in very heavy shoes. Breathing, too, ragged, hissing.

He fired his last shot as Darkman jumped for him, Darkman a frozen picture of orange and red in that brief illumination, Martinez a man made of sweat and fear. The flash died a quick death, but the bullet zoomed harmlessly into a wall.

Martinez bubbled out a wheezing scream as bony claws clamped over his mouth. After that he fainted into a blessed oblivion where anger was not known, and death a fantasy.

35

Grouchy

THE FORMER SMILEY heard Martinez's screams stab through the dark from the other side of the massive building, and his grouchy frown turned down even farther, looked even grouchier. He could no longer remember why he had been smiling these long years, for it was a greater pleasure to wear a frown than an idiot's grin. The boss man, Durant, was no stranger to trouble, not much of a smiler, and Smiley had been no stranger to trouble, either. But Durant's little messes had a way of getting cleaned up almost by themselves—a little blackmail here, a bit of torture there. Only this deal with Westlake had been absolutely botched, and there was no one left to blame but Durant. It had been his goofy idea to leave the scientist guy alive and make fireworks out of him; it had been his idea to turn a simple hands-up, gimme-the-paper routine into a double murder accompanied by torture. And who had to pay the price? Everybody except Durant, the greasy slug.

Martinez screamed again. Grouchy found that he did not care that much, because Martinez was a spick, first of all— and he was always trying to be a hotshot and pretend he was in charge. The slimy bum had been a lousy boxer, and was a lousy crook as well. Surely Durant knew the man was a phony, and most surely he believed that Smiley had the brains to be second in command. And as Smi—oops—Grouchy knew quite well, Durant's criminal shoes were just panting to have a new boss inside them.

But Martinez was still screaming, as if he had stepped on a nail, which didn't seem unlikely in this dump. Sighing, reluctant, the newborn Grouchy plodded toward the place from where the screams were coming, his shotgun lounging on his shoulder, his mind free of burdens. What would Strack say when Durant, under questioning, burst into tears and begged him to let him give up mobstering forever? Strack would say, "Smiley"—not knowing the new moniker— "Smiley, my boy, I need a good man with brains and talent. Care to be my top dog, since the former one turned chicken?"

He got to the place where Martinez had been screaming. There was a door keeled over on edge, its bent lower hinge catching small sticks of light and reflecting them dully into Grouchy's wide eyes. He took a firm step forward, determined to make this the best night of his life, the one that would get him promoted.

As is often the case with stupid people, he was fooling himself and no one else. What happened was that he stumbled across something that was somewhat firm, and picked it up because it was warm. It was a boot. Grouchy stuck his nose in it. Martinez's foot odor wafted out, smelling even worse than that cheap Mexican cologne he liked to wear.

Grouchy dropped the boot to the floor with a soft clunk, wondering. What had happened here? Had that Westlake guy simply *eaten* Martinez?

He heard muted footsteps coming from dead ahead, where the blackness was complete except for one miserable shaft of dying daylight poking through a knothole in the sagging wall. Grouchy moved his shotgun down to waist level, ready to mutilate whatever walked through the weak beam of light. Like Martinez, sweat oozed out of his forehead, dripping and tickling his eyelashes on the trip down his face. He shook his head, flinging drops from the wet strings of his hair, internally cursing it and the scalding fear that was forming in his guts and brain.

Worse yet, who in the hell was that man standing with his head right in the light, the guy swaying on his feet like a drunk?

Grouchy squinted. By all that was holy, it was *him* standing there, a copycat Smiley with one corner of his lips hiked up into a sneer, his eyes full of torment and fear, just like Grouchy was feeling about now.

His finger tightened on the shotgun's broad trigger. "Wha, wha—who are you?"

No reply, or at least not a good one. The other Smiley wobbled on his feet, making small moaning noises.

"Westlake?" Grouchy demanded in a voice full of the bravado of stupidity. "You sure as hell can't fool me!"

He jumped forward and smashed the butt of the shotgun against the mouth of the "fake" guy, who staggered back and hit an unseen wall. Decrepit tools clanged and rattled to the floor. He fell to his knees, then toppled over, his face cut in half by the gray beam of light. Blood was oozing out of his mouth.

Grouchy went into a squat beside him. "You ain't so tough, and you ain't so smart, Westlake. We know about your fancy masks and all. The boss figured it out in a second. So now all I have to do is fill you full of buckshot and drag your ass out. Get it?"

The fake Smiley rolled left, then put his hands on the floor. Blood dripped out of his mouth in large clots as he found his feet. He began waving his arms, speaking muted mumbo jumbo.

"So long, fucker," Grouchy said, and blew his chest apart with a shotgun blast that sounded as loud as an atomic bomb in these confining walls. Fake Smiley flopped backward in a splash of his own blood, his head once again landing—hard—in the pitiful beam of light. Grouchy watched Westlake die with great relief.

Something at the base of the dead man's neck began to wrinkle where the light hit it. It smelled bad, smoked a little. Grouchy frowned, then used the hot barrel of his gun to worm under the mushy fake skin. With a flick he pulled the mask off, more interested in seeing Westlake's dead face than anything else.

All his hopes of someday being head honcho vanished forever.

Martinez lay there dead with a large wedge of wood stuffed

into his mouth, his eyes open and locked forever in an expression of manic surprise.

Grouchy stumbled backward, thudding into things that hadn't seemed to be there before. Panic was rising to a boil in his feeble mind. He had shot Martinez. Nobody shoots Martinez—or Skip or Durant or anybody else—without permission. Martinez had been a damn good man, an asset to the team. With Pauly and Rick gone forever, he was irreplaceable. So what would the boss have to say about this?

"Nice shooting," someone said behind him, and Grouchy spun in the air, twirling like a master of ballet, and landed back on his feet, agape with fright.

Durant was standing there. A familiar shadow, no more. But the voice was his—no doubt about that.

"Boss, boss," Grouchy said, already switching his voice into the high range that customarily indicated remorse. "Westlake put a new face on his ass. No, wait. He had a different face, you know, like . . . my face. I knew it wasn't me, so I shot him. Jeez, boss, anybody could fall for that."

Grouchy stared hard at the dark figure. The aroma of expensive cigars drifted over as Durant got one out of a pocket and bit off the end.

"You know, of course, that what you did is wrong," Durant said gravely.

Grouchy nodded, suddenly wet with sweat and dread.

"The repercussions of your little disaster here will be severe, Smiley. Very, very severe."

Grouchy—not even worthy of that name anymore—stood in the dank heat and waited for his sentencing.

Durant lit his cigar. His face shone briefly in the light, a bit smudged and strained. He sighed. "Do I do it, Smiley, or do you?"

The man who had no name left began to blubber, shoulders hunched, tears coursing down his cheeks. "Please, boss," he said, sobbing. "One little mistake. Okay, two, yeah, the one a minute ago and then this one. But haven't I been faithful? Haven't I always done what you said?"

Durant nodded. "Fine, then. You must now do as I say."

The wretched husk that had been Smiley and Grouchy nodded vigorously, nearly snapping a neck bone. "Anything, boss. Anything!"

Durant must have smiled, because Smiley–Grouchy–Nobody caught a wink of light off a tooth and grinned back.

"Blow your stupid fucking head off," Durant said, his voice smooth and reassuring and deadly. "Right now. Do it and I won't have to have you killed the slow way, the way I like."

Smiley's bowels went loose. To the sane and healthy, death is something confined to hospitals and nursing homes and graveyards. This new Smiley was now thrust into the stark border zone between life and death, and he didn't like it one bit.

"Y-you can't make me do that," he said, stammering.

"Watch me," Durant said. *"Just watch."*

Durant turned and walked away. On the trip outside he stopped and puffed his cigar, eyes fastened on Smiley, a hint of a smile moving his lips. Smiley had seen the look before. It was the same look he had worn on the day they quick-fried Westlake and exterminated his chink pal. It was the same look he had had when Pauly sailed through a really nice window and dropped seventeen floors, whooping and screeching.

He would never get out of this dark hole alive.

The distant door was pulled open, letting in the weary light of dusk. Then it was shut. Darkness.

Smiley sat on the dirty floor with Martinez's body behind him and his own executioner waiting out front.

He put the barrel of the shotgun between his eyes—hot, bony flesh against cold steel—and before he pushed the trigger with his thumb, he hoped that when he entered hell, he would not find his dead baby sister there, because she had been a real pain in the ass.

36

Durant

OF COURSE, THE real Robert G. Durant was still up on the roof in his pal's helicopter, sitting Indian-style behind the .50-caliber gun, its barrel pointing at the strips in the tar that indicated a trapdoor. The tarred roof itself was flat and dotted with stagnant puddles. Their resultant mush of leaves, bugs, dead birds, even toads and frogs, and don't—for God's sake— forget the mosquitoes that bred there by the millions and feasted on the blood of suburbia, not so far away smelled awful.

Durant, in the belly of the copter, heard a muted bang that indicated a gun in action. He cocked his head, wanting to hear more but hearing instead only the horrible whining of mosquitoes as they buzzed around him by the hundreds, miniature Draculas feasting on his blood. He slapped at them, occasionally getting a few, but these were swiftly replaced by more and more and more.

"Get this bird in the air!" he shouted, whacking at his tormentors. The pilot, Steve Dalton, recent widower worth a million bucks, gave the bird some power, and up it rose. It drifted sideways, away from the roof, hovering over the street. Durant glanced down and saw himself walk out of the soap factory, puffing a cigar. His bewilderment lasted only a second, and then he was pointing and shouting.

"Turn around, Dalton! Goddammit, turn this turkey around so I can get a shot!"

Dalton, no slouch in the pilot department, complied by spinning the craft in a swift half-circle that left Durant feeling quite nauseated. On the ground, even over the whapping and whining howl of the copter, Darkman could hear Durant shouting. The copter bobbed in the air while Durant raked the .50-caliber's cocking handle back, and then the machine gun was pounding the rutted sidewalk at his feet, the huge bullets smashing inch-deep craters in the cement before rebounding away, singing the high song of multiple ricochets. Darkman danced for a while, not expecting this kind of high-powered technology from a goon like Durant. It was when Durant quit shooting and began firing grenades from an actual grenade launcher that Darkman decided the options here were limited, and that if he were to die today, he might as well die in the dark that had been his prison these long weeks.

He ducked back inside. Durant went back to the machine gun, pounding the steel door with bullets, shouting inventive curses and gripping the .50-caliber hard enough to break its wooden grips. With a snarl he socked the hot barrel with a fist, got hurt by the steel and burned by the heat, gave up, and crawled forward to the cockpit, where Dalton was busy doing nothing. "Get me on the ground fast!" Durant shouted, and pulled his pistol out of his belt. "That bastard is one dead motherfucker."

The copter fell from the sky. At the last moment Dalton yanked on the collective joystick, the one that made the bird go up or down. Durant's queasy stomach bottomed out and threatened to slide out of his asshole to complain in person, but he held on, gritting his teeth. When the craft was firmly on the ground, he hopped out and went to the door of the soap factory, his greased-back hair flying wildly and his eyes glistening with pure animal hate.

He swung open the door, went inside. The good people of Fresh Splash Soap welcomed him with the cheery sign overhead, the one caked with dust and yellow varnish. Beyond that, things were dark. Durant began to sweat immediately.

"Westlake!" he shouted, and was answered by echoes. "Westlake, I'm not here to kill you! I have someone you ought to meet!"

More echoes, more silence. Durant scowled. This wasn't

going to be easy. The heavy artillery was in the chopper, currently useless. Here, in this darkness, it would be man against man. Durant's little revolver only held the usual six bullets. His pockets were empty except for the usual coins and keys, and the cigar snipper. So what did Westlake have? An atomic bomb, probably.

Something thunked off to the right, where the light was a weak haze. It sounded like a large slab of metal falling on edge, ringing. Then, rapid footsteps.

Durant ran toward the noise, tripping and falling just as Martinez and Smiley had done, banging his shins on invisible obstacles, getting a spluttering faceful of cobwebs now and then. He stumbled over something soft and yielding and stopped, going down on one knee.

It was a body. Smiley's body, by the smell of it. All that was left of his head was the lower jawbone. The rest was large, wet spillage on the wall where flies buzzed as they ate what had been his eyes and brain.

Durant stood up. Okay, no problem. Smiley bought the farm, no big loss. Martinez was worth two Smileys.

So, like, where *was* Martinez?

He took two steps and found him. Martinez's stiffening corpse exuded the smell of ruined guts and, below that, the Mexican cologne.

Durant straightened, edging close to panic. Where did he stand? Rick: gone. Pauly: gone. Smiley: gone. Martinez: gone.

Westlake: alive. Here and alive.

"Westlake!" he screamed, rattling loose things throughout the factory. *"Come out and fight me!"*

Silence. Nothing else.

Durant raised his pistol overhead and fired three shots at the black ceiling as fast as his finger could move. The staccato bursts of fire lit everything a weird orange, showing dangling wires and intricate doilies of spiderwebs. A rat was nestled beside Martinez's head, frozen with fright, black blood hanging from its whiskers. A portion of Martinez'a left eye had been gnawed out.

Durant shot at it, succeeding in mangling Martinez even more. The rat trundled off, squealing.

Durant realized he was losing it, that Westlake was stealing from him, stealing his men and his confidence and his exalted position with Louis Strack. The wimpy college boy had become as dangerous as a viper, a man who lived in the dark and hid in its protection while he murdered man after man. How was he doing it?

Durant was shaking now, swallowing with a throat that was parched, breathing with lungs that wanted to lock up on him forever, thinking with a brain that was whirling in insane circles. The factory was dusty and dead, the walls seeming to pulse in and out, as if the factory itself were a part of this monstrous conspiracy to rob Durant of everything he had, including his sanity.

A door opened behind him, letting a large wedge of light streak in. Durant spun around, sweat flipping off him in salty drops, his revolver held in two hands that were greasy with sweat, trembling with fear and this crazy new claustrophobia. He fired at the light and then it vanished. The door banged shut, leaving him alone with his frightened self and no one else.

He ran for the door, sliding, tripping, moaning, desperate to get out where the air was not sticky and hot. He ran headlong into a giant machine full of spikes and cogs and fell back with a shriek, his body shallowly punctured in a dozen places, bruises welling up on his forehead and ribs. His pistol skittered away and pinged against something. Durant did not care. He found his feet, ran some more, and got to the door just as the thin thread that held him from the abyss of insanity was about to break.

He jerked it open. Cool fresh air and welcome light drenched him, never tasting better. He stepped sideways and slumped against the building, sweat raining off his face and fingertips, eyes closed with thankfulness and relief.

The Dalton guy's helicopter began to howl, whining with fresh power, ready to lift off. Durant glanced over at it, squinting against the wind.

He was inside it, riding shotgun, his face very clear through the copter's bubble of Plexiglas. The other Durant turned away and shouted at the pilot.

Durant pushed away from the wall and ran for it, expensive

224

shoes slapping the street, all worries of sweat, fear, and claustrophobia left behind. That bastard, Westlake, had pulled his last impersonation. It was time to die.

The copter was four feet off the ground when Durant dived inside, sliding on his belly across the smooth aluminum floor of the cargo bay and conking his head on the far door, the unopened one. He struggled to get to his knees, but his pants, torn now, were hung up on the .50-caliber's tripod.

The wrong Durant turned and looked at the right Durant. So did the pilot. He gaped in amazement at these strange twins, one wearing blue polyester, the other maroon polyester.

I believe we have done this before, Durant thought, and ripped his pants free, exposing a black sock held up with a garter. For a short instant he felt embarrassed by this, but then it was gone, and he was lunging for Westlake's throat, grappling at it, managing to get a handful of some slimy, cold stuff. He jerked at it and came away with a familiar-looking mask in one hand, a wig in the other.

"Gotcha!" he shouted, and pulled Westlake backward, out of his seat. He thumped to the floor on his back, writhing and twisting. Durant, experienced at this, gave him a karate chop to the throat, a tactic meant to crush a man's Adam's apple and ruin his whole day in the process. It worked. Westlake let Durant loose and clutched his own throat with his claws, making thin, croaking noises.

Durant, panting, looked down at him. "You are," he said with a satisfied grin, "the ugliest motherfucker I have ever seen." He peeled off Westlake's artificial hands, grimaced with disgust, and tossed them out to the street below.

"It's just you and me now, my friend," Durant said, and then, to the pilot, "Crank this bitch up as high as she'll go. We're about to make a Westlake pancake."

The pilot did just that.

225

37

The Man on the Flying Trapeze

OF ALL THE things he had been deprived of by the burning—
his hands, his face, his career, his fiancèe, his self-control—
until this day, air had not been high on the list. But it most
certainly was now, because Durant's crashing karate chop had
made his larynx slam shut, and the tattered, scorched remnants of his facial skin were turning pale blue between the
charred edges as he slipped into oxygen starvation. Durant
stared down at him with a small half smile curling his lips.
The helicopter was barreling straight up, seeming to want to
touch the clouds, which it probably could.

Durant bent over him. "I hope you regret the day you met
me, Mr. Big Shot Westlake, because I am going to enjoy this
very much, and you will not." He looked up at the pilot.
"How high?" he asked above the noise.

Dalton checked his altimeter. "Twelve hundred feet, Mr.
Durant."

"Sounds perfect, my friend. Let's level off here and look
for a fitting burial site for Mr. Westlake."

He looked back down at him. "You see, Westlake, I happen to know that you have already been declared dead, so no
one will care when you wind up ten feet underground from
the force of the impact. Remember all the old cartoons? Road
Runner? Daffy Duck? Sure you do. Every time somebody fell
off a cliff, they punched a hole ten feet deep in the ground.

As a child I often doubted this, but now we will find out for sure.''

He jerked Darkman to a sitting position and began pushing him toward the open side door, where evening's bright colors were still patched into the fabric of the sky. Darkman struggled uselessly, laboring to live, feebly kicking and waving his crippled hands. One shoe caught on a thick white rope near the edge of the door. The rope was snapped out by the wind, spooling in fast motion, as well as the shoe, which tumbled twelve hundred feet to the ground.

None of this was of the slightest interest to Darkman, because his legs were dangling in the wind and the tips of his finger bones were sliding across the floor of the copter, as if it were made of glass and grease. With one gigantic shove Durant pushed him out. There was a moment when Darkman seemed to be floating, airborne, kicking, and flailing, and then gravity took over and he zipped out of sight.

''Survive *this* one.'' Durant chuckled, and told Steve Dalton to make a beeline for the Strack mansion on the outskirts of town.

Darkman did fall, his fear draining him of everything but the will to survive this latest in a series of catastrophes that had started so long ago—the day he was born and did not die. As he fell, an inner voice, silent until now, told him that his life had been a brief, tumbling fall from darkness to darkness, not knowing where he came from, not knowing where this fall would end. It was a philosopher's idea, a philosopher's dilemma. Could life be so meaningless, so worthless, to be ended for no reason at all?

A dim part of his mind took over the power of his sight while the Peyton that had been fell to his death. His eyes registered a flapping series of white ropes directly in front of his face: a rope ladder made of sturdy white nylon. He counted the rungs as he fell, still another part of his mind wondering if this were an accident or Providence or not worth a dime. He reached out to the last rope-rung with both mangled hands, still drifting in fear and in misery and the knowledge that death was the only real truth and monster and demon: the only thing truly to fear on Earth.

227

The ladder snapped taut, making his shoulders pop as his own weight pulled against it, and his fall ended and became a flight as the helicopter surged forward. He looked up at his hands and realized in a strange and disturbing way that if these had been ordinary fingers, they never could have held. His bony claws did not feel the pain that real fingers would have. *Thanks again, Mr. Rangeveritz,* he thought. *And this time I mean it.*

Durant stuck his head out of the helicopter, already frowning. They had felt the heavy jerk up there, which Darkman knew had made the copter wobble. Durant's eyes opened wide with disbelief. If Darkman could have drawn enough air through his swollen larynx, he would have laughed up at him while the wind shooshed past his remaining ear and flapped his polyester suit against his bones. It was definitely no joyride, but it beat the hell out of making that ten-foot-deep man-shaped hole Durant had promised.

Durant's head pulled back in. Darkman thought he heard shouting. Suddenly the copter began to descend, still making good speed but falling.

He looked down. Colorful lights, the crisscrossing of streets, skyscrapers, big city. They were headed to the new downtown, away from the dead wreckage previous generations had left in the belly of the old city. The fresh, clean buildings below were a gigantic aerial postcard from this height, and it rushed up as the copter fell, becoming large and very real. Darkman swallowed, knowing that what came next might not be fun.

They dragged him along a high rooftop decorated with TV antennas. The aluminum poles and struts snapped as he was towed through this forest of metal, Darkman emitting *oofs!* and *oogs!* as these blunt spears slapped against him at high speed, too dull to puncture him but not all that pliable, either. He grabbed the next rung on the rope ladder and pulled himself up one step.

The antennas slipped behind, replaced by wide streets farther below. The copter began swaying from side to side, creating a deadly whiplash effect, still descending. The gritty limestone wall of a huge bank swept into view, ready to slam against him, and he stuck out his feet, one shoe on, one shoe off, and kicked it away. This made him swing wildly, spinning, too confused to get his bearings. He was reminded of the toy drinking bird that had evaporated in the explosion. He was the bird now, bobbing ever closer to danger, a big kid on a park swing that had gone out of control and might bash him against the pipes and make him cry.

He caught a glimpse of something large. As he spun again he saw the gigantic face of a woman drinking iced tea. He blinked, not understanding. As he spun back he tried to make sense of it again. The word *Lipton* swooshed by.

He clenched his eyes shut as he smashed into the huge billboard, shattering wood, tearing free huge slabs of paper, breaking electric floodlights and making glass crash down to the freeway below. One car spun out of control, its headlights dancing against the dark. Another car plowed into it. The explosion was loud; Darkman looked back, full of regret.

Durant leaned out again, this time from the cargo door. He swiveled the machine gun down and began to fire. The long black barrel sprouted flowers of orange and blue, but Darkman was directly below the copter, nowhere in range, and it was useless. Durant fired wildly, trying to shoot straight down, able only to puncture a variety of cars and make them swerve and crash. He screamed in rage and defiance, firing now toward the first evening stars.

The machine gun tipped over the edge of the cargo floor. Darkman saw a foot clad in a patent-leather shoe, one of the angry Durant's feet, shoving the gun out. It swept past Darkman on its way down, a strange, gawky contraption full of gizmos and gadgets, clattering noisily while trailing a shiny ammo belt to a new existence sixty feet below. Darkman hiked another rung higher.

Durant leaned out with the grenade launcher, his hair a flapping black flag. He aimed the top end of the black tube skyward and dropped a grenade in, then jerked it downward to aim at Darkman. Militarily speaking, this was not a recommended tactic, for an upside-down grenade launcher will lose its grenade, much as a can of soup will lose its soup if turned upside-down. Darkman saw the grenade slip out and tumble past him. It exploded on the freeway, causing more cars to smash into one another.

Durant shrieked. He began throwing grenades at Darkman by the handful. One actually came close, and Darkman snapped a hand out, snagging it in midair. He chucked it upward, not expected anything miraculous and not getting it. Durant looked absolutely insane now. He ducked back inside. Almost immediately the helicopter jumped downward again.

Darkman climbed up, and up. The rope ladder twisted and flapped below, sometimes dragging on the cement of the freeway. Cars honked and swerved, as if driven by drunks, some of them taking the bumpy ride into the median strip, others spinning in circles while smoke belched off their tires. Red and blue lights began to flash in the distance. Police were on the way, but Darkman doubted if they could do much, unless they contacted a police helicopter and got it here in ten seconds, which wasn't likely. As soon as Darkman had been killed, this copter might well vanish to Mexico.

An old white Delta 88 was coming at him. The helicopter dipped low, dropping him so close to the highway that he had to raise his legs. The oncoming car honked, as if this were all Darkman's fault. He felt a driving rage to kill the knucklehead, but then he was scrambling up more rungs to get out of the way. The car honked without pause, sounding normal, then passed, sounding low as it receded. The Doppler effect, Darkman thought almost hysterically, wondering if he really had been a scientist named Peyton or if his entire life had been preparation for this moment.

The copter swerved left, descending on the outbound lane. Darkman was lowered over the roof of a green car, then jerked up and down, pounding him against the paint and steel. Dalton was a fine pilot, no doubt of that.

The driver of the green car hit the brakes and the copter moved on. Darkman was up on the third from the last rung. The lack of Durant poking out the door began to worry him. What if he had gotten a bright idea and decided to cut the rope ladder?

What if he doesn't have a knife?

What if the ladder is tied to something he could untie?

What if this huge truck in front of you hits the brakes and you slam into its ass end? Doesn't that warning label on the back say anhydrous ammonia? That's not exactly Kool-Aid.

Darkman worked himself higher, was forced to cock his head sideways as it jammed under the copter's belly. Dalton let the craft cruise a little faster than the truck, bringing it directly under Darkman's feet. The rest of the rope ladder twirled and thunked against the shiny aluminum skin of the truck's ammonia tanks.

Darkman crawled back down the ladder. His feet bumped into the top curvature of the truck's rearmost tank while the cool evening wind blasted against his head, where a happy little grin could be found, if only he had a face. There was a large steel hook atop the tank, though Darkman had no idea what it was for. Still holding the rope ladder, he knelt down and gave it a tentative pull.

Solid. Perhaps useful. Perhaps . . . very useful.

He pulled the flapping tails of the ladder together and tried to straighten out the tangles, gave up, and stuck as many loops as he could under the hook. As far as rescue devices went, it looked horrible, a bundle of rope tied into a Rubik's Cube of knots. Darkman let go of the ladder entirely and plopped himself down onto the smooth metal tank, hugging it like a child might hug a horse the first time he rode bareback. This was going to be close, or not at all. He looked up and saw a reflective green sign that proclaimed AVENUE A, NEXT EXIT.

"Please don't exit there," he said aloud. "One last favor."

The truck began to slow. The rope ladder grew taut as the copter tried to fly over the tanker. Darkman pounded the shiny hide of the tank he was riding, begging the driver not to take the exit.

It changed lanes. The final exit sign swept past, and ahead was the overpass that allowed Avenue A people to go west. Fortunately for those lucky people, they were not on the bridge when the truck passed beneath, towing a helicopter that was already filled with shouts and screeches. Darkman caught one voice—"*Pull her up! Pull her up!*"—and it sounded very, very much like Robert G. Durant shouting the last words he would ever speak.

The truck was big, more than six tons of anhydrous ammonia sloshing inside, moving fast. The copter was light, an easy tow. The truck passed under the huge concrete overpass, as it would a thousand times more before it was retired, but the helicopter ceased to fly and was dragged into the bridge in a huge yellow fireball of destruction, death, and brilliant light that would be talked about for weeks by those who witnessed it.

Darkman looked back at it as the driver slowed to see just what the hell had happened. When the truck was safely parked on the shoulder and the driver was gone, Darkman jumped down and slipped out of sight.

There was only one thing left to do, and that was to rescue Julie. After that, he promised himself, he would buy a bottle of the world's cheapest whiskey and drink himself into oblivion.

38

Skip

WHILE ROBERT G. Durant was being incinerated, the last member of the motley group that had killed Yakky and nearly killed Peyton, Mr. Skip Altwater, was watching television while smearing Noxema on the stump that used to be his right leg. He had not had the dignity of losing his leg in Vietnam, for he was far too young, though he usually told the young ladies he dated that he had sacrificed it for his country, which always went over big. Tonight, though, he was taking it easy, no company, letting the old stump take a break. Cutting the grass yesterday with the balky old mower had started the pain. Hauling that she-devil Julie around today had jammed the skin tight against his wooden leg, crunching it into the amputated bone. Because the wooden job was not exactly a normal prosthetic device, what with being a machine gun and all, it was far heavier and had no padding. Wearing it was often excruciating, as it was today.

He massaged his stump, which dead-ended at the knee, thinking for the billionth time of the accident that had cost him his leg. Too simple, it had been; too avoidable. Skip had grown up on a farm in Indiana. His dad, a crusty old buzzard, made Skip work in the fields, drive farm machinery too big for him, slaved him from dawn till dusk during summer vacation while the other boys did fun stuff. On a Wednesday the thresher he was driving caught on a thick chunk of old wood, halting the blades. Skip, ten years old, had gotten down and kicked out the soggy piece of wood. Instantly the thresher worked fine again, dragging Skip's foot in, amputating it, dragging his shin in, amputating it, dragging his knee in, amputating it. It was a process that Skip had found revolting but not yet painful. The thresher's big blades were sparkling red and wet under the afternoon sun, twirling merrily. Skip tore free and hobbled home, got yelled at by his father for being such a stupe, and then was driven to the doctor with a plastic trash bag tied to his stump to catch the blood. His dad was already fuming and roaring about how much this disaster would cost him in doctor bills.

Skip tore his mind away from the subject, trying unsuccessfully to get interested in the program on TV. He looked around for the remote control, couldn't find it, didn't feel like getting up from the couch, so he slumped sideways instead and drifted off to sleep . . . and woke up two hours later when his television exploded. He jerked upright, frowning. The TV was a smoking shell with a pink wooden leg sticking out of its shattered face. He wondered instantly if he had done this in his sleep, heaved his shoddy prothesis into the TV from the sheer hatred he felt toward it and the misery it caused his stump.

The television burped and rattled. Lazy flames waltzed in its bowels, sending black tatters of smoke to the ceiling. Skip looked around, dazed. Except for the TV, nothing else was amiss.

But the front door was standing fully open.

Skip stood up and hopped to it, beginning to cough on the smoke. As far as nightmares went, this one was a dandy, if it was indeed a nightmare. He shrugged to himself and swung the door shut.

Darkman was waiting behind it, a dark hulk in a cheap suit. Skip emitted a squawk and fell backward as the door thumped shut.

Darkman stood over him, a living skull capped with a bit of scruffy hair in spots, blackened bone and burned flesh, the hint of decay wafting off him. He bent down and stuck a finger bone against Skip's forehead. Skip tried to wriggle away, eyes stupidly crossed as he took in the sight of the Darkman's rotting hand.

"Where did you take her?" he said in a grating, tortured way, as if his lungs were dying inside him while Skip watched.

"Tuh-tuh-tuh-take who?" Skip said, gurgling.

Darkman hoisted him off the floor by the front of his shirt. "Julie Hastings, you bastard. You stuck her in your trunk. She's not in there now, and I ought to tell you your old Javelin will never be the same. *Where is she?*"

Skip squinched his eyes shut, not able to look at this monstrosity anymore, not able to stand the smell of putrefaction that was carried on the outrush of its hot breath. "I took her to Strack's house!" he shouted. Fingers bone clamped onto his throat and shook him.

"What is a Strack?" the monster barked in that queer, strangled voice. *"Who in the fuck is this Strack?"*

"Just a guy." Skip whimpered, almost slipping into the comfortable, dreamy world of shock. He was slapped across the face, making his eyes pop open. "Rich guy," he said. "Big in real estate. Louis Strack."

"What does this Strack have to do with the Bellasarious memo?"

Skip almost wet his pants, for this answer would not satisfy the creature that was about to kill him. "I don't know about any memo."

"Liar! You were there when Durant took it out of my pocket. How does Durant tie in with Strack?"

"The big boss," Skip answered immediately, not wishing to die a hero's death. "Strack runs the crime in this city, uses Durant as a front man. Strack stays clean as a whistle while Durant and the rest of us get dirty. Okay?"

Darkman deliberated. Was it okay? Did it make sense? What value did Julie hold for Strack? Enough to kidnap her, obviously.

"What about your old buddy Rick? Why didn't he tell me this?"

Skip shrugged as he tried to get up. "Rick was a loser, man. Durant wouldn't trust him to keep his mouth shut even if it was Superglued."

Darkman pulled Skip upright. Skip wavered on the edge of

235

collapse, standing on one leg and clutching Darkman's lapels for balance, his head rolling on his shoulders like a drunk. "Got a phone in this dive?" Darkman snarled.

Skip lifted one weak hand. "Over there."

Darkman shoved him toward it. Skip fell, moaning, onto his remaining knee. Darkman kicked him in the ass. "Call Strack. Find out what he's done with Julie. Mention my name and I tear your throat out. Understand?"

Skip nodded as he crawled to the phone on the wall in a corner of the living room. He clawed his way up the wall, eventually finding the phone, and punched the buttons. Darkman waited, growing angry at this small-town punk who walked on a machine gun and did everything he was told, even if it was murder. The scrawny bastard had no right to live.

"Sure," Skip was saying into the phone, trying to keep his voice level. "The new building going up at the waterfront? No, no, not that. She hurt my bum leg so bad today, I'd like to be there when you shove her off."

"Tell him to wait," Darkman snapped, his heart speeding up. "Tell him it will take an hour or more to get there."

Skip put a hand over the receiver. "It's only a twenty-minute drive!"

"Then make something up!"

Skip went back to the phone. Sweat was running down his temples and his hands were shaking. "Um, my stump's been bleeding a little. Not real serious, but it hurts. I'll patch it up and come over in, say, an hour?"

Relief transformed his face. "Thank you, Mr. Strack. Thank you very much."

He hung up. "You've got your hour," he said wearily, wiping a hand across his wet forehead. "Riverfront construction, over where the docks used to be. There's a high rise going up, twenty-two stories done already. Just steel, though. Think you can find it?"

"Don't worry."

"Well, then," Skip said, swelling up a bit, "get out and leave me alone. In an hour Strack's gonna kill that bitch. You wanted a ringside seat, you've got one. So go the fuck away. And send me a check for the TV you busted."

236

For Darkman that gnawing hint of anger at this kid roared alive, a beast waiting to be let out, demanding it. Just to look at this young man's defiant face was enough to set the red rivers in motion, the anger, the hate, the raw lust to kill, three rivers fusing into one and blotting out reason. The little piece of Peyton that had survived through all these ordeals begged him, screamed at him, to control it, control that anger and that hate.

No more, Darkman thought savagely, and jumped at Skip. Skip's eyes only had time to open wide in fear and surprise before Darkman was on him, pulling hair out by the handful, ripping skin into bleeding shreds, gouging his eyes out, grunting with animal satisfaction as Skip screeched in agony and tumbled to the floor. Darkman stepped back, his heart racing, his breath pumping up and down and scorching his wounded throat.

Skip was a skinny man made of mangled clothes and bloodied skin, writhing on the floor, clawing at the bleeding holes that had been his eyes. Darkman's blood lust grew as the smell of blood drifted up to his gaping nostrils.

He jumped to the television and snatched the burning leg out, madly out of control, seeing only hate and death in a world gone insane, himself gone insane. He jiggled the leg and a handgrip flipped out, complete with trigger. He aimed the absurd contraption at Skip's head and jerked the trigger back.

Skip screamed for the last time as the rapid-fire bullets sizzled through his skull.

The gun ran out of bullets. Darkman howled with rage and smashed it through a window. He squatted, got hold of the couch Skip had been dozing on so peacefully, and flipped it over. He stumbled into the kitchen, no longer himself, no longer anyone in particular. He yanked drawers out and hurled them away. A flying fork pinged off the counter and ticked against his forehead, where rage was a monster as big as the universe. He found the fork and stabbed it through the refrigerator door a dozen times, bending it, breaking it, panting and shrieking in this orgy of destruction.

He was about to snatch the clock off the wall and toss it through a window when it struck him that time was passing—

yes, time was passing—and he had much to do before meeting the estimable Mr. Strack. The rage was dwindling, leaving him sick and shaken, confused, almost spent. He staggered out of the kitchen and saw anew what he had done.

A small aftershock of his rage told him that this was good and real and nothing to trouble himself about. The rest of him informed him that he was a murderer, a monster on the loose, a beast created by the science he used to worship and teach. Careening into walls that dripped with blood and gore, he found the door and shambled out into the night, then threw up on the lawn that Skip had mowed only the day before, and would never mow again.

39

Darkman and Julie and Louis

SKIP ALTWATER MADE it to the riverfront construction project barely one minute before Louis Strack's limousine drove down the winding, muddy strip of road that had been mashed into the ground by bulldozers and cranes over the last weeks. Construction was moving at a frantic pace, obviously: The last time Darkman had been here to salvage parts from his old lab (now bulldozed into mud and dust), the huge steel construction had been only two stories tall. Now it was twenty-two, a giant Erector Set reaching to the moon and partially blotting it from Skip's sight.

The white limousine's headlights caught Skip in their glare, making him squint. He raised a hand to shield his eyes just as the headlights snapped off. The driver got out stiffly and opened a rear door of the giant cruiser. The fake Skip, watching everything with the sick memory of the real Skip's barbaric slaughter chasing through his mind, did his best to control the pace of his breathing; Skip's battered Javelin was parked on the street two blocks away, and it had been a hard run down this weedy slope. But it was nicely dark, the artificial face that had been hurriedly stuck into place had little chance of melting, and the wig that was most suited to match Skip's motley haircut was pulled tight over his head.

The impostor Skip shuffled forward uneasily, his feet wrapped in the foul-smelling steam that drifted up from the surface of the river. The steam pooled in recesses in the damp ground like a mysterious glowing gas and entwined the trunks of the scrappy trees that poked up here and there, trees doomed to die as they absorbed the poison that once had been river water.

Darkman arranged his face in a way he hoped duplicated the real thing. He had not had much time to study Skip, to learn his quirks and his posture. It seemed that next to Rick, Skip had been a fairly useless prop in the game of crime, his only talent being his magical mystery leg.

Suddenly a woman dived out of the car, nearly falling in the muck. Faint moonlight told its tale: Julie. A man in a dark suit stepped out with more dignity than Julie had, and took her arm. Together they walked toward Darkman while the driver eased himself into the limo and slammed the door. Darkman's rage rose up in an instant tidal wave, his dead fingers wanting only to rip and tear and kill the man who had created this hell for him, and for Julie.

But he stopped the emotion before it could expand out of control, because it was almost certain that Strack, and maybe even the limo driver, had guns, and the purpose here was not to get himself and Julie killed but to save the one who deserved to live most.

Darkman gimped toward them, wishing to all the patron saints that he had had time to practice Skip's voice. He was no Rich Little, no impressionist, no one at all. Strack drew close, just a figure in the dark shadows cut by the huge steel beams, but Julie was still Julie, looking terribly frightened, her hands tied behind her back, a red cloth stuck in her mouth.

"Well, Skip," Strack said casually, "do you want to go topside and help push her off, or stay down here to hear the splat?"

Rage.

Strack continued.

Darkman pointed up.

Rage.

"Right this way, madame." Strack swept an arm toward the skeleton that someday would be a building. It was surrounded by a moat of cast-off steel beams, silent trucks awaiting morning, huge tools that defied explanation, rods and pipes and barrels that stank of oil. The odor of recent cement work hung in the air, smelling like chalk dust, competing with the oil fumes and the stink of the mud and the river. It was not a pleasant combination.

"Over there," Strack said, aiming Julie toward what looked like a large steel-and-plywood box. Darkman tripped over something sticking out of the ground and nearly went down.

Rage.

"When you work high steel for a while," Strack said, "you acquire a certain sense about things. What you just broke your last foot on, Skip, was a piece of re-bar that was most likely tossed down here from high above. When you're dancing on a beam twenty-two stories high, it's fun to watch things fall. I'd estimate that piece of re-bar was over ten feet long when it was dropped, and you saw how little of it was still sticking up. Weird stuff, that re-bar. It's used for reinforcing poured concrete, just an iron bar about an inch in diameter, so weak that a big man might bend it over his knee. But without re-bar there'd be no construction. Know much about construction, Skippy, my boy?"

Darkman shrugged. They were close to the steel-and-plywood box, stepping around huge slabs of concrete where re-bars stuck up twelve feet high, awaiting their entombment in cement. Now he could see a set of taut cables attached to the roof of the structure, balefully reflecting in the moonlight. It was a construction elevator, the kind with no front door.

Strack unhooked the chain that was the elevator's ersatz door. When they were inside, he clipped it back together and worked a lever on the wall.

Gears clanked. Something whined. They rose with a heavy lurch.

"It is the tragedy of my life," Strack said suddenly, as if asked, "that I must kill the ones I love most. My father's death nearly stole my heart away, but it was a necessary evil to have him killed."

Wild-eyed Julie moaned something as the layers of pitch dark and moonlight zipped past the steel girders and rolled down her face.

241

"My wife," Strack went on, "the one who died so tragically, well, she held deeds to certain properties I needed. I sent her on a plane trip over the Great Smoky Mountains, and, well, let's just say the pilot and I landed on our feet."

He chuckled as the steel beams whizzed past. It occurred to Skip that he ought to be laughing, too, so he did. The rage seethed inside, a giant tapeworm of hate gnawing at his guts. Julie moaned again.

"Ah," Strack said, turning to her, "not to worry. Your boyfriend pops up when he's least expected. I'm sure he'll be here shortly. It seems he created an amazing amount of chaos today. The hospitals are full of his innocent victims, and many have died. He has killed at least five of my most trusted associates, and is determined to kill me. Imagine this, Julie! Your bumbling, educated boyfriend is a mass murderer! Skip, tell her what happened to our friend Durant."

Darkman squirmed, his mind suddenly blanking out. Wait a minute, wait a minute . . . how did Strack know Durant was dead? Evening news? A late paper? That innocent?

"His chopper got blown to shit," Darkman said, sounding, to his own ears, a lot like John Wayne and nowhere close to Skip. He put on a feeble grin and massaged his throat with his cool fingers.

"You betcha," Strack said, and then the elevator clunked to a stop and he unhooked the chain. "Now, Julie," he said, pulling her out onto a plywood floor, "you have a rendezvous with Mother Earth. Skip? Your pleasure or mine?"

"Do your dirtiest, boss."

Strack produced a pistol from somewhere inside his jacket and edged her out onto a single beam, like a lady condemned to walk the plank. Behind the mouthful of cloth, she wept and screamed, staggering on the narrow beam.

Rage.

"Just jump right off, Julie. Ours could have been a lasting relationship, if it weren't for your high moral principles. Baby, I despise principles, and I can't stand morals. So do us and everybody else a favor and take a long hike on a short beam."

Darkman . . . *rage.*

Darkman . . . *rage!*

Darkman . . . *RAGE! RAGE!! RAGE!!! RAGE!!!!*

242

"*You murdererrr!*" he screamed, nearly tearing all the cords in his neck and throat. His rush job of a Skip-face split from the real skin at his neck and began to peel upward like cheap wallpaper.

Strack turned. He smiled knowingly. "Ah, Mr. Westlake. You make a lousy Skip because, though you look like him—and the voice isn't all that bad—the real Skip would not know what happened to Durant because I, myself, didn't know what happened to him. And most importantly, the one-legged slob never would wear a suit."

He took a breath, smiling hugely. "Time for the unmasking, Westlake. Show us just who you really are."

Darkman walked toward him on a long and solid beam, where two hundred feet below the dirty river reflected colorful lights. Vertigo swept over him like a wave of terror, and he sidled back, panting.

"So glad my father made me work high steel," Strack said. "At the time I hated him. Now I love him for it. Watch what I can do."

He jumped up and clicked his heels together, then landed solidly on both feet again, arms outstretched for balance. "It took me sixteen months to get the courage together for that. Do you know what it's like now? Death ready to grab you at any moment? Sure you do. So come on and get me."

Darkman ground his teeth. The rage was still there. But so was the fear, and if it were up to him, he would flop down on the girder and hang on until the crew arrived in the morning.

But . . . it wasn't up to him. It was up to a man named Rangeveritz.

Darkman jumped for Strack, launching himself skyward, a flying wonder in a cut-rate suit, parts of his face disintegrating in the cold wind. He smashed down onto the girder where Strack had been, but Strack was gone and Julie was alone on this bleak beam, wavering and bobbing to stay in place, her eyes twin lamps of terror. Darkman swung around, hands ready to stab and claw, but Strack was in the moon shadows of the interior, chuckling.

"Bravo, Mr. Westlake. I applaud your clumsiness. I would love to shoot you right now, but for all the trouble you've caused me, I will wait to hear your screams when you fall. Know how long it takes to reach the ground in free-fall? A long time, Westlake. A long, long time. Plenty of time to consider what I did—with Julie—while you were away. Did you know about the mole on her inner thigh, the left one? I know. I know a lot of things.''

Darkman jumped toward the voice, a ragged scream of hate barreling past his lips. He landed hard on a stack of plywood, breaking another finger bone. He went up on all fours and searched the dark with Skip-eyes that were small and slitted.

''Look around yourself, Westlake. Look at the new construction going up. Remember when this place was a pile of filth where the drunks came to puke and sleep and get rolled by teenage punks? All of that is changing. Someday this river will run pure and clear, good enough to stick your face in and drink forever. This is the dream. And here you are, a circus freak let out of its cage, a murderer, a destroyer trying to crush my dream. What do you really look like, Westlake? As bad as the riverfront used to be or worse?''

Darkman swiveled his head, noting that Julie was sidestepping back off the plank, retching on the red cloth with saliva dripping from the corners of her mouth, moving slowly. For now, at least, she was okay.

''You want to know how I look?'' Darkman shouted into the darkness. ''I look like you, Strack. You hide behind money and lies and false faces, and all I've got is the false faces.''

There was a pause. Then, gently: ''I guess we both belong to the same club, Westlake. Let's call it the pretenders' society. I pretend to be nice and admirable and generous. You pretend to be human. I live a lie, you live a lie. Who's worse?''

Damn, Darkman thought, damn, damn, damn. The bastard had brains, unlike his partners, and he knew how to use the shadows. ''Why are we arguing morality, Strack? I believe you said you don't like the word.''

Silence. Julie came to a vertical beam and leaned against it, a white ghost against the sky and the stars. Strack was silent, possibly moving, possibly not, possibly anything.

''Strack!'' Darkman shouted.

The reply sounded weary. "You are a killer, Westlake. I live only to build—skyscrapers, malls, office buildings, whole towns. I put stuff up, but all you can do is tear stuff down. But you know what?"

"What?" Darkman answered, swiveling his head to find that voice. "Go on, what?"

"No one ever said being bad didn't feel good. It grows on you, gets better every time. Pretty soon you're hooked on it, needing to shape the world just the way you want it, eliminating anybody who stands in the way, feeling oh so fine. If I guess right, you've killed all five of my men. Skip was the last one, right? What did you do to him? Stab him? Smother him? Does it even matter to you?"

Darkman kept his mouth shut, looking without seeing.

Seconds passed. A minute. Two minutes.

Strack sighed. "I've got a little job for you over in Atlantic City. I want you to do your mask thing, impersonate someone for me. If you do it right, I'll pay you a quarter of a million dollars and give you Julie as a bonus. Sound good?"

This time Darkman waited, still madly trying to pinpoint that voice.

Something winked in the darkness just to the right, some golden metal touching a moonbeam. A cuff link? A belt buckle? A ring? The gun? "Not even if you could give me back my life, Strack," he growled, then gathered himself and pounced toward the light.

His fingers brushed against soft fabric, and then there was nothing but air. He snatched out wildly and caught the side edge of a girder. The moon was a cold white beacon, the man in the moon looking on without interest as Darkman tried to keep his artificial finger pads from slipping. Strack leaned over and began pounding his hands with the butt of his revolver. Slivers of bone burst past the slipping skin, raining down on Darkman like ghostly sawdust. He looked down, looked for something to land on, but there was only cold air and steel and one hell of a drop.

He tried to pull himself up. Strack kept pounding his fingers. It was a minor irritation, not painful at all, but when Darkman brought his head into range, Strack started pounding it too. It didn't hurt much, but it was growing very tiresome. He swung out and captured one of Strack's ankles with a fist. Strack let out a whoop and grabbed a vertical beam while Darkman clambered onto the girder, breathing hard, balanced between rage and fear.

Strack jerked, trying to free his foot. Darkman pulled, managing to tear Strack's shoe off. It tumbled out of sight. Nice going, Darkman thought sourly, chiding himself. The poor bastard will certainly miss that wing tip.

He tore Strack's sock off, just for the hell of it. Strack grunted, stretched taut between his captured girder and Darkman's hands. The artificial skin ripped free with a squelch, and the mushy Skip-hands pinwheeled out of sight. Strack looked at Darkman's scorched claws, his eyes growing wide in the moonlight.

"If your face looks as bad as your hands," he said, noisily straining to stay in place, "I'd sure hate to see it. You are just a damn carnival freak."

Darkman growled. It's not nice to call a freak a freak. He pulled one hand free of Strack's bare foot, beginning to feel the extra strength, the partner to his anger. He considered twisting Strack's foot until something snapped, but a better idea surfaced, a more fitting punishment for this creature made of money and lies.

He tore the Skip mask and wig off, glad that the moon was shining directly in his face. Strack let out a loud gasp.

"Go ahead." Darkman sneered. "Pass out, go blind if you want to. You did this to me, Strack, stole my future and my girl. I hope you're happy with the results."

Strack put on a false smile. "They have a carnival going in town, part of the Octoberfest. You could get a job, a free cage, straw to sleep on."

"Never lose your nerve, do you? Mr. Smart Guy to the end."

Strack nodded, his own face strained as his grip on the girder weakened. "Get yourself a bag, cut an eyehole in it, and you can be the Elephant Man. Of course, a big jug of formaldehyde would preserve you longer."

Darkman twisted his foot. Strack groaned, his hold on the girder getting weaker. Anklebones crunched as Darkman rearranged them. Strack gritted his perfect white teeth, the pistol still in his fist but quite useless unless he let go.

Walking practically on tiptoe, Julie edged toward them, the front of her white blouse stained from the flow of saliva, the wind blowing her hair, making it shift and billow. Darkman turned and saw her. He turned his head quickly away, not wanting her to see him unmasked.

"Stay away," he said, unconsciously easing his hold on Strack's foot.

With a huge jerk Strack pulled himself free. He aimed the gun, hopping on one leg. "Say good-bye, Westlake," he crowed triumphantly. "This bullet's for you!"

Darkman ducked in time. The bullet thunked against steel and bounded away, whistling crazily. Both Julie and Darkman went into a squat while Strack fired again, and again. Julie wobbled, retching against the cloth, almost ready to fall. Darkman reached out and caught her elbow, steadying her.

The moon showed her eyes as they shifted down to his hand. She emitted a bloated, terrified screech.

"Do you see now?" Strack shouted at her. The wind picked up, whooping past the unyielding steel, moaning with a hundred cold voices. "He isn't a man anymore, Julie. He isn't even human. Look at him!"

Darkman snatched his hand away from Julie and covered his head and face with his arms.

"A freak, Julie. A nightmare, a spook. Is that what you want? Come back to me and we'll forget that this Peyton creature ever existed. Forget, too, that damn Bellasarious memo that caused all this." He extended a hand. "Together, Julie. You and I, just us. All grudges set aside. In other words, a declaration of peace."

She stared at Strack with her hugely gaping mouth drooling, her hair tousling back and forth. Darkman peeked through his arms and saw her nod. She sidled toward Strack, stopping where Darkman blocked her path on the beam. Strack reached out and steadied her as she stepped past him. Strack was smiling gently. He pulled her close and jerked the soggy cloth out of her mouth. He tossed it away while she recovered.

"Mr. Westlake," he said, "I believe our business is almost

ended. There is only one more thing to do and we will all be released from this silly bondage.''

Darkman turned his back. Julie should not remember him as Darkman but as the Peyton she had loved.

"Only one thing left to do, Mr. Circus Freak," Strack said. "Julie will live, but only if you can prove your love for her."

Darkman shuffled around, uneasy, shielding his face from the light.

"You will take an extended hike off this building, Mr. Nobody. I want you to jump."

He spun Julie around and hooked an arm around her neck. "Either you jump or she does. Which will it be, Romeo?"

Darkman stared at him.

Anger . . .

"Once you are in the coffin you deserve, I will make Julie my bride." He stroked her breasts with his free hand. She stiffened but said nothing.

ANGER . . .

"These are my treasures now, a bit wet, but still mine, you ugly son of a bitch. Remember that mole on her thigh? I will be seeing it again and again and again, while you rot in the hell you came from."

RAGE!!!

He jumped at Strack, no longer afraid of the height, no longer afraid that Julie might see his face, no longer afraid at all. Strack swung the gun up, too late. Darkman smashed it aside and tore Julie from his grasp. She wobbled, arms pinwheeling, a high-pitched scream of terror slipping out, but Darkman pulled her so she could regain her balance, and stood face-to-face with Strack, boiling with hatred for this human swine.

"Now who jumps, asshole?" He snarled in Strack's face and grabbed him by the hair. With one overpowered move he yanked him some ten feet in the air. For a moment Strack was outlined against the moon, a windblown scarecrow with its legs and arms wildly flailing, a thin scream of fright bursting out, and then he was falling and falling.

Darkman reached out as he passed. He snagged him by one ankle, the bare one, gloating inside that as Darkman he was stronger than Charles Atlas, stronger even then Schwarzenegger, the victim of a mutation that had made him powerful and deadly. He laughed at Strack.

"If you can't fly, you'd better learn how, Strack," he said, chuckling. "Better learn pretty fast too."

"Wait," Strack screeched, upside down, the change in his pockets clattering out. "Listen to me! If you kill me, you've become as bad as I have. Maybe worse. If you drop me, you'll be the monster you look like. I know you. Julie told me a lot. If you kill me, you'll never be able to live with yourself. Right?"

Darkman dropped him. *"Wrong."*

Julie gasped.

Strack screamed for a remarkably long time before stabbing through the re-bar and splatting against the cement that his own men had poured just two days ago.

"I'm learning to live with a lot of things," Darkman whispered, and covered his face as he walked to the elevator, afraid only that the moon would show his face to Julie and end forever the memories she already had.

Epilogue

Nobody

JULIE WAS WAITING by the crude elevator, tears sparkling on her cheeks, her hands still tied behind her back. Darkman walked toward her, his emotions draining, replaced by a numbing weariness and dread for the future.

She unhooked the chain and backed inside, her face becoming a black mask. Darkman stepped in beside her and turned his face to the plywood wall, feeling that even in the darkness his mangled features could be seen. He reached to the lever on the wall and the elevator started down.

"Peyton?"

He didn't respond.

"My hands?"

He turned a bit and untied her. The thin white rope dropped to the floor. She wrapped cold fingers around his forearm, trying to pull him close, but now he had become a statue.

"Peyton, look at me. I can help. The burns don't matter to me."

He laid a claw on her hand. Sudden nausea rose up her throat as the cold, pointy things touched her skin, skeleton fingertips that were broken and spiky and smelling vaguely of rot.

"Look at me," she said evenly, almost sternly. "Peyton, turn around and look at me."

He shuffled around. Bars of light and shadow swept upward on his . . .

face?

She clenched her teeth together to capture the gasp that had welled up in her throat. In the stuttering darkness a savage monster was encaged beside her. She gave herself a mental slap.

"It's only a burn," she said, hoping to convince herself as well.

He let out a miserable chuckle and spoke. "Don't you think I've told myself the same thing, night after night? A burn. Only skin-deep. I could make masks to fool you, but it only made the disaster worse. I wanted you to love me without pity. But just when I got the masks down pat, something strange happened."

"What?" she asked. "What happened?"

He clutched his head, groaning. "I'm not Peyton anymore, Julie. I live in the dark like a vampire. I have no future left, nothing. I won't drag you down with me."

The elevator jerked as it touched the ground. Julie unhooked the chain and guided Darkman out of his cage, pulling him by one elbow. He had begun to make wrenching sounds of despair. Her stomach gave another lurch. He was crying.

"I want our old life back, Peyton," she said, pressing herself close. That aroma of slow decomposition enfolded her and she nearly retched. "I want our lives, our careers, our nights—Peyton, wear a mask if you must, but for God's sake don't leave me again."

He sighed heavily, shaking his head. "Ninety-nine minutes, Julie. A chance to pretend nothing happened, no fire, no explosion, no nothing. But I can't spend the rest of my life making Peyton masks that self-destruct every hour and a half. I don't belong in the real world anymore. I've changed—been changed—and I can never go back."

He started to walk away. She grabbed him and flung her arms around his neck, crying herself. "You can't leave me again. I can't take it anymore! Jesus, Peyton, I can't live without you!"

He pushed her away gently, stroking her cheek with what

251

was left of his fingers. "These hands used to caress you, but now they can only kill and destroy. Julie, Peyton did die. He will stay dead forever. I do not know who I am, but I do know who I was—and never will be again. Good-bye, Julie."

"*No!* Don't leave me!"

But he was already walking away.

It began to snow, but by then she had crumpled to her knees with her hands clasped over her face, and didn't notice the snow, and didn't care.

Winter was here at last.